Shake Up & Smell the Coffee

AVERY KANE

KISSINGSHARK PUBLICATIONS

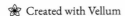 Created with Vellum

Prologue

NICK-2011

"Widen your hips."

Nick Griffith squared off with his best friend, Maya Markham, on the basketball court in the dark parking lot behind the high school. He was serious as he regarded her, but a hint of amusement glinted in his eyes. He knew how she felt when he told her how to play basketball, and it wouldn't end well if he didn't watch himself.

"They are as wide as they'll go," Maya snapped. "Why are you always so bossy?"

"I'm not bossy. You just get so intense when we play. You're shorter than me, which means you have to use your hips to block me. Otherwise, I'll cream you every time."

Maya narrowed her blue eyes and swiped at the fall of sweaty blonde hair that clung to her cheek. "You're bugging me."

Nick laughed, the sound filling the air in Bellaire, a small town in northern Lower Michigan. They'd both grown up there and become best friends despite the other kids making fun of them over the years for their closeness. Bellaire was their home, yet they were both eager to leave one day.

1

"I'm not trying to bug you." He was almost a foot taller than she was, but her personality was big enough to erase their size difference. "I'm trying to make you a better player."

"Why? It's not like I'm going to go pro. Heck, it's not like I'm even going to play in college. I would need another five inches for that. I'm just playing for fun."

"But you're a poor loser."

"I am not. Why would you even say something like that? I'm gracious in defeat. It's just that I never lose."

Nick's heart rolled at her earnest expression. "You don't actually believe that, do you?"

"Of course I do. I always congratulate the victor, don't I? When you win, on those rare occasions it actually happens, don't I always congratulate you?"

Nick arched an eyebrow. He wasn't just tall—he was muscular. It came from playing sports every season, something he loved, although he was under no delusion that he would ever be able to go pro. Sports would always be part of his life. So would Maya. That was why he paused before responding.

"Oh, come on," Maya whined. "I always congratulate you."

"Sweetheart, I have some bad news for you. Whenever I'm winning—which I only allow to happen on rare occasions because you're such a poor loser—you normally pitch a fit and walk off before the end of the game."

Maya's jaw dropped, making her even cuter for some reason Nick couldn't identify. She was beautiful and not just in a best-friend sort of way. She was a knockout, which was something she didn't see. One of the things Nick loved best about her was how animated she was, and that was on full display at the moment.

"You take that back," Maya insisted. "I never pitch a fit."

"Right." Nick let out a chuckle.

"I don't." Maya strode toward him, not stopping until

they were chest to chest—or more like face to chest, but Nick didn't comment on the height differential. "Admit that I'm an awesome loser." She poked him for emphasis. "Admit. It."

He held strong for as long as he could, but her finger was vicious, and he caught her hand before she could poke him again. "Just so we're clear, you're saying you want me to lie to you. That's what you're getting at, right?"

Nick didn't think Maya's mouth could open any wider, but he was wrong.

"You take that back," she hissed, using her slim hips as a weapon and knocking them into his thigh. "I'm a total sweetheart when I lose."

Nick dropped the ball. He was no longer interested in the game. In truth, he only came to the lot to play because he enjoyed spending time with her. When he was serious about competing—and winning—he played with the other guys after school. Their game was just for them, and it wasn't about the basketball, at least for him. He had no idea if it was about the basketball for her.

"Maya, I'm not going to lie to you." He caught her around the waist, doing his best to ignore her weaponized hips. When he dragged her to him, their bodies touching, his heart momentarily clogged his throat. He'd been feeling differently about her for almost a year, though he couldn't identify it because it was so alien when it came to his best friend. If he were with another girl, he would've assumed it was attraction. But that wasn't a word he could use when dealing with Maya. It just ... didn't fit. It couldn't fit.

"I'm not asking you to lie," Maya insisted. "I'm asking you to tell the truth."

"The truth is that you're a crappy loser." Nick's face broke into a grin when she grew outraged. God, she was cute, so much that he couldn't stand it sometimes. She'd gone through the awkward stage all kids went through early, meaning by the time she hit eighth grade, she was already a knockout. He'd hit his awkward stage later, which had given her the upper hand in their relationship for years. They were eventually on even footing, but he often questioned how their relationship would all play out over the long haul. She would always be in his life, but he wasn't sure how.

"I'm a good loser," Maya insisted, jutting out her lower lip. "You have to say it. If you don't, I'm going to be so mad that I won't talk to you for the whole weekend."

They both knew that was a load of crap. They never went a full twenty-four hours without at least talking to each other on the phone. Heck, she technically lived across the road from him—although there was a huge field between them—and at the very least, they waved when out in the yard.

"You're a poor loser. But you're a great friend."

Maya rolled her eyes. "You suck." She pushed away from him, and Nick instantly regretted the loss of warmth her body produced against his. "I'm practically perfect, and you know it."

Nick's heart panged. Maya *was* perfect. She would be somebody else's perfect person one day, though, and he didn't know how he would deal with it.

"I was just trying to help. You do whatever you want, though." He turned to retrieve the ball. "You are a poor loser, no matter what you believe." He couldn't stop himself from lobbing the dig in her direction. "Maybe you'll outgrow it."

"Oh, those are fighting words." Maya let loose a shriek and started to give chase, causing him to laugh as he caught her before she could jump on his back.

For a moment, his breath refused to come, and his chest expanded as he looked into her eyes. *Could she be mine one day? Do I want that?*

Don't be stupid, his inner voice chided. *You don't date your friends.*

That voice had been growing quieter lately, and when it did speak, he could easily ignore it. For the moment, however, he decided to listen and kept his thoughts to himself. The fear of losing her friendship was the only thing that kept him in check lately.

"Do you want to keep playing or go for ice cream?" he asked finally, when he was reasonably certain he could speak without sounding squeaky.

"How is that even a question?" she demanded, seemingly unaware of the inner turmoil he was constantly grappling with.

"Ice cream, it is."

"Right?" She bobbed her head. "You have to buy, since you called my sportsmanship into question. You know that, don't you?"

"I'll buy, if only to shut you up."

"Listen to that ego. You're so cocky these days."

"I'm not cocky. I'm just honest."

"Yeah, you keep telling yourself that."

MAYA-2015

"You look handsome in your robe," Maya announced as she straightened Nick's graduation cap. They'd somehow managed to make it through four years together at Central Michigan University, and they were going to graduate together, which was exactly how it should be.

"I look handsome all the time," Nick replied with a wink, although his attention was quickly diverted by a pretty brunette across the aisle.

She waved at him, swished her hips, and blew a kiss. He pretended to catch it with the sort of smile that turned Maya's stomach. Then he sent it back to the other woman.

"That was unbelievably gross," Maya complained when he

looked in her direction again, planting her hands on her narrow hips. "I can't believe you just did that. Worse, I can't believe you're dating her."

"Who?" Nick was the picture of innocence.

Despite everything, like living across campus from each other for years, they were still incredibly close. Sure, they'd taken tentative steps away, but when one needed the other, they were always there to act as a pillar of support.

"You know who." Maya darted a death glare at Camille Burton. She was one year younger than them but was somehow graduating at the same time. It made Maya's stomach burn to think about her, but she couldn't say exactly why. She wanted Nick to be happy, of course—she always wanted that for him—but she couldn't help but wonder why he'd been finding his happiness with Camille over the course of the past nine months.

"I don't understand why you have such an attitude about Camille," Nick complained. "She's been nothing but nice to you."

Maya remembered it differently. Camille, who'd grown up in Central Lake, only fifteen minutes from them, had only tried to ingratiate herself with Maya because she wanted to make sure that the claim she was staking on Nick was acknowledged. Maya was used to people not understanding her relationship with her best friend. She'd been slapped in the face with jealousy more times than she could count. Camille's approach was different, more manipulative, and Maya genuinely disliked her because of it.

"What did you say?" Maya asked when she realized it had been quiet for a long time. When she dragged her eyes back to Nick, she found him watching her with an unreadable expression. "What?"

He gently brushed her hair away from her face. "I was just thinking about tomorrow."

"We're having brunch with our parents."

He smiled. "Yes, and I can't tell you how much I'm looking forward to that. Have I mentioned how well my parents are getting along these days?"

Maya's stomach constricted. The constant battles playing out between Nick's parents had left him feeling uneasy. He liked when things were on an even keel, and she was afraid— just as much as he was—that the fights signified something bigger was going to happen down the line.

"They'll be fine," she reassured him. "Your parents love me."

"Yes, they're still convinced we're going to somehow get married and pop out grandkids for them. I've tried telling them friends don't get married, but my mother refuses to listen."

"Yes, well, my mother is feeding into that delusion." Maya made a face. "I wish she would stop. It makes meals so uncomfortable when they look at us like we should be making out."

"Right?" Nick let loose a laugh that turned into a sigh. "I'm not thinking about the brunch, though. I'm thinking about what comes after."

"What do you mean? What comes after?"

"That's just it. We don't know. Neither of us has a job."

"We're staying in town together," Maya said. "You're moving into my apartment so that we can afford the rent for the summer." Panic licked at her heart. "I thought you were on board with that."

"I am. Don't freak out."

"I don't freak out."

"Right, not my Maya." His grin was cheeky. "I just mean, we're going to spend the summer working odd jobs at the college, but by fall, we're supposed to know what we're doing. We're supposed to have jobs lined up. We're supposed to have our futures set."

Maya nodded. "I know."

"What if those futures are in different places?" Nick sounded as if he was the one panicking. "Maya, we've never lived more than ten minutes apart. What if you get a job in Detroit, and I get one in Traverse City or something? That's five hours driving time. We can't see each other on a regular basis when we're five hours apart."

He wasn't saying anything that hadn't been plaguing her dreams for months. Still, she forced a smile. "We'll figure it out. We have phones."

"I know." He looked momentarily morose.

"I mean, maybe we'll be the ones who get jobs in the same location, and Camille will be far away." Maya brightened considerably at the prospect. "That could happen."

Nick chuckled. "Will you just leave her alone? She's not so bad." He lowered his voice. "Besides, she's a college girlfriend. It's not going to last forever. We're not that serious. Chill out."

Nick had never voiced his opinion on their longevity odds, and Maya couldn't help but be relieved. "Are you going to break up with her?" She struggled to keep the hope from her voice. Ever since she'd broken up with Blaine several months before—the distance after he graduated and moved north to work had been too much for them to overcome despite a two-year relationship—she'd been feeling things she'd never thought possible when in close proximity to Nick. They were the sort of emotions she didn't want to dwell on, especially when they had so much going on.

"I'm not going to break up with her," Nick replied, dashing hope Maya didn't even know she needed. "She's going to be here over the summer, looking for a job too. There's no sense in ending it before I have to." He averted his gaze.

"You mean you don't want to give up the regular sex," Maya replied darkly. "Just admit it."

Nick lifted one shoulder in a shrug and grinned. "Does that make me a tool?"

"You've always been a tool." Maya flicked his ear. "It seems like a lot, doesn't it?" she said in a low voice. "You want to work in a sports setting, even if it's a smaller league. I want to eventually own my own restaurant. It was easy to make up scenarios when we were kids that involved both of us getting our dream jobs and still living across the road from each other."

"Yeah." Nick fixed the way her cap was sitting on her head. "We're still going to figure it out, Maya. We've been together for seventeen years now, ever since I stole your heart in kindergarten. Nothing can tear us apart."

"Do you promise?" Tears threatened to spill, and she had a strange lump in her throat.

He nodded solemnly. "Even if we have to spend a year apart, getting experience on our résumés, we'll talk on the phone and plan weekends together."

"That's not the same."

"I know, but I believe we're going to end up where we belong. Don't let the fear get to you now. We have our whole lives in front of us. This is just the beginning. We're going to figure it out."

"I would feel a lot better if we could figure it out without Camille giving me death glares," Maya muttered.

Nick snorted as he pulled her in for a hug. "Ignore Camille. I think you're seeing things that aren't there. It's always going to be you and me, Maya. The fates decided that a long time ago."

Maya briefly closed her eyes, listening to the steady beat of his heart. "You're right. I'm just nervous. I can't believe we're graduating. We always talked about it, but now it's actually happening."

"I know. It's weird, but we're going to be fine." He pulled

back far enough to stare into her eyes. "We're ride or die, right? That means we're always going to be in each other's lives."

"I hope so."

"I *know* so." He lightly kissed her forehead. "Don't doubt us now, Maya. We're meant to be best friends forever. I know it, and you do too."

"I'm just afraid. I'm sure I'll feel better after a few cocktails tonight. We're still going out, right?"

"Yeah." Nick bobbed his head. "Camille and a few of the others are coming too."

Maya stiffened. "But..."

"It will be fun," Nick insisted as he pulled away. "We're graduating. That means we're going to have a huge party, one we'll never forget."

"Fine. I still don't like Camille, though."

"You'll get over it."

"No, I won't. I just want you to get over her."

"I'm sure it will happen."

Maya could only hope that was true. Her traitorous heart wouldn't rest until it did.

One

"I like this color." Maya held up a muted-purple vinyl swatch. It was more silver than pink, and she loved the rich undertones. "What do you think?"

Lindsey Torkelson, holding a to-go cup of coffee, cocked her head as she regarded the sample. "Sure. Why not?"

Maya, her long blonde hair pulled back in a loose braid, made a face. "Come on. You're supposed to be helping me. This is a big deal."

"It's purple," Lindsey replied.

"Yeah. Purple is my favorite color."

"I like red."

Maya shook her head. "I don't like red, especially for a booth color." She gestured around the construction site that would one day be her cafe and made a hurry-up motion. "Can't you see how cute this will be? I'm doing cream walls, slate-gray trim, and purple booths. It's going to be magical." She paused, thinking of the future. "You know I've always wanted to own a cafe," she added when she'd shaken herself from her reverie.

"No, I actually remember you saying you wanted to own a

11

restaurant." Lindsey was the pragmatic sort. She didn't believe in wasting time saying things that weren't important—she had too many kids for that. "If that's what you want, you should go for it. This is your coffee shop."

"Cafe," Maya corrected automatically, turning sheepish when Lindsey gave her a dark look. "What? I'm going to be serving soup and sandwiches. It's a cafe."

"You're also going to be closing at three every day," Lindsey reminded her. "That sounds more like a coffee shop to me. This place used to be a coffee shop ... before you came in and totaled it." She wrinkled her nose. "How long until this place doesn't look like a total wreck?"

Maya sighed as she shoved the vinyl sample aside. "Weeks. It's already way better than it was, though. I mean, to say it was dated before I got in here would be an understatement."

"Oh, I don't know. I liked the knotty pine and vinyl flooring. I thought it added a touch of seventies elegance to the place."

Maya choked on a laugh and shook her head. "It's going to be great, right?" Normally, she wasn't an insecure person. Owning her own business had made her edgy, however, and she couldn't help asking the same questions over and over again. She knew Lindsey found it annoying. There was no turning back, though.

"It is going to be great," Lindsey agreed, not missing a beat. "I'll be here on a daily basis. I'm going to leave the kids with Bear and make this my new hideout. I've already told him."

Maya let out a low chuckle. She'd been close with Lindsey in high school—not joined at the hip or anything, but still close—and she was trying to wrap her head around Lindsey's choice of husband. "I still can't believe you married Brian Torkelson."

"Hey, I love that man!" Lindsey extended a finger in warning. "He's the love of my life. I'm totally going to have him fixed, though. It seems the love of my life is a giant sperminator. We're done having kids, and he's getting snipped. Once he does, life will be perfect."

Maya had only been back in Bellaire for two weeks, but she'd seen Lindsey and Brian—or Bear, as he was known affectionately because of his size—interact enough times to know their marriage was far from perfect. Despite that and the gaggle of kids they hauled around with them wherever they went, genuine love bubbled between them, and they seemed head over heels for each other after ten years of marriage. In truth, Maya was a bit jealous of their easy rapport. She would never say that out loud, though.

"Does he know he's getting fixed?" she asked as she picked up the purple vinyl sample. She couldn't get it out of her mind. She knew exactly how she wanted the interior to look, and the purple was a big part of it.

"No, I haven't broken that little detail to him," Lindsey replied, then sipped her coffee. "I thought I would wait to spring it on him. Like ... on our anniversary, I'm going to make him a big cake shaped like a penis, and I'm going to write the words *snip, snip* on it and yell, 'Surprise' when he can't figure out the message."

Maya was glad she hadn't been drinking, because she surely would've spewed coffee all over the floor. "Well, please film that for TikTok. You'll become an internet sensation if you do."

"Oh, I've already got that covered. Trust me." Lindsey sipped her coffee again, her eyes contemplative when they landed on Maya. "You know, not to beat a dead horse..."

Maya stiffened. She knew what was coming.

"I never thought you would come back to Bellaire," Lindsey continued. "I always thought you would at least move over to Traverse City so that you could own a restaurant on the water there. You always dreamed of it."

"I didn't specifically dream about Traverse City," Maya hedged.

"You dreamed about having a restaurant on the water."

"Yes, and Bellaire has a lake."

"But—"

"I have to be realistic." Maya shook her head. "A restaurant is expensive. The outlay is massive, especially for the sort of restaurant I want. I need to save up. We're talking at least three hundred grand here. I need to make this business a success and prove myself a good risk for a mortgage before I can even consider an actual restaurant."

Lindsey nodded. "I get it. I'm still sad. That was always your dream."

"Well, sixty percent of new restaurants fail in the first year. Almost eighty percent are gone in the first five years."

"Yeah, but this is a tourist community," Lindsey pushed. "We have a lake ... and a resort ... and a huge tourist population in summer and winter. Heck, when the leaves change, it's packed up here for fall too. That cuts down on the risk."

"There's still risk." Maya had done her research. She knew the industry backward and forward. "Up here, by March, the skiing and snowmobiling have dried up. There's no good golf until mid-May because the greens can't dry out and perk up until the sun is making regular appearances. So that's two and a half months of downtime right there. Then once September hits, golf is usually done by the end of the month. We get a burst of tourists for the fall color tour in October. Then November is a dead zone. That's another six weeks of downtime. Depending on when the snow comes in, business picks up, so that's still late December at the earliest and more likely early January. That's another four weeks. So that's five months of downtime when you add it all together. That leaves seven months of good business."

Lindsey worked her jaw. "Since when are you a math wizard?"

Maya huffed a laugh. "I'm not a math wizard. But I did talk to an accountant about opening a restaurant before I came back. Given the money I managed to save when I was working in Birmingham, I thought I would have a shot. He was fairly brutal when making me see exactly what I could accomplish. It wasn't nearly what I thought."

"So basically, you're saying he crushed your dreams," Lindsey surmised. "What a tool."

"He was just being honest. It was better for him to be brutal and keep me from losing a hundred grand than to sit back and watch me throw it all away. Can you imagine if I'd opened a restaurant and lost it in six months? I would never have recovered from that. It's better to start small and build myself up than go big and watch all my dreams tank."

"Well, if you're going to be realistic about it," Lindsey said slowly, eliciting a giggle from Maya. But she sobered quickly. "Have you seen Nick yet?"

Maya was expecting the question and thought she was braced for it, but her shoulders subtly jerked all the same. "Not yet." She avoided eye contact. "I'm sure he's busy."

"Yes, being the high school gym teacher and basketball coach is the stuff eighty-hour weeks were made for. He barely works forty hours a week. He could easily stop by if he wanted to."

Maya ran her tongue over her lips, debating. Lindsey was hardly the first person to question her relationship with Nick. Half the town had stopped her to ask how things were going. Unfortunately, she didn't have an answer for them. Things with Nick were going nowhere.

"I guess he doesn't want to stop by," Maya said stiffly as she held up the vinyl sample again. "I'm totally going with this, no matter what you think. I have a vision, and it's going to be great."

"Cool." Lindsey shot her a sarcastic thumbs-up. "I don't want to talk about the booths, though. I'm going to sit on anything you pick. I want to talk about Nick."

Maya bit back a sigh and turned her back to Lindsey. She didn't want to talk about Nick. Lindsey, however, would push and push until she got her way. That was simply how she was built.

"Come on, Maya," Lindsey wheedled. "When you guys went to college together, everybody assumed you would finally get together and live happily ever after. The whole town was on pins and needles, watching you guys as teenagers—and I include myself in that group because we were friends, and even I couldn't figure out your dynamic—but you guys held strong and were just friends. Now you're not even that."

Maya ran a hand over her hair to smooth it, being careful to avoid the braid so that she wouldn't inadvertently snag it. "We were never going to be a couple." Even as she said the words, they rang hollow. Looking back at college graduation, she realized she'd been trying to figure out a way to tell Nick she had feelings for him. She'd thought she would have a chance that summer when they were living together. It never came to fruition, though.

"Of course you were. You guys loved each other beyond reason. You just couldn't be together here because everybody was watching. Nobody expected you would fall out of touch and ignore each other when you both landed back in town. I mean, nobody had that in the pool."

Maya jerked up her head. "There's a pool?"

Lindsey was the picture of innocence. "Who said there was a pool?"

"You just did."

"Well, don't listen to me. I'm twenty-nine and have four kids under the age of ten. I'm clearly not the brightest light bulb in the pack."

"Plus your husband's name is Bear," Maya muttered.

"Hey, you leave my cuddlekins alone." Lindsey's tone was stern, but her eyes twinkled. "I'm being serious, Maya. You and Nick were like conjoined twins who wanted to have sex with each other when you were teenagers. Now you've been back two weeks—he's been back a full year—and you haven't even seen each other. What's up with that?"

Panic grabbed Maya's stomach and twisted. She'd expected questions and even had plans to sidestep them. Lindsey was relentless, however. "We just fell out of touch. That happens."

"Not to you guys, it doesn't." Lindsey folded her arms and glared. "You and Nick love each other." She softened her voice. "I mean, you *loved* each other. Even if you never got together—which seems ridiculous when I think about it—how could your friendship fall by the wayside? You guys couldn't even go an hour without checking in with each other back in the day."

"Things change." Maya had to blink back tears. She didn't like thinking about Nick, and it wasn't because there was some horrific story to explain away the loss she still felt like a dagger in her heart whenever she thought about him, which was daily. No, the truth was more mundane than that, and it felt like a tragedy. "I don't know what to tell you." She held her palms out and shrugged. "It didn't happen all at once. It just ... happened over time."

"Meaning you called less and less until you just stopped calling?" Lindsey was dubious. "You guys were so codependent, though."

Maya exhaled heavily to center herself. Lindsey wouldn't just let it go. She had to tell her the truth, just once, and hope that it would be enough to placate the masses when

Lindsey started running her mouth. "I was in Detroit to start, and it was hard. I got hired to work in that restaurant in the Renaissance Center, the one I told you about, and because I was low woman on the totem pole, that meant working like sixty hours a week ... and at night. I was grateful for the learning experience, but Nick got a job in Grand Rapids at that sports rehab center. He had to start at five in the morning, and sometimes he went until eight at night. I slept until noon every day. It was hard to schedule calls."

Lindsey looked momentarily sad. "I'm sorry. This is clearly hard for you."

"It's fine." Maya forced a smile. "It is what it is. We tried to keep in contact, but it became impossible. Before I realized it, a month had gone by. We talked, but we were always distracted. He didn't know the people in my life, and I didn't know the people in his. We just fell out of touch."

"I really am sorry. That must have been painful."

"It wasn't painful until the point when I realized we'd gone five months without talking," Maya replied. "We weren't even texting. We just stopped communicating. It happened out of nowhere." *And I was to blame. He was still with Camille, and I was bitter. I let my jealousy get between us. It's on me.* "I thought about calling him that day, trying to get our friendship back on track, but I didn't. I figured if he was fine going five months without talking to me, I should let it go."

"Have you let it go, though?" Lindsey cocked her head as she studied Maya's face. "I see you sometimes, when there's a shadow passing the front window. It's always a man who gets your attention, and you jerk your head up to look. When it's not him, you seem sad. Then you pretend you're not upset and go back to work."

"He knows I'm here," Maya reminded her. "He could stop by. Even if he didn't know where I rented my cabin in town, he could ask my mother. It's not like he doesn't know where she lives."

"You could do the same for him," Lindsey pointed out. "If you're wondering, he bought a house on the east side of town. I hear he's looking to buy bigger than he has now, but the market is a mess. I could find the exact address from Bear, if you want. He and Nick hang out all the time."

"No." Maya shook her head. "I don't want to track him down like a freaky stalker. How awkward would that be?"

"Probably pretty awkward," Lindsey conceded. "The thing is you're living in the same town again. It's not a big town either. There are two freaking traffic lights. There's no way you won't eventually see each other."

"Well, I'll just let it happen naturally. That will be easier than ... chasing him down. Less embarrassing too."

"Yeah, but you're Maya and Nick. Will it really be embarrassing? All you guys need to do is be in the same spot. You're going to fix everything that's wrong in five minutes flat, if you just lay eyes on each other."

Maya didn't believe that for an instant. They had too many hurt feelings—on her part as well as his—and it wouldn't be fixed in the blink of an eye. "You know what? I need to go to the hardware store and grab some paint samples. I lost the cream ones I had and need to pick a color. Can you hold down the fort? I'll be right back."

Lindsey's gaze was speculative. "Yes, I can hold down the fort," she said after what felt like a long time. "I don't think anybody is going to bother coming in here when it's clearly under construction, but I can handle anybody who braves the mess."

"Thank you." Maya started for the door.

"We're not done talking about this, though. I'm going to put together some talking points while you're gone. I'm not just going to let this go."

"Great," Maya gritted out. "I can't wait to have this conversation yet again." Rather than wait for Lindsey to respond, she pushed through the door and ran smack dab into a wall of flesh.

"I'm so sorry!" Maya splayed her hands against the man's chest, hoping she wouldn't fall backward and break a hip. That would be just her luck.

The man grabbed her before she could topple, making a grunting sound, and when Maya regained her senses enough to look up, she stared into the depths of Nick Griffith's silver-green eyes. He looked as surprised as she was.

"Nick," she squeaked, dumbfounded.

"Maya." He almost looked like he was in pain. "I guess this was bound to happen."

Maya nodded, her heart threatening to shred at his proximity. "I guess it was."

They fell into silence. The awkward encounter she'd been fearing had finally arrived, and she had no idea how to deal with it.

Two

NICK

Nick's heart skipped ten beats when he realized whom he'd crashed into. He hadn't been paying attention, instead studying the text his father had sent him regarding groceries. Nick grabbed Maya's shoulders without thinking to make sure she wouldn't get knocked over, then he sucked in a breath while taking her in.

She was still beautiful. *Why couldn't she have suddenly turned ugly or something?* That would've been better, at least for him.

"Maya." Her name came out as a breathy whisper.

"Nick." Maya's expression was hard to read as she regarded him.

"Maya," Nick repeated, mostly because he didn't know what else to say.

"Nick." She laughed with genuine warmth. It put Nick at ease, although only a little.

"Maya." A reflex had him smoothing her hair, then he quickly drew back his hand. *That's inappropriate,* he scolded himself. *You're not sixteen any longer.* "Sorry."

Her smile didn't waver. "It's fine. I ... um... How are you?" She seemed to gain control of her faculties through sheer force of will.

Nick was determined to emulate her. If she could be polite and go through the motions of a conversation, so could he. "I'm good. How are you?"

"Busy." Maya gestured toward the old coffee shop, which had brown paper covering the windows. "I'm opening a cafe."

"I heard." Nick smiled. "You're finally making your dreams come true."

"Well, I'm starting. I mean, I still want that restaurant I always talked about when we were kids."

"One day," Nick said.

"One day." Maya licked her lips. She wasn't wearing any makeup but still looked almost exactly the same, which was frustrating because it catapulted Nick back to a time when they had constantly been together. "So, I hear you're a teacher at the school."

"Who told you that?" The question came out more accusatory than Nick would've preferred, but he was still wrapping his head around seeing her. He'd known it would happen eventually, of course—Bellaire was a tiny town—but he wasn't prepared for it to happen right then. He had other things to do that day.

"Um ... just about everybody I've run into," Maya replied. "My mother told me. My aunt told me. Maude Phillips at the bakery told me. Sandy Capshaw told me. Oh, Lindsey is inside, and she told me like ten times. She thinks you look great in the shorts you wear when conducting your gym classes out on the soccer field, by the way."

Nick let out a low chuckle. "Right. Lindsey."

"She's been helping." Maya gestured toward the coffee shop again, seemingly at a loss as to what to do with her hands.

Nick understood why she was so fidgety. He was having the same problem.

"She's a great helper," Nick said, internally cringing. *She's a great helper? Could you be any less interesting?* "As for teaching, I've been at the high school for several months now. It's not my dream job, but it pays the bills, and it keeps me close to my dad."

Maya's expression warmed at the mention of Hank Griffith. She'd always been fond of him. "How is your dad?"

Nick shrugged. "He's ... been struggling. Ever since my mother ... did what she did, he's been having a tough time of it." He couldn't bring himself to say the actual words. He didn't want to talk about his mother.

Maya nodded. "My mom told me about your parents splitting up. I'm so sorry." She didn't press further, something Nick was grateful for.

Nick held out his hands. "It is what it is. She made her choice. Now we all have to pick up the pieces of the life she left behind."

"It can't be easy." Maya wet her lips and looked up and down the street. "So ... um ... it's been a long time."

"Eight years," Nick confirmed. *Eight years since you decided you no longer cared to put in the effort on a lifelong friendship.* He almost jolted at his thoughts but held it together. Getting bitter about something that couldn't be changed was useless. The friendship he'd thought would last forever had turned out to be more temporary than he envisioned. Life was disappointing, though. It wasn't just her. He was disappointed in himself too. "I'm actually surprised you moved back here. I didn't think you wanted to live up here. You were always talking about running big restaurants in big cities."

Maya worked her jaw.

"I'm sorry. You obviously don't want to talk about that."

"No, it's fine." Maya exhaled heavily. "There's nothing to apologize for. I just don't know what to say."

"Eight years is a long time."

"It is, but I was actually talking about the restaurant thing." She looked sheepish. "I didn't think I wanted to be here. I spent all of my teens convinced I wanted to be anywhere but here. Oddly enough, though, when I was in the city, I started thinking about home more often. It didn't happen overnight and wasn't a knee-jerk thing. Eventually, I realized that I wanted to be here, so here I am."

"To stay?" Nick tried to hold himself in check as he waited for the answer. Why it was important, he couldn't say. But he wanted to know.

Maya nodded. "Yes. At least, I think so. I can't control some weird catastrophe or something unexpected that forces me to move. Like if I were to lose the cafe and couldn't pay my bills, I might have to move. There aren't quite as many options here as in the city."

She looked so forlorn at the prospect that Nick couldn't stop himself from reaching out to touch her shoulder. "You're going to do great, Maya. This is what you've always wanted to do, and I know you're going to be good at it. You'll figure out a way to get that restaurant you've always wanted at some point, and you'll be everybody's favorite businesswoman before you know it."

After letting out a hollow laugh, Maya replied, "Yeah, I don't think it's going to be that easy."

"Sure it is." Nick bobbed his head. "You've always been destined for greatness."

The softness in Maya's eyes unraveled some of the barbed wire Nick had wrapped around his heart over the years. "Do you really think so?"

"I *know* so." That time, when Nick reached out to stroke her hair, he didn't feel guilty. Sure, he was confused, but despite his anger with her over the years, the old familiarity remained. They'd touched each other's lives for a very long time. It had been painful when they pulled apart, but that pain had ebbed some. It no longer felt like a dagger between his ribs. "I've always had faith in you."

"Nick." Maya took a step toward him, causing his emotions to start churning. Before she could say whatever she was going to say, however, a shadow fell over her, and she looked to her left, to a man who was watching her expectantly.

Slowly, Nick tried to shake off whatever Maya had been about to say to him. If it was important, she would find another way to say it. They were living in the same small town again. The odds of running into each other were astronomical. No one could avoid someone in a town with two stoplights.

Then he registered who was standing next to Maya, and all he could think about was wearing a bag over his head so that he would never have to see her again.

"Blaine," Nick blurted, dumbfounded. *Blaine Carter? How is this even possible?* He hadn't seen the man since he graduated two years before them. He'd disappeared from Maya's life, left her crushed, and never looked over his shoulder when making his escape.

In truth—and Nick would never admit it to anyone other than himself—he'd been secretly glad when Blaine broke Maya's heart. He'd never liked the guy. Not that he was jealous or anything—people didn't get jealous when their best friends dated—but he'd never thought Blaine was good enough for Maya. *So what is he doing here?*

"Nick." Blaine's lips twitched as he regarded him. They'd never been friends, only tolerated each other because of Maya. "How's it going? I guess I should've known you would come around eventually."

Nick narrowed his eyes. *What's that supposed to mean?* "I guess I can't say that about you. What are you even doing here?" Something horrible occurred to him. "Are you two together?"

Blaine snorted then made a face. "Yeah, I'm here to show her trim samples." He held up a big bag. "I got three in each price range, Maya. You need to make a decision today so that I can order it and have time to paint it."

Maya nodded. "Okay, um ... Lindsey is inside. I'll be there in just a second."

Blaine glanced at Nick again, as if debating whether he wanted to keep pushing things, but instead, he nodded. "Okay. Try to be fast. I need to run some errands."

"I won't be long," Maya promised. Her eyes were on Nick, but she waited until Blaine disappeared inside to speak. "So, he's helping with some of the details for the cafe. He owns his own construction business in Kalkaska and has been a great help."

Nick had had no idea Blaine was back in Kalkaska. "I thought he went to college for communications. Wasn't he going to be a radio personality or something? Didn't he move to Grand Rapids after graduation for that?" *And that's why he dumped you, because he was having too much fun in Grand Rapids.*

"We don't always get to fulfill the dreams of childhood," Maya reminded him. She looked uncomfortable. Nick was making her that way, and he quickly regretted it.

"It's none of my business." Nick held up his palms and took a step back. "I'm sorry I said anything."

"No, you can say whatever you want." Maya moved toward him to make up for the distance he'd created, but it was too much for Nick.

"I have to go."

Disappointment flashed in the depths of Maya's eyes, but she shuttered it quickly. "Of course."

"I was actually on my way to meet someone," Nick explained.

"Of course." Her voice was small.

For some reason, Nick was irritated by her response, although he couldn't quite identify why. "I really am meeting someone. Bear is down at the basketball court. He's meeting me."

Maya blinked several times, then smiled. "The basketball court, huh? We used to spend so much time there. Is it still the same?"

Nick shrugged. "The lines have been freshly painted, and the nets have all been replaced. They've also updated the shrubbery around the parking lot. It's the same but different."

"Nothing ever truly stays the same, I guess."

"No," he agreed. "Nothing is forever."

She opened her mouth to respond, but Nick decided that he was either unable or unwilling—likely the latter—to hear her out.

"I have to go." He raised a hand in a casual wave. "Good luck, Maya. I know you're going to do great."

"Thank you, Nick." She looked pained as he started to move off. "It was nice to see you."

"You too. I'm sure I'll see you again eventually."

"Yeah. Eventually."

Nick turned his back on her and broke into a jog. He couldn't get away from her fast enough. Since it was hard for him to wrap his head around what he was feeling, he did the thing he'd done during his teen years when he needed an emotional break—he ran. The reaction was both physical and emotional, something he recognized but didn't want to dwell on.

His feet pounded in tandem with his heart, and he focused on the noise, the rhythm. He was a creature of habit, and he ran five miles a day. The simple act of embracing the ordinary was enough to calm him by the time he reached the basketball court in the parking lot of the high school. There, Bear was dribbling a ball as he aimlessly circled the court.

Nick grinned when he saw his friend. It was impossible not to smile at Bear. The dude had charisma to spare and didn't care what anybody thought about him. *We should all be more like Bear,* Nick thought.

"Are you eager to get your ass handed to you or something?" Nick called, drawing Bear's eyes to him.

"Oh, please." Bear puffed out his chest. He wore a pink tank top with a pineapple with sunglasses under his hoodie, and his ridiculous chest hair poked out—the reason he'd been nicknamed Bear at a young age. "I could beat the snot out of you with one arm tied behind my back."

"Uh-huh." Nick grinned then drew his shirt over his head. "Let's play."

Bear frowned when he caught sight of Nick's cut torso. "Dude, you're dolphin smooth. Where is your chest hair? Also, why are you shirtless in December? I know it's a warm day for this time of year but come on."

Nick frowned at him. "Why does it matter?"

"Because real men have chest hair."

Nick rolled his eyes. "If you say so."

"You're one of those manscapers." Bear didn't look thrilled at the prospect. "I'm appalled on your behalf, man. That is just ... horrible. I mean, you look like you're going through a health emergency."

Nick glowered at him. "You go through this routine whenever we play."

"That's because you look like a hairless monkey, and it's such a horrible sight that I block it from my mind until we do it all over again."

"Whatever." Nick blew out a sigh and planted his hands on his hips. He'd meant to push his reunion with Maya out of his mind, but he couldn't quite manage it. "I saw Maya." He purposely kept his voice even, but it took effort.

"Oh yeah?" Bear's expression was blank. "How did that go?"

"About how you would expect. Well, other than the fact that her ex-boyfriend is doing trim work for her." Nick was desperate not to think too hard about what sort of other "trim" work Blaine might be doing for his ex-best friend.

"That Blaine guy?" Bear made a face. "I'm pretty sure he's just doing carpentry work for her. I don't think he's actually checking any other trim or anything. Lindsey would've told me if he were."

Nick tried to tamp down the hope that spread through his chest. *Where did that come from?* "They're not together?"

"I'm almost positive they're not. Lindsey likes to gossip. She tells me things I don't care to know and would've mentioned if Maya and this guy were knocking construction boots. She's been going on and on about how Maya needs to get laid for two straight weeks now."

"She thinks Maya needs to get laid?" Nick couldn't help laughing. "And why is that?"

Bear lifted one beefy shoulder. "I'm not sure. Lindsey says she's wound tight. We have four kids, and Lindsey is more relaxed than she is. She said Maya seems intense, like to the point where she needs fifty orgasms to loosen up. That's Lindsey's opinion, mind you, not mine. I don't care if Maya is wound tight. She's always been that way."

Nick's frown was instantaneous. "She wasn't always wound tight. She was fun."

Bear snorted. "She was fun to you. To the rest of us, she was a bit of a pain. I mean, has that girl ever met a to-do list she didn't want to foist on everybody else?"

"That was funny," Nick insisted.

"You found her funny because you had a thing for her.

That meant everything she did was cute, in your estimation. It wasn't funny for the rest of us when she demanded we start color-coordinating for the away games so that you would know we were rooting for you."

Nick was taken aback—not about the color-coordination thing, because he'd always been aware of it. But the other thing Bear had said threw him for a genuine loop. "I didn't have a thing for her."

"I can't believe you just said that with a straight face." Bear huffed a laugh.

"I didn't. She was my best friend. There were no *things* being had. You don't have things with your friends."

Bear looked calm as he pinned Nick with a "You've got to be kidding me" expression. "Dude, I don't know who you're trying to convince when you say that, but it's not going to work on me."

Nick made a protesting sound.

"I'm being serious. You guys kept calling each other friends back then, but everybody knew. We took bets. If one of you had just admitted to the other that there were actual feelings there, the other would've fallen in line, and you guys would've been married eight years ago.

"You couldn't do that, though," he continued. "You couldn't risk being the vulnerable one. She couldn't either. And I'm guessing you're not liking where you guys are right now."

Nick had no idea how he was supposed to respond. "None of that is true," he said finally.

Bear looked as if he wanted to argue further, but he just shrugged. "Fine. Are you ready to play? I have exactly one hour before I have to pick up the littlest drooler. I don't have time for being sensitive."

"I didn't have a thing for her," Nick snapped.

"Okay." Bear held up his hands in supplication. "You

didn't have a thing for her. Now, let's play. There's no reason to dwell on high school, regardless."

Nick agreed, yet he couldn't shake the niggling feeling that Bear had hit a nerve and exposed it in such a way that it would never be covered again. *How did that happen?*

Three

MAYA

Maya did her best to push her awkward interaction with Nick out of her head and focus on what needed to be done. They were on a timetable, after all. The grand opening of Red, White, & Brew was only weeks away, and even though she wouldn't admit it to anybody else, she was nervous. If she failed, there would be no restaurant in her future, so she *had* to make it work.

Despite that, her mind kept drifting to Nick as she prepared to lock up the shop for the day. *Why was he so cold? Why did he refuse to make eye contact for more than a few seconds? Why has the best friend I've ever had turned into an awkward acquaintance?* She was bothered by it all and too afraid to do anything about it.

What is there to do? You guys aren't friends any longer. You had as much to do with it as he did. He's not to blame. Nobody is to blame. Some friendships don't last.

It made her bitter to think about it, so she ruthlessly shoved the notion aside and prepared to head out. Then a noise in the kitchen reminded her she wasn't alone.

"Are you finished?" she asked when she checked on Blaine,

who was replacing the trim on the door that led to the small office behind the kitchen.

"Almost." Blaine drove a small finishing nail into the trim then stood back to admire his handiwork. "This is up, but I ran out of the smaller nails. I'll bring more of what I need tomorrow. This won't fall, but don't go tugging on it or anything."

Maya shot him a withering look. "Yes, because I so often go around tugging on trim."

Blaine's lips twitched. "You have an attitude this evening. I wonder why that is."

"It's because I almost locked you in here. You're so quiet that I forgot you were in the building. I almost jumped out of my skin when I heard you."

"Yeah, that's not it."

Maya frowned. "Of course that's it. What else would it be?"

"I saw you with Nick outside."

"Oh, here we go," Maya grumbled under her breath. "I don't want to hear about how much you dislike Nick. I had to listen to that for two years in college. It was freaking painful. I'm not listening to it again."

"I didn't hate Nick."

"Of course you did. You kept telling me not to spend so much time with him."

"That was because I was jealous." Blaine's gaze was pointed when it landed on her. "We're adults now, not under-developed morons, so I can say this without feeling like an idiot. When we were together all those years ago, I didn't understand how you could have a male best friend and have it be completely platonic, especially a guy like him."

Maya made a face. "What? Why would you think there was something going on between us?"

"Because there was."

"Oh, geez." Maya was at the end of her rope. "Nick and I never touched each other. Give me a break."

"You guys touched all the time. They were just innocent touches ... that you somehow couldn't stop yourselves from making." Blaine held up his hands when it became apparent Maya was close to exploding. "There's no need to make a thing out of this. We've both moved on. We're not young and stupid. I can see the truth of the past, and I'm fine with it. Maybe you should try to see it too."

Maya was beyond annoyed. "And what is the truth of the past?"

"That you both wanted to take your friendship to another level, but you were afraid. That's what I saw back then, though I didn't know what I was seeing. I just knew I didn't like it. Since I was attached to you, I had to show my dislike for the situation by giving Nick grief."

"How healthy," Maya said primly. "I'm so glad you've figured out your old issues."

"Don't." Blaine extended a warning finger. "I'm not trying to start any shit. I'm just saying that I understand what was happening back then, even if you don't."

"Nick and I were just friends, and we're not even that any longer."

"Uh-huh." Blaine didn't look convinced. "You might want to think long and hard about why you guys fell out the way you did instead of dwelling on the fact that it happened in the first place. Maybe you'll figure things out faster if you go that route. I'm not an expert, though."

"You sound like an expert, Mr. Know-It-All." Maya knew she sounded petulant but couldn't stop herself. "Are you done here?" She didn't want to drag the conversation out a moment longer than necessary.

"Why?" Blaine's lips twitched. "Do you have somewhere to be? Are you going to track down Nick and have a fight?"

The suggestion was absurd. "No, and why would you think that? Nick and I aren't even friends any longer. Why would I track him down?"

Blaine's disappointment was obvious, but he shuttered it quickly. "It was just a suggestion. I thought maybe you would like to put an end to your misery sooner rather than later. It's obvious you want to be a masochist, though."

"I have no idea what that means."

"You'll figure it out eventually." Blaine tossed one more look at the trim then grabbed his toolbox. "I'm heading out. I'll be back tomorrow."

"Joy." Even though she was being pouty, Maya smiled. "Thanks for helping me."

"It's what I do for a living."

"Yeah, but I know you're giving me a break on your rate."

"I have a friends-and-family rate for a reason." Blaine flicked her ear and smiled. "You're always going to be my friend, even though we were young and dumb together. I happen to like you, even if you are being willfully blind."

Maya opted not to focus on that statement and instead give herself an easy out. "I'll bring coffee and doughnuts tomorrow."

"See? And you didn't think you were paying me enough." Blaine winked, then took off toward the parking lot across the street. "Find him," he ordered, not looking over his shoulder. "Things will get better if you guys scream at each other and get it out of your systems. Until one of you admits you're angry, things are going to continue to be uncomfortable."

All Maya could do as she watched him disappear into the dusk was shake her head. "I'll take it under advisement."

"You do that."

.   .   .

RATHER THAN THINK ABOUT NICK, Maya decided a visit to her mother was in order. Catherine Markham had been less than subtle at a family barbecue the previous weekend when mentioning that her only daughter's visits had been few and far between. Maya wasn't deaf or ignorant, so she took the pointed comment for what it was ... a demand. Rather than ignore her mother and wait for the inevitable explosion, Maya decided to head off any problems with an impromptu visit. What she hadn't expected was to find Melanie Griffith— Nick's mother and not *that* Melanie Griffith—having chocolate martinis with her mother on the back porch.

"Oh, hey." Maya felt unbelievably awkward when staring into Melanie's eyes. As a kid, she'd absolutely loved Melanie and not just because she served as such an effective distraction for her own mother. No, Maya loved her energy and smile, even when she was obviously unhappy with how her life had turned out. Maya had started noticing her frown in middle school, which had been caused by Nick's father. Apparently, she'd remedied that situation within the last eighteen months, because she'd moved out of the house and was living with another man, even though she hadn't divorced Nick's dad.

"Maya!" Melanie hopped to her feet and threw her arms around her. "I heard you were back in town, and I was heartbroken you hadn't stopped in to see me yet. What's up with that?" She lightly slapped Maya's wrist and giggled.

Maya couldn't hold back her smile. "How many chocolate martinis have you guys had?"

"Don't worry about it," Catherine shot back. "We're adults. We decide how much we can drink. We don't need input from daughters who can't be bothered to visit their mothers, even though they only live twelve blocks away. Yes, that's right, twelve." She bobbed her head. "I counted."

Maya held back a sigh but just barely. "You're still aces

with the guilt trip, Mother." Turning to Melanie, she said, "As for stopping in for a visit ... um ... I don't know where you live now."

"Oh." Melanie's hand flew to her mouth, and she let loose a giggle before sliding back into the patio chair she'd been reclining in when Maya arrived. "I didn't think about that. I'm over on Aspen Lane, down by the park."

"Oh." Maya nodded. "Okay, well, I'll try to figure out a time to drop in and hang out."

"She's very busy," Catherine added. "She doesn't have time for her own mother, let alone you."

"Oh, can we not do this?" Maya's irritation was on full display as she planted her hands on her hips. "I said I was sorry. I'm doing the best I can. I have a deadline I have to hit, Mother. I'm trying to be responsible by devoting the necessary time and attention to my new cafe, and that might not mean you can have every single one of your needs met at the exact time you want them to be met. I'm sorry."

"She's basically telling you to stop being a pill," Melanie offered helpfully.

"Yes, I figured that out myself." Catherine inclined her head toward one of the open chairs. "Sit."

Maya knew better than to argue. She was essentially stuck on her mother's patio until she could make an escape, and that wouldn't happen anytime soon.

"Do you have enough money?" Catherine asked, her expression impossible to read.

"What?"

"Do you have enough money?" Catherine enunciated each word with precision. "If you need a little extra to stop panicking—and perhaps visit your mother more often—I'm sure your father will help."

Maya had to bite back a growl. *How can she not realize that is the last thing I want?* "I've got it, Mother. I just need to stick to a schedule. I don't need help."

"I wish you wouldn't say 'Mother' in that manner."

"You *are* my mother."

"Yes, but when you say it the way you do, it makes me think you want to add another word behind it."

"Trucker?" Maya couldn't contain her grin.

"Essentially." Catherine flashed a smile, then shook her head. "You came at a good time. Melanie and I were just discussing your relationship with Nick. We think it's high time you got your heads out of your asses and made us grand-mothers."

Maya blinked rapidly several times. "Um…"

"You're embarrassing her," Melanie said with a playful slap. "Look at her face."

"Nick and I aren't exactly close any longer," Maya offered, grappling for the right thing to say. She had no idea what Melanie was and wasn't aware of, because Lindsey had told her that Nick essentially cut off contact with his mother when she left his father, who still lived across the street from Maya's parents. The whole thing was awkward.

"Oh, give me a break." Catherine snorted. "You guys are just messed up right now. You'll sort things out now that you're back in the same place. We have a bet as to when it's going to happen and everything."

"Is that a fact?" Maya asked, annoyed. "When do you think we're going to make up?"

"I have Friday," Melanie volunteered. "Your mother thinks you'll be more stubborn than that. She has next Wednesday."

"Well, awesome." Maya flashed a sarcastic thumbs-up. "I'm glad to see you guys have taken such an interest in something that doesn't concern you."

"Oh, don't take that tone with me," Catherine warned her, her eyes flashing. "It's not our fault you and Nick let your immaturity take the lead. It's not as if we didn't warn you what would happen if you moved to different cities after graduation. You just thought you knew better, and now look at the mess we're in."

"He's the one who stopped calling," Maya snapped before she could bank her emotions.

"Yet he says the same thing about you," Melanie mused, grinning. Her smile only lasted a few seconds. "At least he said that when he was still talking to me."

Maya had a million questions, things she'd always wondered. Melanie's marriage—or lack thereof—was none of her business, however. She had a right to privacy. Plus, there was no way for Maya to ask questions without looking like an idiot.

"Oh, it's going to be okay," Catherine reassured her, leaning closer and gripping her friend's wrist. "Nick is just going through something. He feels he has to stand with Hank because it's disloyal otherwise. Besides, Hank isn't holding it together. Nick is all he has right now. Things will work out."

Maya's heart constricted, but she didn't say anything.

"I mean, Maya is here now," Catherine continued, barely taking a breath. "She and Nick are going to make up. Then she'll fix the problem. We all know it's going to happen. They're not going to be able to hide behind a friendship any longer because they ruined the friendship. It's going to be different this time. You'll see ... as long as Maya doesn't screw it up."

"And on that note..." Maya pushed herself to a standing position. "I think I'm going to go."

"Oh, you don't have to go," Melanie protested, wiping away her tears. "I didn't mean to drive you away."

"It's fine. I have things to do." She pinned her mother with a serious look. "It's not my fault you were ass deep in chocolate martinis when I got here. I expect a credit on my ledger."

Catherine's eye roll was pronounced. "Just go. If you're not going to help, you're going to be a hindrance. I don't have time for that."

"I love you too, Mother," Maya sang as she headed out.

"Don't forget your father's birthday is in two weeks. You'd better get him something good, and the potential for grand-children with Nick sounds like the perfect gift."

Maya thought her stomach might actually twist so tightly that it could explode. "I'll give it some thought."

"That's exactly what I want to hear."

MAYA COULD'VE GONE HOME TO THE cabin she was renting, poured a glass of wine, and enjoyed the beautiful night from her teeny-tiny patio. Instead, she headed for the high school parking lot. She had no idea why she picked that location, but she couldn't stop herself.

She walked because there was no reason to drive in Bellaire unless it was raining or you were in a hurry, and when she got to the paved parking lot, it was quiet. The only sound came from the nesting birds and the bugs in the distance.

"And here we are," she murmured as she stood in the middle of the court. "Here we are again."

Briefly, she pressed her eyes shut and thought of high school. A memory quickly filled her head. Nothing about it stood out, yet she would never forget it.

"Hand me that ball," Nick growled, wrestling with Maya. Her back was pressed to his chest. "It's my turn. You're cheating."

"Oh, I would never cheat." Maya was all smiles despite the sweat rolling down her face. "You're just a poor loser."

"Oh, that's rich coming from you. Give me that ball!"

"No. It's my turn. You're cheating."

"You're the cheater."

"Oh, I never cheat. I'm as loyal as the day is long." When she turned, she found her mouth was directly in front of his. "It's my turn."

"Oh yeah?" Nick's eyes flashed with something she didn't recognize. Heat? Annoyance? Both? *"What if I keep you like this and don't let either of us shoot?"*

"Just like this?" Maya pressed closer to him.

"Yup. Just like this." Nick licked his lips.

They stared at each other for a long time, to the point that Maya wondered if she'd forgotten how to speak. The air between them was supercharged, as if it might catch fire, and Maya had to wet her lips if she didn't want to be singed by it.

"Nick..." Whatever she was going to say died on her lips thanks to new voices, the sounds of friends rushing in from the darkness to take over the court.

Nick looked torn when he released her, but he had a smile on his face as the others approached. "You're late. We should do teams. Maya is on mine."

"Maya is always on your team," Bear shot back. "You guys never separate. That's hardly new."

"Well, it's also not going to change." Nick smirked. "We'll be skins. You guys can be shirts."

Maya slapped his arm, sending another jolt through her at the contact. She forced herself to speak calmly despite her fluttering emotions. "That's the stupidest joke," she said. "I'm never going to be skins."

"Never say never." Nick's smile was beautiful. "There's always a first time for everything."

Maya was lost in the memory, to the point that she didn't realize she was no longer alone. Then she heard a throat clearing, and she didn't have to turn to know who had joined her.

"Nick."

"Hey, Maya," he said quietly.

Four

NICK

Nick's heart stuttered as he took in Maya's surprised face. *What is she doing here?* He rubbed his hands over the front of his jogging pants and regarded the woman who used to be his best friend.

"Is this yours?" Maya held up the ball. She looked flummoxed.

Nick shook his head. "No. I was just out for a walk."

"At night?"

He shrugged. "I like to walk when it's quiet."

"I can see that." Maya held the ball against her hip. "We used to play basketball when it was quiet. I guess things really do change."

Nick gave a small smile. "Pickup games still happen here. Daily. I played with Bear earlier. The kids don't come here after dark any longer, though. The new hangout place is the eighteenth green on the golf course."

Maya's eyebrows rose. "Seriously?"

He laughed. "Yeah. They think they're the first to ever do it. They hike in the long way too. They don't know about the ambulance codes for the property owners."

"Oh, what amateurs." Maya's laugh made his stomach constrict. He remembered the sound so well. It almost hurt to hear it.

She tossed him the ball. "How about a game for old times' sake."

"You want to play a game with me?"

Maya hesitated. "A game of one-on-one," she clarified. "I haven't played in forever."

"I bet that means you're rusty." Nick dribbled the ball three times then pulled back to shoot. The audible *swish* filled the air. "I'm not rusty. I think I'm out of your league now."

Maya had always been competitive, unhealthily so. When playing basketball with the boys—an everyday occurrence during her teen years—she'd insisted they not treat her any differently. She'd earned a reputation as an aggressive player, something Nick encouraged because he enjoyed watching her victory dance on a regular basis.

"How about we play Horse?" he countered after a few seconds. "You need to get back in shape if you want to play one-on-one."

Maya frowned. "I can play one-on-one. Just because it's been years doesn't mean I'll be bad."

Nick made an exasperated sound deep in his throat. "Some things never change. Can't we just have a lighthearted game? I'm not sure we need to add the intensity of your refusal to lose to ... this." He didn't come right out and say what he was thinking. He didn't have to.

Maya clearly understood, because she nodded. "Fine. You go first."

Nick eyed her for a long beat then moved to the free throw line and threw up an arcing shot that ended with nothing but net.

Maya frowned. "Even I can still make that one," she

groused as she collected the ball and moved to take his spot. "Slide over, you ... you."

Nick couldn't stop a grin from taking over his features. "You really haven't changed." He moved because it was expected. If it had been a decade before, he would've made her move him just so that he could feel her body close to his. They weren't in that place at the moment.

"I don't know about that." Maya's expression contorted in concentration, and she took a little time when aiming. Her ball banked against the board before going through the net, and she let loose a breath when she didn't miss. "Definitely rusty."

Nick smiled. "It's okay. You'll be back to fighting form in no time." He took the ball to the far side of the court, to where the darkness swallowed him, and let loose another shot. That one rimmed away. Truth be told, he hadn't put that much effort into it. He would never admit that to Maya, though.

"Denied," Maya trilled as she grabbed the ball and studied the court. She opted for a shot from the right, inside the three-point line. She obviously wasn't comfortable enough with her abilities to go for a long shot just yet. That one swished. "See? I still have what it takes." She swung her hips.

Nick smirked as he took the ball and moved toward her. "You still have the dance down. That's for sure." He waited for her to move. When she didn't, he inclined his head. "It's my turn, Dancing Queen."

She snickered and stepped away from him. "So, you're working for the school, huh?"

He'd been expecting the question. "Yeah. It just sort of worked out that way. I wanted to make a name for myself in sports rehab, but the jobs were few and far between. Then my parents ... well, I'm sure you've heard."

Maya nodded.

"I needed to come home for my dad," Nick explained as

he lined up his shot. "The only job opening I was qualified for was gym teacher. That was humbling, but I kind of enjoy it. Plus, now I get to be a basketball coach. It's not so bad."

"I'm still sorry that you didn't get everything you wanted," Maya said as she watched him sink the shot. "It's hard to accept when dreams die."

Nick sent her a sharp gaze. "Did your dreams die?"

She took the ball and dribbled it to the other side of the court, showing Nick her back. He didn't think she was going to respond, but then she finally answered, "I think everybody has to readjust their dreams at some point. I thought I would get in at one of those expensive Detroit restaurants—you know, one of the ones in the Renaissance Center or out in West Bloomfield—and I would be able to save up money for my own restaurant in five years or so because I was just that good."

"That didn't work?"

"No." When Maya turned, anguish lined her eyes. "It turns out I wasn't as good a chef as I thought I was."

"That's crap!" Nick exploded.

Maya jolted at his vehemence.

"It's crap," Nick repeated, adjusting his tone. "You used to cook for me all the time. I happen to know how talented you are. I've never had food that good since ... since..."

"Since?" she asked with a small smile.

Nick wasn't in the mood to talk about their past. He needed to make sure she didn't broach the subject, because he simply wasn't ready. If talk turned to their breaking apart, he wouldn't be able to take it. He'd shoved Maya into a little corner of his heart long ago, and accessing that corner seemed like a big hassle he wasn't ready to brave. "Just suffice it to say you're a good cook."

Maya gave a little laugh before moving to the top of the

key to throw up a shot. She missed, and the frown that marred her face upon realizing it tugged at Nick's heartstrings.

"It sounds to me like you're being smart about things," Nick said as he retrieved the ball and debated his next shot. "Restaurants are iffy propositions. I saw a documentary on one of the streaming channels—I think it was Netflix—and they said the bulk of new restaurants fail within five years. The ones that survive are the ones where the owner knows the market and gives customers exactly what they're looking for."

"You saw a documentary on Netflix?" Maya chuckled. "That sounds like a weird watch for you. I get it, though. I saw the same documentary."

Nick couldn't admit—even to himself—why he'd watched the documentary. He decided to ignore the statement. "I think a café is a smart move. This town hasn't had a good coffee shop in two years. It's too small for a Starbucks, but you could provide exactly what we need. I think you'll do well right out of the gate."

"I hope so." Maya's earnest gaze locked with his. "I figured that everybody loves coffee. Young. Old. In-between. Everybody needs their daily caffeine fix."

"It's definitely smart." Nick absently sank a shot. "I think you're going to do well."

"I hope so." Maya took the ball and moved to stand next to him. "My mother doesn't think I'm doing the right thing. She believes I should take money from my father and open a restaurant willy-nilly without putting the proper research in."

"Your mother has always been impulsive," Nick countered. "The thing is she has faith in you. You should've heard her when she announced you were coming up here to open your own place. She was so proud. Sure, she doesn't always show her pride in the right way. But that doesn't mean she doesn't feel it."

Maya's jaw dropped. "You talked to my mother about my moving home?"

Nick was caught, and he knew it. Sheepishly, he slid his eyes to her. He might not have wanted to talk about their past, but there was no way he would get out of the conversation completely unscathed. "I ran into her at the park. They were having a festival, and I heard her talking. She said you were coming back. I might have questioned her about it."

"*Might* have?"

Nick's lips curved. "Fine. I asked. Sue me."

Maya's laugh somehow arrived from the past on a rocket ship that was aimed straight at his heart. "I asked about you before I came back too," she admitted. "I knew from my mother that you'd come back about a year ago. It hurt when I heard about it from somebody else."

Nick touched his tongue to his top lip and thought hard about what he was going to say next. "I don't know how to feel about you. All my memories of this place are wrapped around you, yet I'm really mad at you, Maya."

Maya's head bobbed. "I feel exactly the same way. It's like I need to know you're okay, but I'm still really mad at you. I don't know how to explain it."

"Why would you be mad at me?"

"Um ... because you stopped calling."

Nick made a strangled huffing sound. "You stopped calling first."

"No, it was you." Defiance lit Maya's eyes as her hands landed on her narrow hips. "I was so tired back then. You remember Sergei? That guy I was working for? He just would not let up. He was constantly berating me. I wanted to call you, but it was always so late at night when I got a chance, and I knew you had to be up in a few hours. I didn't want to wake you. I don't know if you recall it or not, but you're cranky when you get woken up in the middle of the night."

Nick wanted to argue with her, but he knew she was speaking the truth. Besides, the anguish on her face was enough to check his righteous indignation. "The same thing happened to me. I had terrible days. I hated the head of the clinic where I was working. By the time I was finished with my shifts, though, you were at work. I knew I couldn't call you before work, because you were tired and needed your sleep."

A rueful expression crossed her face. "The truth is those are excuses. There was more."

"More?" Nick's heart rolled. *What is she talking about?* "What more?"

"I was embarrassed." Maya looked as if she was struggling to get out the words. "I was embarrassed about being on the lowest rung on the totem pole and about Sergei sexually harassing me on a daily basis. I was just ... embarrassed, and I didn't want you feeling sorry for me."

Nick's eyes filled with fire, and he thought his heart might pound right out of his chest. "He sexually harassed you?"

Maya groaned. "I probably should've kept that to myself."

"No." Nick vehemently shook his head. "Why didn't you tell me? I would've made time to drive to you and handle the situation."

"And get me fired?"

"I ... guess." Nick's shoulders slumped. "You were afraid I would go after him and ruin everything you'd been working toward."

"Maybe a little."

"It's still annoying you went through that without me," he growled. "If I ever see that guy, I'm going to pop him in the face. I get it, though."

"You do?"

"I do." Nick regarded her. "I really and truly do. I didn't want you to know how badly I was struggling, either, although it was nothing compared to what you were dealing with. I just felt like I couldn't keep up. I had a lot to learn, and I wasn't retaining the information very well. With the added pressure I was feeling because of Camille, something had to give."

"Camille." Maya made a face. "I'm so glad you chose her over me."

"I didn't choose her over you," Nick shot back. "She was there. With me."

"Because she invited herself along," Maya muttered.

That elicited a smile from Nick, the years of separation falling away. He remembered every single one of her expressions. They still had their rapport. It felt as if nothing had changed, yet everything had.

"At first, I was glad she was there." Nick struggled to get the words out. "I was in a new city. You were always my safety blanket. At least I knew her."

"But?" Maya prodded. "You obviously didn't get married or anything. Which ... good job." She flashed a cynical thumbs-up.

Nick barked out a laugh. "But I came to realize she wasn't a substitute for you. I was miserable not being able to talk to you. It felt like my right arm had been amputated. You were always my best friend, and I needed you. Losing you made me bitter."

"What did losing her make you?"

"It was easier once I ended things with her," Nick admitted. "She ... got a little full of herself at some point. I was struggling with our friendship falling apart. She seemed giddy about it. Cutting her out of my life wasn't difficult. I just ... did it."

"Then you started over without anybody to help," Maya mused.

"You did the same thing, didn't you?"

"Yeah, but it was hard. I don't recommend it. Zero stars."

Nick smiled again. "We might've technically been adults,

Maya, but we were still kids. We were grappling with stuff we didn't know how to deal with. I think being able to resent you and blame my unhappiness on you made it so that my life in Grand Rapids was more palatable."

"But eventually, you realized you didn't want to be there," Maya noted. "You came home."

He wet his lips as he searched for the right words. "When we were growing up here, all I could think about was getting away. When I was there, alone, all I could think about was coming home. And when I got here, it was a struggle. People were always asking me about you."

"Yeah." Maya looked morose. "I've had at least thirty people ask me about you since I got back. I think they know we're not talking. They just want gossip."

"Aren't we, though?" Nick gestured between them. "We're talking right now. That's more than we've done in eight years."

"It *is* more than we've done. It feels natural too."

"It does, and I'm kind of angry with myself for not reaching out to you years ago." Nick had thought it would be difficult to admit but being with her felt effortless. That made him angry, but mostly with himself. "Yeah, we had a rough year. Maybe we were always going to end up splintering for that year or even two. That doesn't mean I couldn't have called you three years after the fact. I bet you still have the same freaking phone number."

Maya nodded. "Yeah. Do you?"

He nodded.

"That makes me sad," Maya said softly. "I was going to call you so many times. I just wanted to hear your voice. The longer it went, though, the harder it got. Then eventually, I knew I couldn't just pick up and call you out of the blue. It was too late."

"Maya, I don't think it's ever too late. We're adults now—

like, real adults—but that doesn't mean it's too late to capture the magic of our childhood. Maybe we're both here now for a reason. Maybe that reason is to be friends again.

"I'm not saying it's going to be easy," he continued. "It's not as if that bond is going to instantly spring back and be as strong as it was. We can start over, though. We can try again. I mean, we're here together right now. What is this if not trying?"

A tear slid down Maya's cheek.

"Oh, none of that." Nick dropped the ball and moved closer to her, his thumb instantly swiping at the errant tear. "I hate it when you cry. How can you not know that? Also, it was just a suggestion. If you don't want to try, then we don't have to."

"God, you're so stupid." Maya slapped his chest. "I'm not crying because I don't want to try. I'm crying because that's exactly what I've wanted to hear for eight freaking years."

"Oh." Nick was taken aback as he regarded her. "So, this is good, right?"

She nodded and sniffled. "It's good."

"Great. I guess that means we should hug. I mean, friends hug." He opened his arms before she could respond, and Maya automatically stepped into them.

Nick closed his eyes when she melted against him, and he was rocked by the sense of rightness that flowed through him. *Why did I wait so long? Why didn't I call her sooner? Why did I punish myself rather than admit I need her in my life?*

He didn't have answers to any of those questions. All he knew was that they were finally ready to put the past behind them. For the moment, that was more than enough.

Five

MAYA

Maya was feeling lighter after her time with Nick. It didn't feel quite like old times, but it was better than it had been. They'd cleared the air, both taking responsibility for the end of their friendship. Maybe they could get back on track. They'd made enough progress for her to get worked up and start cooking, which was why she had to make three trips into the coffee shop from her vehicle the next morning. She'd decided to do a sample tasting with her friends, and that required free food, which she had in spades after her marathon cooking session.

"Wow." Lindsey, a thermal cup in her hand, looked surprised when she slid into the shop. "Somebody has been busy."

"It's a taste extravaganza," Maya announced with a grin. "I had some extra time on my hands last night."

"Have you tried sex?" Lindsey shook her head as she approached. "Or at least maybe some strenuous masturbation? I mean that's a lot of free time there, my friend."

Maya shot Lindsey a withering look. "I want a firm idea of

what I should be serving when I open. There's not much time."

"Hey, I'm never going to turn down free food." Lindsey hopped onto one of the stools and pulled one of the huge Tupperware containers toward her. "What are our options?"

"Most of it is baked goods today. The kitchen will be finished in three days. That's when I'm going to do a similar sampling for breakfast and lunch sandwiches."

"Ooh, make sure you remember me that day." Lindsey pulled a pastry out of the container and took a bite. Her mouth was still full when she spoke again. "So, I hear you and Nick made up last night."

Maya froze, dumbfounded. "How...?"

Lindsey smirked. "I know all and see all."

"How really?"

"I sent Bear out for milk last night," she replied. "If there's not milk for cereal in the morning, then I have a gaggle of unhappy kids. If the kids aren't happy, then mama isn't happy, and if mama isn't happy, the world burns."

Maya had to swallow a snort. "You know, you really make the idea of having kids one day sound divine. I can't tell you how much I'm looking forward to motherhood."

"You'll be fine. Just don't have a baseball team. That was my mistake. Also, don't teach them to talk. There's nothing better than a pile of adorable mutes. It's when they start talking back that things fall apart."

"Uh-huh." Maya knew Lindsey loved her children. "You just talk to hear yourself talk sometimes, don't you?"

"Pretty much." Lindsey finished off the first pastry. "That's a keeper." She reached for another. "So, back to Nick," she prodded.

Maya had known that moving back to Bellaire would mean a change in lifestyle. Bellaire was a small town. Everybody knew everybody. That meant keeping secrets was virtually impossible. Still, she hadn't expected news to travel quite so fast. "What do you want to know?" she asked, resigned.

"Well, for starters, how much tongue was involved?"

"I don't understand."

Lindsey waggled her eyebrows.

"Oh, don't be gross." Maya made a face. "Why does your mind always go there? Nick and I were never that way with each other."

"No, you never *admitted* you wanted to be that way. There's a difference."

"Well, I don't know what to tell you." Maya held her palms out. "There was no tongue action. Other than talking, I mean." She braced her hands on the counter as she thought back to their conversation. "We kind of made up."

"Kind of?" Lindsey arched an eyebrow. She had frosting on her cheek but made no move to wipe it off. "I'm going to need more than that."

"We both took responsibility for what happened and agreed that maybe our being back here in Bellaire at the same time was fated or something. We want to see if we can salvage the friendship now that we're together again."

"You both took responsibility, huh?" Lindsey's expression was hard to read. "And what exactly did you take responsibility for?"

"You know, falling out of touch."

"Actually, I don't know. You've been less than forthcoming when it comes to telling me what happened."

"Nothing happened. It wasn't some big blowup. We just lost contact."

"That is the most boring rom-com plot ever. You're going to have to do better."

A chuckle escaped as Maya opened the other pastry containers. "I'm sorry to disappoint. And this isn't a rom-com."

"No? What genre is it?"

"Horror?"

"Please. You'd both be the first to die in the zombie apocalypse. You have no idea how to survive when the world is falling apart. This isn't a horror novel."

"Then what kind of novel do you think it is?"

"Um ... romance. You guys are hitting all the tropes. Sure, your backstory is weak—I mean, there has to be more than you're telling from the fight eight years ago—but the tropes are all there."

"I don't even know what you're saying."

"This is a friends-to-lovers story. It's one of the most popular tropes for a reason. I should know. It's one of my favorites."

"You read romance books?"

"I have more kids than I can keep track of. Of course I read romance books. Heck, Bear reads them, although he just likes the sex scenes. He also says they give him ideas when I'm mad and he needs to get me to forgive him."

"Bear has issues."

"Bear is a man's man," Lindsey replied. "He's not like Nick, who has a lot of feelings. Bear either doesn't recognize he has feelings or doesn't care. Nick thinks about his feelings, and he holds grudges—just look at his poor mother—and he spends all his time remembering the one who got away."

Maya focused on the pastries, unsure how to respond.

"That's you, in case you're wondering," Lindsey pressed. "You're the one who got away."

"Have you ever considered that you're just making that up in your head?"

"Nope. Everybody saw it when you guys were teenagers. Heck, the adults started making jokes about it when you were in middle school. We all knew you were destined for each other. Then when we heard you were going to the same college, we assumed that was where it was going to happen. Once you were away from the prying eyes and ears of the town, you were finally going to get your shot, then you didn't."

"I feel like I should apologize for disappointing the entire town," Maya mused.

"Don't worry about that. It's enough that you apologize to me." Lindsey winked, then sobered. "I know you don't want to hear it, but have you ever considered the real problem you and Nick had back then was that you both wanted to be together, and you didn't know how to tell each other?"

"No." Maya shook her head. "That never once entered my mind. We were friends. Nothing more."

"Oh, right," Lindsey said, obviously annoyed. "It's going to take you forever to figure things out. I just know it. I could really use the money from that pool too. You're totally going to screw things up for me."

"Well, I would hate to screw things up for you," Maya drawled, resting her elbows on the counter. "How do you feel about the second pastry?"

"Dude, it's a pastry. I'm going to eat it regardless. The only way I wouldn't eat it is if it had cherry flavoring. You know how I feel about cherry flavoring."

"Yes, it's rubbish. I know. I—"

The sound of the door opening made Maya look up. More than once, somebody from town—and sometimes tourists—had entered the shop, assuming it was open. Her admonishment that they were closed died on her lips when she saw Nick, however.

"Hey." Her cheeks burned at his smile.

"Hey." He looked just as awkward as she felt. "I ... um ... thought I would stop by and see the place. You've done a lot."

"Yeah." Maya wiped her hands on her jeans as she emerged

from behind the counter. "It's coming along. I'm going to do slate-gray trim with grayish purple booths."

"And she won't stop talking about it," Lindsey added as she licked her fingers.

Nick shot her an amused look. "Good morning, Lindsey."

"Oh, so formal. I think it's funny that you're greeting me that way when you were drinking beer with my husband until two in the morning this weekend, not caring in the least that Sundays are Bear's mornings to feed the kids, and he was too hungover to do it."

"Yes, this feels like a conversation I don't want to be having." Despite his words, Nick ambled over to Lindsey and pressed a friendly kiss to her cheek. "Bear is a lucky man."

"He is," Lindsey agreed. "Speaking of lucky men, I hear you and Maya made up last night."

"Really?" Nick's eyes slid to Maya. "Talking about me, are you?"

Maya practically tripped over her tongue. "She knew. Bear saw us on the basketball court last night."

"That's true," Lindsey added. "Bear did see you. Apparently, he didn't spy for very long, though, which is totally a failing on his part. He was afraid the milk would go bad. I have no idea how much tongue was involved in your reunion, and I'm dying to know."

Nick made a face. "Why do you always have to take it there?"

"That's what I do," Lindsey replied. "So, how much tongue again?"

"Knock it off." Nick lightly flicked Lindsey's ear, causing Maya to marvel at his easygoing demeanor despite her busybody tendencies. "What's all this?" he asked as he looked over the containers.

"Maya is doing a taste test," Lindsey replied. "She thinks

there are people out there who are actually going to dislike certain types of pastries. As if that's really a thing."

Nick chuckled. "Right? Who doesn't like anything that falls in the pastry group?" He slid his eyes to Maya. "Can I have one?" He almost looked nervous to ask the question. "I haven't had your cream cheese Danish in so long that I think it might shock my system. I'm willing to risk it, though."

Maya chuckled. "That always was your favorite."

"See, I could go so many ways with him regarding the withdrawal because he didn't have access to your cream cheese Danish that I think my head might implode," Lindsey complained.

Maya shot her a quelling look. "How about you don't go there, huh?"

"No, I just need to sort my thoughts to come up with the right zinger. You guys carry on doing ... whatever it is you're doing. I just need a moment."

Maya didn't bother to hide her eye roll as she focused on Nick. "I've changed the recipe a bit since we were in school." She was suddenly nervous, although she had no idea why. "You'll have to tell me what you think." She shoved the container with the cream cheese Danish in it toward Nick. "You were always my guinea pig. I bet there were some of my pastries you were happy to say goodbye to."

"It's like you just keep giving me openings, and I have no idea what to do with them," Lindsey lamented. "This is so unfair."

"Eat your pastry," Maya growled. Her attention was solely for Nick, who looked unbelievably happy when he grabbed a Danish.

"Oh, I've had dreams about your Danish," Nick said.

"Good grief!" Lindsey smacked her forehead. "Why are you torturing me with an overabundance of material?"

Maya decided to ignore her and instead focused on Nick as

he took a bite. Her heart pounded as he chewed, then her stomach constricted when he didn't immediately respond. "You hate it."

"I do not," Nick shot back. "I love it. I just need more than one bite to form an opinion."

"Since when is that the case?" Maya planted her hands on her hips. "You used to tell me your opinion when I was still putting the ingredients together."

"And if I remember correctly, you told me I was wrong for doing that," Nick shot back. "Wasn't it you who said three bites was necessary to acclimate and establish?"

Maya frowned. "Yeah, but you never listened."

"Oh, stuff it." His left hand shot out and covered her mouth as he shoved more pastry into his mouth with his right. "You're ruining my foodgasm."

"And the hits just keep on coming," Lindsey complained.

Nick didn't drop his hand until he'd finished the Danish. "That was better than I remembered. I seriously think I just peaked for the day. There's no place to go but down."

"Oh, and now you're trying to kill me," Lindsey muttered. "I can't believe you just said that with a straight face."

Nick gave her a murderous glare. Apparently, the "going down" bit was too much for even him. "Maya, they're great. I mean, absolutely perfect. I didn't think you could improve on them, and you did. I'm in awe."

Maya rubbed her hands together, pleased. "Thank you. So, you definitely think they should be on the menu, right?"

"I definitely think I'm going to be eating your stuff every single day." He jabbed a finger in Lindsey's direction when she opened her mouth. "You can let some of them go."

"It's like you don't know me at all," Lindsey complained.

Nick smirked. "You know, Maya, I don't know what your business plan is here, but if you want to make some extra money, I think you should go to the high school."

Maya was all for making extra money. In that particular instance, however, she had no idea how that would work. "How am I supposed to make money at the high school?"

"Yeah, she's a little old to be a prostitute," Lindsey offered. "Plus, kids today don't have money. If she's going to go that route—you know, pairing food with porn—then she should probably aim at the parents."

"And just when I think you can't get any worse," Nick complained. "Good grief. I wasn't talking about that. I was talking about a coffee cart."

"A coffee cart?" Maya perked up immediately. "How would that work? Like ... would they let me set up something in the hallway by the lockers every morning?" The gears in her mind were already turning.

"Probably not," Nick replied. "I think the parents would complain about that. It would be a lot of work too. I was thinking more along the lines of bringing a coffee cart to the sporting events. Like ... at home basketball games, you could set up in the hallway and make a mint. People love pastries and caffeine."

"Oh, boy, do we," Lindsey added.

"I'm being serious," Nick insisted. "You're not going to be open nights anyway, right? This would make extra money, and I'm convinced you would double your profits right out of the gate if you made the effort."

"Wow." Maya had no clue what to make of the idea. "That's really smart." Her eyes locked with Nick's concerned ones. "I don't know what to say."

Confused, Nick glanced around. "Say about what? It was just a suggestion."

Maya didn't respond immediately. Instead, she threw her arms around Nick. "It's a great idea, and if I can get the school to agree, that eases my fears a great deal. I can't believe I didn't think of it."

She held him tightly, closing her eyes. When his arms came around her to return the hug, a jolt ran through her. Their bodies melted against each other, warmth passing between them, and for a moment, Maya wondered if Lindsey was right. *Did the friendship fall apart because we were destined to be more?* She almost immediately pushed the notion out of her head. That was ridiculous. She and Nick thrived on being friends. It could never be anything more between them. When she moved to pull back, Nick held on longer than she was anticipating. That meant she had to hold him again, or things would turn awkward.

When they finally pulled back at the same time, Nick smiled softly. "You're going to have to get permission from the school to sell on the grounds. I can't grant you permission for that."

"I know." Maya's smile was so wide that it almost swallowed her face. "It's something that could totally make things easier for me, though. I can't tell you how much I appreciate the idea."

"Oh, geez," Lindsey complained as she started rooting around in one of the pastry containers again. "You guys are turning this into a mutual-love society and not one of the fun ones. How long is the awkward phase going to last?"

"Until you stop talking," Nick replied.

"Oh, so forever." Lindsey's lips quirked. "Honestly, it's a really good idea. I wish I'd thought of it. I don't think you'll have any trouble getting clearance."

"No?" Maya looked hopeful. "I don't know how to thank you for this, Nick."

"I think I do." Nick searched through the cheese-pastry container and came back with five Danish. "This should do it."

Maya chuckled. "Would you like a bag for those so that you can take them to school with you?"

"That would be great." Nick beamed at her as she moved behind the counter. "As for you, stop making things weird," he ordered Lindsey. "We're working things out. That should be enough to shut you up for the foreseeable future."

"Yup, you don't even know me at all. It's hurtful. That sounds nothing like me."

"You'll survive."

"I guess we'll have to see, big boy," Lindsey countered. "Just FYI, though, nobody is going to believe you're just working on your friendship when you hug each other like that."

Maya fixed her friend with a scowl. "I would really appreciate it if you didn't make things weird."

"I can try," Lindsey replied. "But I can promise nothing. You guys are the ones setting the tone, and I can tell right now that this thing is going to take on a life of its own before it's all said and done."

Is she right? Maya didn't want to know the answer. For the moment, things were coming together—on more than one front—and that was all she cared about. "Do you want a bear claw too?" she asked Nick.

His smile told her everything she needed to know. "What do you think?"

"I think you're going to be running on sugar all day."

"There are worse things."

Six

MAYA

Maya was excited about the prospect of having a coffee cart at the school. Sure, she didn't have a cart, but that was one of those little details she would tackle after handling the big one. Once she'd cleaned up after the pastry tasting, she headed toward the high school, smiling as she walked up the front walkway and remembering her time there.

She took a breath when she walked inside and soaked in all the memories. Everywhere she turned, all she could see was Nick—well, and herself, of course. The school was full of memories, as was the town, and she was grateful she and Nick had taken the first step toward making up. That would make things easier.

Next, she needed to take a step toward her professional future, and she was all smiles as she headed toward the main office. As she walked in, a willowy brunette was coming out, and it wasn't until Maya was almost on top of the woman that she recognized her.

"C-Camille?" she sputtered. She hadn't seen the woman since a few weeks after college graduation, when Maya had managed a visit with Nick before her schedule got too busy and they'd fallen out of touch.

"Oh, hello." Camille stood ramrod straight, evidently surprised. "Maya, right?"

It took everything Maya had not to frown. No way was Camille having trouble placing her. They'd shared time with Nick for years, which meant they were forced to go on outings as a group on a regular basis.

"Have I really changed that much?" Maya forced out, keeping her expression neutral.

"I have no idea. I can't really remember you." Camille's smile was friendly enough, but something else lurked in her eyes.

You remember me, you wench. Camille was so superior. She'd been impossible to deal with when they were both in their early twenties and Camille was desperate for Nick's attention. Maya had hoped Camille would outgrow that. *Obviously not.*

Actually, if Maya was being honest with herself, she had hoped to never see Camille again. Apparently, she wasn't that lucky.

"I had no idea you were living here," Maya said when neither of them had spoken for a full ten seconds. She was bad with uncomfortable silences. "I thought you lived over in Traverse City or something."

"Well, the nice thing about being an adult is you can move wherever you want." Camille showed her teeth when she smiled, reminding Maya of a mean dog—one of those yippy ones that humped legs and bit by way of greeting.

"Okay, then." Maya forced herself to smile. "It was great seeing you." She moved to edge around Camille, but the brunette readjusted so that she had no room to navigate.

"I heard you were back in town," Camille started.

"Yet you couldn't remember me."

Camille pretended Maya hadn't spoken. "I understand you're opening a hot dog stand."

Maya didn't consider herself a violent person—well, mostly—but for a moment, she imagined jumping on Camille and ripping out all that perfect hair, shoving it into her mouth, and gagging her. "Coffee shop," Maya corrected sharply. "I'm opening a coffee shop."

"Caffeine is bad for your skin."

So is my cutting your skin off and feeding it to zombies. It took everything Maya had to refrain from yelling at Camille. The woman pushed every single one of her buttons. "There are trade-offs in life," Maya replied sweetly. "Caffeine is one of them. If you'll excuse me." She gestured toward the office.

"Are you here to see Nick?" Camille looked smug. "He doesn't work in the office."

"I'm here to talk to the principal about something that doesn't concern you," Maya fired back, finally allowing her annoyance to creep into her voice.

"Nick isn't in there. He's in the gym. He's the gym teacher."

"Thanks. I wouldn't have been able to figure that out if you hadn't talked to me as if I were four," Maya shot back before she could gain control of her tongue. "Now, if you'll excuse me." She was more forceful when she pushed past Camille to enter the office. Then something occurred to her.

"Did you move here to be closer to Nick? I mean, are you being a creepy stalker or something?"

Camille shot her a withering look. "Are you being serious right now?"

"It's just a question."

"I'm here because this is where I got a job. I happen to love the town—the lake is amazing, and I enjoy skiing and golfing —and this is now my home. I don't chase men ... unlike you."

Maya briefly saw red. "What now?"

"Nothing." Camille gave an imperious hand wave. "I really need to be getting back to my class."

"Yeah, you do that." Maya glared at her retreating back in an attempt to manifest superpowers and burn her from afar. When that didn't work, she shook her head and walked into the office ... and ran right into another blast from the past.

"Carrie?" Maya laughed when she saw the strawberry blonde she'd graduated with behind the front desk. "Carrie Conners? I didn't know you worked here."

"Maya?" Carrie hopped to her feet and hurried around the desk for a hug. "I heard you were back in town. Also, it's Carrie Hamilton now." Carrie's cheeks reddened. "I married Brett Hamilton."

"Really?" Maya tried to wrap her head around that. Brett had been two years ahead of them in high school and something of a jerk, if she remembered correctly.

Carrie, clearly understanding where Maya's thoughts had gone, made a choking noise. "He's not as bad as he was. He was just a blowhard back then because he was insecure. He's cool now."

"Well, as long as you're happy." Maya meant it. "I didn't realize you worked here."

"A lot of our graduating class is still in town," Carrie replied as she returned to her chair. "Only a few people got away, including you and Nick. Now you're both back." She looked momentarily thoughtful.

"I guess we are," Maya agreed.

"I hear you're opening a coffee shop." Carrie switched gears fast. "I can't tell you how badly this town needs one. I'm excited that you're doing it. So much that I can't even say."

"I'm excited too," Maya admitted. "That's why I'm here. I was hoping to talk to the principal. Nick had an idea about my opening a coffee cart at games and stuff, and I wanted to see if it was a possibility before I spent any money getting a coffee cart made."

"Oh, that's a great idea." Carrie's eyes sparkled. "Kids today are different from us. You know how we always hid underneath the bleachers to smoke pot and went into the woods to drink? These kids drink coffee and look down their noses at stuff like that."

"They sound fun."

"Oh, they're real little shits." Carrie's ski-slope nose wrinkled. "I think they might be more tolerable if they bothered to have a drink or two. They're too good for that, though."

Maya worked her jaw, debating. "Do you and Brett have kids?"

Carrie snorted. "We have a daughter. She's three and has her daddy wrapped around her little finger. She's not a teenager yet, so she still has time to turn into a little shit too."

"Maybe just have the one kid," Maya suggested.

"It's been discussed. Brett wouldn't mind another, but I'm not so sure."

"Go with your gut." Maya turned the conversation back to her reason for being there. "So, who is the principal these days? Do you think he'll be open to my coffee suggestion?"

"Well, up until a year ago, it was Jethro Carmichael."

Maya frowned. "Really? The old science teacher with the glass eye that he popped into his mouth, then smiled with the eye staring back at us?"

"That would be the one. He retired, though, because he also thought the kids were little shits, and it didn't go over well with the parents. You're in luck because his replacement is Will Baxter."

A smile spread across Maya's face. "No way."

"Yes, the Will Baxter who was great friends with Nick while harboring a secret crush on you."

Maya shook her head. "He did not have a crush on me."

"Oh, *puh-leez*." Carrie rolled her eyes so hard it was a miracle she didn't fall over. "Will practically drooled whenever you were in the room. He just didn't make a move because he didn't want to step on Nick's toes."

"Why would that be a thing?"

Carrie's eyes narrowed. "Seriously?"

Maya held out her hands. "Yeah, seriously, why would Nick have cared?"

"*Seriously?*" Carrie repeated.

"Yes," Maya insisted.

"Girlfriend, you're a moron." Carrie made a ridiculous face, then pressed a button on her phone.

A man answered after two rings. "I'm busy."

"You're doing your stupid fantasy football stuff, and you shouldn't be gambling on the taxpayers' dime," Carrie fired back. "You have a visitor anyway."

"Is it Helena Cartwright? I don't want to see her. That kid of hers is a menace and deserved his two-day suspension. She frightens me, though. She has those weird fingernails that could put somebody's eye out. I don't want it to be my eye, Carrie. I wouldn't look good as a pirate."

Maya had to stifle a giggle. Will sounded exactly the same.

"It's not Helena, and you're on speakerphone, dumbass," Carrie snapped.

Maya could practically hear Will panicking.

"Take me off speakerphone," he ordered.

"No. Don't you want to know who's here to see you?"

"Knowing you, I'm sure it's someone horrible. Tell me again why I haven't fired you."

"You're afraid of me."

"That would be the reason. Who is it?"

"Maya Markham."

After a pause, Will's voice lightened. "Well, why didn't you say something sooner? Let her in."

Carrie rolled her eyes and ended the call. "If you go in there right now, you'll find him sucking in his gut and fixing his hair because he's so excited."

"You're really mean to him," Maya chided as she walked toward the door.

Carrie didn't look bothered by the accusation. "It keeps me young."

"Come by the coffee shop one morning. I've been testing pastries to decide what I want, and people have been stopping in left and right."

"Nick?" Carrie's eyes gleamed with curiosity.

Maya hesitated, then nodded. "He was there this morning."

"Good. I'm glad to see you guys are getting things back on track."

"Geez. Remind me never to get on your bad side."

"That would be best."

When Maya walked into the office, Will was already on his feet to greet her—he was indeed sucking in his stomach, because he gasped when he couldn't hold his breath any longer —and they embraced.

"It's so good to see you." Will placed his hands on her shoulders and pulled back to look her up and down. "You look exactly the same."

"So do you."

"Um ... not quite." He pointed toward his middle, which had spread just a little. "Nick keeps trying to get me to play basketball with him and Bear a few nights a week. I think I like my potato chips a little too much to put them down, though."

"Don't do anything you don't want to do." Maya sat in one of the chairs across from his desk. She figured it was best to get straight to the point. "So, I have a favor to ask."

"Okay." Will sat, then steepled his fingers as he waited. "You look a little intense. Is this favor going to hurt?"

"I have no idea. It was actually Nick's idea."

"Of course it was. Way to throw him under the bus, by the way." Will shot her a thumbs-up that made her grin.

"I was thinking I might try to open a coffee cart at the games and dances. Teenagers like coffee, and since I only plan on opening the coffee shop until three every day—I think I'll lose money staying open at night—I thought it might be a good way to supplement my income."

"Kids do like coffee," Will agreed.

"Do you think it's feasible, or should I let it go before I get too attached to the idea?"

Will cocked his head, considering, then smiled. "I think it's a great idea. I'm more than willing to grant you a license to operate on school grounds—I'm the only one who can do that —but I want one thing in return."

Maya was suddenly leery. Carrie's opinion that Will had a crush on her caused her heart to skip a beat. *Is he about to ask me out?*

Will barreled forward without realizing anything had changed inside Maya. "I want twenty-five percent of the money to go to the boosters. I know that might seem like a lot, but we're trying to make it so that kids who don't have money at their disposal can play sports. This pay-to-play shit sucks. Do you think you can manage that?"

Maya was so overcome with relief that at first, all she could do was nod. "I can totally manage that, and it seems more than fair."

"Great." Will beamed at her. "I'll send you our standard contract with the details for you to look over."

"Awesome." Maya let out a breath as she stood. "Well, I guess Nick had a good idea after all."

"He did," Will agreed. "Don't let it go to his head, though. He's already unbearable."

"I'll try to refrain."

"He's in the gym if you want to see him before you go."

Maya hesitated. *Is that a good idea?* She loved the thought of seeing Nick in his new environment. "I just might do that."

She picked up the sound of a ball hitting the hardwood before she turned the corner to the gym. Nick had propped open the doors that led to the hallway, and she could hear him ordering the kids around. When she poked her head in, she found Nick pairing everybody into teams.

"Free throws," he said as he tossed a ball to one of the kids. "I want you to practice until it hurts. And only minimal trash-talking. The team with the most free throws doesn't have to clean up. That's the prize."

One of the boys, a tall one with black hair and green eyes, was the first to see Maya looking into the gym. "Can we have her as a prize instead?" he asked confidently.

Nick jerked his head toward Maya, perhaps expecting one of the school's female teachers, and smirked. "Dakota, you couldn't handle her even if you were an octopus," he chastised the boy. "Everybody, get to your free throws."

As he approached Maya, he asked, "How did it go?"

"It was great," she replied. "I just stopped by to thank you. I didn't realize Will was the principal, and he didn't give me any grief at all. He just wants twenty-five percent for the boosters, and that's more than fair."

"Will is a good guy. He's always willing to help."

Maya considered bringing up Camille, then decided against it. She didn't want to ruin what had otherwise been a magnificent day. "As I said, thank you, Nick. Being able to sell at the games will help me financially in ways you can't possibly imagine. I really appreciate the idea."

"That's what friends are for, right?" He unleashed a charming smile on her, and it was enough to rock her back on her heels.

"I missed you," she blurted.

Nick's eyes were soft when they locked with hers. "I missed you too. But we're together now. We'll figure this stuff out." He chuckled. "Don't cry." He brushed a small tear from her cheek.

The boys, who were supposed to be focused on their free throws, were fixated on Nick and Maya instead, and a series of wolf whistles echoed throughout the gym. He immediately pulled his hand back and made a face.

"What did I say?" Nick demanded.

Maya giggled. "I guess that's my cue to go. I didn't mean to disrupt your class. I just wanted to thank you."

"No thanks are necessary, Maya. You're the one doing the work. I just made a suggestion."

"Well, it's one that's going to stop me from waking up in a cold sweat every night. I really appreciate it."

"Don't be weird." Nick shook his head. "I didn't do anything."

More whistles pierced the air when Nick shifted.

"*What did I say?*" Nick bellowed.

Maya laughed again. "You seem to have firm control over your class."

"I did before you showed up. I think you got their hormones racing."

Maya tried to ignore her own racing hormones, which had made an appearance out of nowhere when he touched her. "I'll let you get back to it. Thanks again."

"I'll see you."

"You definitely will."

Seven

NICK

"I saw Maya today," Camille announced as she met Nick in the parking lot after he finished his day. If he didn't know better, he would've guessed she was waiting for him, something he wouldn't put past her. She'd managed to show up more than once when he wasn't expecting her over the past few months.

"Yeah?" Nick arched an eyebrow. "I've seen her too."

"She came in to see Will."

Nick wasn't certain what she was getting at, but he figured it was nothing good. Age had given him a better understanding of exactly who Camille was, and he didn't like anything about her. "I know. She poked her head into the gym on her way out."

"And?"

"And what?" Nick readjusted his gym bag. He changed his clothes when he finished teaching most days because he was often active with the kids.

"What was she doing here?" Camille demanded.

Though that was none of her business, it was hardly a secret either. Still, he was careful when responding. "I believe she wanted to talk over a business opportunity with him. That's my understanding anyway."

"What sort of business opportunity?"

Nick had to bite back his exasperation. "Why does it matter to you?"

"I'm just curious about whether she's going to be hanging around or not."

"And again, why does that matter to you?"

"I feel I have a right to know what's going on in my school."

"Your school?"

"I work here. It's my school."

"Whatever." Nick was too tired to deal with Camille. "She wants to run a coffee cart at games. She talked it over with Will. He thought it was a great idea because part of the money will go to help the booster club. It's not a big deal."

"I see." Camille's expression made Nick leery. "Have you two been hanging around again?"

"Why do you care, Camille?"

"I'm just curious. I never thought she was good for you. She was far too demanding. Your friendship was always ... weird. You didn't reach your full potential until she was out of your life."

"That's a load of crap." Nick made a face. "Maya never held me back. You, on the other hand..."

Camille was glowering when he risked a glance at her. "Well, that was just hurtful."

"I didn't mean for it to be hurtful. I just don't understand why you're so interested in Maya and what she's doing. It doesn't affect you."

"If she's going to be hanging around, it affects me. It also affects you."

"Yes, but I'm none of your business. This entire conversation bothers me. I think we should end it."

"Well, I'm not quite done yet." Camille kept following him toward his vehicle. "I heard you and Maya were seen together at the basketball court last night."

"You heard?" Nick slowed his pace, his brow furrowed. "Where did you hear that?" The only person he knew of who'd seen them was Bear, but he couldn't fathom a reason for his old friend to be talking to Camille, especially about anything that involved Maya.

"They were talking about it in the teacher's lounge this morning," Camille replied. "Apparently, you were seen together ... and looked chummy."

"We looked chummy?" Nick found her attitude ridiculous. "Well, if you heard it from random people in the teacher's lounge, it must be true." He threw his gym bag in the back seat of his truck. "I need to head out."

"Are you saying it's not true?" Camille pressed.

"I'm saying it's none of your business. Maya and I have been friends since we were kids. What we do in our free time isn't any of your concern."

Camille's expression darkened. "We're friends, right?"

Nick wouldn't use that word to describe their relationship. In fact, the only reason he would even say they had a relationship of any sort was because at one time, they'd been in a romantic one. He didn't have a lot of time or energy to spend on Camille, however. He had other things to worry about. "We're colleagues," he said finally.

Camille ignored his word choice. "Well, since we're friends, I think I have a right to worry about you. I just don't want you getting hurt. Maya has never been good for you."

Nick felt the exact opposite, but he didn't need to justify his feelings to Camille. "I have to go. Have a nice night." He pulled open the driver's-side door and hopped in. "Also, mind your own business. What I do is none of your concern."

He didn't look, but he knew Camille was watching him as

he drove out of the parking lot. She was a never-ending problem in his life, and he had no idea what to do about it.

"HEY, POPS." NICK LET HIMSELF INTO HIS father's house without knocking. There was no point, since he knew where he would find his dad and exactly what he would be doing.

"Nicky!" Hank Griffith raised his glass of bourbon and toasted his arrival with a huge smile.

Nick kept his face impassive as agitation regarding his father's drunken state rolled through him. "How's it going?" Nick moved a pile of takeout bags from the couch so that he could sit. Whenever he visited his father, it was always the same. The house was a mess, and his father was an even bigger one. When Nick left, he felt depressed. It would be the case again that evening.

"Well, I heard your mother was over visiting Catherine Markham last night." A muscle worked in Hank's jaw as he stared at the television. "They were drinking on the back patio."

"And how do you know that?" Nick asked, tossing a cursory look toward the hockey game on the screen. The Red Wings hadn't been good in years, yet Hank never gave up hope.

"I saw her car."

"Yes, but the patio is behind the house. How did you know they were back there if you can't see the patio from here?" Nick was almost afraid to ask. He felt he had to, though.

"I have binoculars. If I go to the back corner of the yard and use them, I can see things."

"Well, that sounds healthy." Nick exhaled heavily as he leaned back. "Maybe you should let this go, Pop."

"Let what go? Your mother cheated on me."

"Yeah, but it's not as if you want her back or anything, right?" Nick shared some of the vitriol his father harbored for his mother. When she'd announced she was leaving his father for another man, Nick had done something he never thought he would do and picked sides. Of course his father won out. He was the wronged party. But Nick was ready to stop obsessing about the incident. His father was another story. He was only getting worse, and the alcohol wasn't helping matters. But Nick didn't have a solution to the problem.

Hank made a sputtering noise. "Of course I don't want her back. She's a trollop. You don't take trollops back."

"Trollop?" Nick couldn't hide his grin. "That's an interesting word choice."

"It was on *Wheel of Fortune* earlier."

"Well, at least your television habits are expanding your vocabulary." Nick's gaze skimmed over the mess. "Do you want me to help you pick up?"

"Why would I? It's just going to get messy again."

"I guess I can't argue with that point. Have you eaten?"

Hank shot him a withering look. "I think I'm old enough to handle eating on my own."

Old enough but not responsible enough. "You don't always eat," he argued. "If you're going to drink, you have to eat."

"I'm good."

"Speaking of the drinking—"

"I thought Yzerman was supposed to make the Red Wings better when he got into the front office. That hasn't happened."

"They're rebuilding," Nick said with a sigh. "You have to give them time."

"If you say so." Hank tapped his fingers on his knee for several seconds then slowly slid his gaze to Nick. "I hear Maya is back."

"You live across the road from her parents. I'm assuming you've seen her by now."

"She stopped by when your mother was over there, spent about twenty minutes on the back patio, then took off. I didn't get a good look at her."

"Probably because you had the binoculars focused on Mom."

"That's neither here nor there. I still saw her. She looks the same."

"Kind of," Nick agreed. "She doesn't look exactly the same. It's been years, though. Nobody looks exactly the same year after year."

"Does that mean you've seen her?"

"I've seen her."

"Have you talked to her?"

"I have. We played basketball last night."

That clearly wasn't the response Hank was expecting, because his eyebrows rose halfway up his forehead. "You're with her?"

"What? No, I'm not *with* her. I was never *with* her."

Hank snorted. "Please. It might not have been official, but you were always with her. Your mother and hers were making wedding plans when you were fourteen."

"And did they get to throw that wedding?" Nick challenged him.

"No."

"Then it seems to me they were barking up the wrong tree."

"They didn't think that."

"Well, we're not married. We weren't even friends for a long time."

"But you're friends now?"

"We talked out a few things last night," Nick replied. "We agreed that we were both to blame for falling out of touch."

"Why does there have to be blame? You were adults but still mostly kids and out in the real world for the first time. Of course things changed."

"And that's basically what we agreed. There's no reason for us to be holding grudges, especially when she's back in town and there's no way we can avoid each other."

"Do you want to avoid her?"

Nick took a moment to consider the question. "No," he said finally. "I missed my friend."

"Just your friend?"

"Of course she's just my friend. She's always been my friend and nothing more."

Hank's gaze was appraising, and for once, he was more interested in his son than his bourbon. "I'm of two minds about this," he said finally.

"Well, you don't need to be of any mind about it. It's not a big deal."

Hank looked exasperated. "Do you want to hear my opinion or not?"

"Not really."

"Well, you're going to hear it anyway. I always liked Maya. Even when she was little, she was a spitfire. She had all that blonde hair and those big blue eyes." He smiled as he thought back. "You two were as thick as thieves. You were always playing basketball and running around together. I remember when you taught her to ride a bicycle."

Nick grinned. "She was eight before she learned. I mean, what's up with that?"

"Her father and grandfather kept yelling at her when they were trying to teach her, and she got huffy. She's never liked people telling her what to do. That's why you were patient when you took her out, just the two of you, and taught her with no expectations."

"I kind of remember that," Nick admitted. "I took her to

that road behind the church so that she wouldn't feel self-conscious. Nobody is ever out there. I didn't want the other kids coming by and making fun of her."

"You were always protective of her, and she was always protective of you."

"So it's good that we're trying to be friends again," Nick said. "It's not exactly the way it was eight years ago, but we could get there. We're taking baby steps. I even went into her new coffee shop this morning, and she shoved cheese Danish down my throat."

Hank snorted. "Yes, I'm sure she had to force you to eat those. She was always quite the little baker."

Staring at his father, Nick felt some of the weight he'd been carrying rise. His father had been mired in depression since his mother had left more than a year before. Nick was the one who had to pick up the pieces, and if the state of his father's house was any indication, Nick wasn't doing a very good job of it. Somehow, his father seemed different that night, more like the man he'd grown up with.

"She's even better now," Nick said finally. "She sent me off to school with a whole bag of cheese Danish, and I ate them all day."

"That sounds healthy."

Nick laughed. "Well, one cheat day won't hurt me."

"No." Hank's smile disappeared as he focused on the television. "Do you think you guys will finally get your heads out of your asses and admit you're more than friends?"

"No, because we've never been more than friends. That's all we are."

"Are you sure?"

"I am."

Hank licked his lips, then jerked his chin in agreement. "That's probably good, because as much as I love Maya, I think it's best that you don't open yourself to her. She's just like the others. She'll hurt you. No woman is worth exposing yourself to hurt. Maya might have started out sweet and innocent, but now she's part of the crew."

Nick thought about asking which crew he was referring to, but it didn't matter. "We're friends, Dad. We're not spending all our time together. I expect we'll say hello when passing each other in town and maybe gossip over coffee here or there, and that will be the end of it."

"That's the best decision you've ever made, because Maya has the ability to crush you ... just like your mother crushed me."

Nick briefly pressed his eyes shut. "You don't have to worry about that, Dad," he said when he'd regained control of his emotions. "Maya isn't going to hurt me. We can be friends again. That's what I want. I don't want anything else."

"Well, at least you've got your head on straight. You won't be like me and give your heart to a woman just so she can stomp on it."

"No, Dad. I won't be like you."

AN HOUR LATER, HANK HAD PASSED OUT, and Nick carried him into the bedroom, as he normally did when he dropped by to see his father. Hank was more than happy to sleep in his easy chair, but it bugged Nick, so he went out of his way to make sure his father was horizontal—on his side in case there was a vomit incident—before leaving.

Nick stopped in the living room long enough to pack up all the garbage, and he moved the dirty dishes into the dishwasher and turned it on. After filling a garbage bag, Nick stared at the bottle of bourbon on the kitchen counter. It was almost empty, and there was room in the bag for it.

Nick didn't sweep it in with the other garbage, however. It wouldn't matter. His father didn't think he was an alcoholic.

Hank couldn't see his own faults, mostly because he was too busy obsessing about his ex-wife's faults. He would simply assume he'd finished the bottle and buy another one. Throwing it away would accomplish nothing.

Nick locked the door as he left—although Bellaire was such a small town that it wasn't necessary—and tossed the garbage bag into the bin at the side of the garage before heading to his truck. He would return in two days to take the garbage out himself because his father never remembered.

When he reached his truck, Nick paused and focused on Maya's old house. For a moment, he was swamped with memories. When they were kids, they raced across the field to meet up. When they were teenagers, she climbed out her window to hang out with him after midnight, even though her parents were sticklers about curfews. That field had been an adventure land for them over the course of their lives.

Sure, it was just a field, but it represented more to him.

Only one light was on at the Markham house, the one in the living room. That probably meant Maya's parents were settling in to watch television, something his parents had never done even before his mother left. The Markham family was a solid unit. His family had always been on slippery footing. That was one of the reasons he liked visiting their house so much, even though there were far more rules to follow than he was used to.

After a few more seconds of staring, Nick let out a pent-up breath. Thinking about what had been lost wasn't going to get him anywhere. Worrying about his father had turned out to be a wasted effort. It was time to put the dregs of the day behind him and head out to have some fun. After all, it was snow party night, his favorite night of the week. He was ready to embrace it.

Eight

MAYA

"I'm sorry. We're doing what?" Maya blinked several times as she looked Lindsey up and down. Her friend appeared perfectly serious, yet what she'd said was ludicrous.

"We're going to the snow party," Lindsey said matter-of-factly. "Don't act like it's a foreign concept to you. You've been to a snow party a time or two."

"Um ... aren't snow parties for kids?"

"Oh, listen to you." Lindsey made a face as she watched Maya stalk the empty coffee shop. "You act as if you're above drinking in a field."

"I'm not above it." Maya wasn't sure that was true. "Well, mostly. Teenagers drink in fields. We're adults."

"Yes, and we've seriously upgraded our partying abilities. It's not just a field now. We have warmers out there ... and a bar ... and a fire pit. It's not like you remember."

"Um, I'm not sure."

"You *are* sure. You've been back in town for weeks and haven't even seen the old crew."

Maya arched an eyebrow. "I've been hanging around with you, haven't I?"

"Yes, and it's a magical friendship. I mean, pixie dust should be flying over our heads. There are more people in this town than just me, though, loath though I am to admit it."

Maya tried to bite back a sigh and failed. "I don't know that I can fathom drinking in a field. Do you know that most people don't do that? I didn't realize until college that it wasn't a normal thing."

"It's normal for here, and that's all that matters. It's the first snow of the year. It won't stick, but the first snow of the year is magical. You can't miss the first snow party when it coincides with magical snow."

Maya had to swallow the urge to laugh at Lindsey's absurd reasoning. "Magical, huh?"

"You know it is," Lindsey insisted. "I remember you and Nick making plans every year for the first snow. It was a midnight walk, if I remember."

Maya's cheeks heated at the memory. Those walks had been some of her favorites. "I recall."

"Well, now that you and Nick are playing nice, I was thinking we would go all the way tonight." Lindsey wasn't used to hearing the word *no*, so she was relentless when pushing forward. "It's time to take the next step in your relationship."

Maya's brow furrowed. "What steps? We're friends again. Isn't that the only step?"

Lindsey shot Maya a withering look. "Oh, you're cute."

"I'm being serious. We're friendly again. That was the goal, wasn't it?"

"Oh, the goal won't be met until you guys are mounting each other in public. You're not there yet, but I know you're going to get there. So that's enough to bolster me this evening."

"*What* did you just say?"

Lindsey gave a dismissive wave. "Oh, clutch your pearls a little less tightly there, Minnie," she drawled. "You know you're curious to see where this goes. Don't bother denying it."

Maya thought about doing just that, but she kept her mouth shut. After several seconds of contemplation, she sighed. "I guess I could go to a snow party. I'm not sure I have anything to wear, though."

Lindsey snorted. "It's a snow party. Anything goes, and that includes chaps, flip-flops, and fringe."

As nostalgia washed over Maya, she smiled. "Ah, the first snow party of senior year. That was fun."

"Wasn't it? Now, finish closing up. I'll go with you to change your clothes, then we'll head to the snow party together."

"It's almost as if you don't trust me to show up myself."

"I don't."

"At least you're honest about it."

"Yeah, I'm hoping we all get honest tonight."

Maya didn't know what to make of that, but she opted to let it go, at least for the moment. *A snow party after all this time? Well, there are worse things.*

MAYA OPTED FOR HER NORTH FACE COAT and her UGG boots. She grabbed fingerless gloves and a beanie cap with a pom as well. The temperature would drop to the thirties that night, normal for the time of year. Locals didn't get cold until it got to the teens. Maya figured that even though she was out of practice, she would be fine once she adjusted to the change.

She was expecting ten people and a bonfire when she

arrived. Instead, there were forty people, four bonfires, and an absolutely huge cabin that included a bar.

"Where did that come from?" Maya asked as she regarded the bar. One wall was clearly a pocket door, and it slid up and down so that people could close the bar area when they were finished using it.

"Duncan Dorsey," Lindsey replied. "He built it because he wanted to be seen as a big shot."

"Dinky Duncan?"

Lindsey smirked at the old nickname. "Yes, and he's still not over being called that name, so if he happens to be here, it's best to pretend you don't remember it. He's done everything in his power to make people forget."

"Have they?"

"Oh, not even a little," Lindsey replied, smiling. "The Dinky Duncan nickname survives. It's been verified by two other people too. We just don't let him know we still call him that. I mean, we're a little old for Dinky Duncan jokes."

Maya didn't disagree. "We probably shouldn't have called him that back when we were in high school. It was mean."

Lindsey didn't look nearly as bothered as Maya felt. "Listen, when you're hung like half a Twix bar and claim you're god's gift to women, people are going to talk. If he'd kept his mouth shut about being a sex god, none of that would've happened."

"Yeah, but that's normal for a teenager. All the boys bragged about that."

"Nick didn't."

An unbidden smile rushed to Maya's lips. "Nick was never a Neanderthal. He was too cool to talk about stuff like that."

"Or he wanted to do it with you and was smart enough to realize that would ruin the mood."

Maya pinned Lindsey with a dark look. "Why do you keep going there?"

"Where?" Lindsey asked, the picture of innocence.

"You know where. I would really appreciate it if you didn't make things weird between Nick and me. We've only just started being friends again. If you push things the way you're clearly determined to push them, you're going to risk us fighting again. I don't want that to happen."

Lindsey snorted. "Oh, stuff it. You guys are clearly on the right track. You're not going to regress now, at least about this. Do you really think people haven't been saying the same things to him?"

"I don't know why they would."

"Because you guys are famous around these parts. Everyone was convinced you would end up together, and they can't get over the fact that you haven't. Now that you're going to get together—granted, years after the fact—the bets are on, and people are invested. You can't shake that."

"You're just pushing my buttons to push them."

"No, I'm helping you achieve your goals."

"Nick is not one of my goals." Maya meant it, yet as soon as the words were out, her stomach flooded with a feeling she couldn't quite identify. *Guilt? Irritation? Something else entirely?*

"Oh, you're cute." Lindsey flicked her ear. "You might not be willing to admit that Nick is one of your goals, but he is. We just have to make it happen for you."

"The coffee shop is my goal," Maya insisted. "Nick is just ... a friend." It felt good to say that again, yet awkward at the same time. "I think you and the rest of the town need to stop making things up to worry about. It's weird, and I get itchy when you won't let it go."

"Fine." Lindsey held her hands up. "Keep denying it. Just remember, when you finally admit what you're feeling and who you want with you at the finish line, I'll be here ... to tell you 'I told you so', then help, in that order."

Maya rolled her eyes. "You really are too much sometimes."

"I am," Lindsey readily agreed. "It's part of my charm."

"'Charm' isn't the word I would use."

"You will when it's all over. Trust me."

MAYA HADN'T BEEN KEEN ON THE IDEA of a snow party when Lindsey first broached the subject, yet she couldn't stop smiling as she ran into person after person from her past. Heather Harper, Brad Dickerson, Dinky Duncan, and so many others hurried over to greet her that she spent the first hour of the party lost in memories—and keg beer—and she was laughing so hard that her stomach hurt when she felt a presence slide in behind her.

Nick.

When she turned, her heart swelled at the sight of him. How she'd gone so many years without talking to him was beyond her. Looking back, she recognized she'd acted like an idiot. She could never get that time back, but she wasn't about to waste another moment of it.

"Nicky." She threw her arms around him, not caring that she spilled some of the beer in her red Solo cup. "I'm so glad you came. Did you know they're still having snow parties, and they're not like the ones we used to have but totally still like them at the same time?"

Nick chuckled as he returned the hug. "I did know that. I went to a few last year."

"Oh, right." Maya's smile slipped. "This is normal to you. I'm the only one somehow excited about this."

Nick grinned and tucked a strand of Maya's blonde hair under her beanie, something he used to do all the time. It somehow felt normal despite the years apart. "I'm excited about it too. You used to love a good snow party."

"Actually, I remember us loving it together," Maya said. "Remember the first year you got the snowmobile?"

Nick nodded. "I do. My father bought it, and my mother melted down. Then your mother joined the party and said you weren't allowed to ride on it without a helmet."

"Gawd, she was so annoying," Maya said, laughing.

"Then we had to go get you a helmet, and you insisted on getting the one with Bigfoot painted on it. When we brought it home, your mother was annoyed because she thought it was stupid, then she didn't want you wearing a helmet."

"At which point I wore the helmet for the entire winter, whether I was on a snowmobile or not. She was always so easy to annoy back then."

"Is she any different now?"

Maya considered the question, then shook her head. "No, she is most definitely not different now."

Then she realized she was still stuck to Nick. His arms were loose around her waist, and her chest was flush with his. It didn't seem odd until she realized it was happening, and she wondered what she should do to rectify the situation. *Should I pull away really fast? Will he think that's weird? Has he noticed we're pressed together?* When she looked over at Lindsey, she knew it was already too late to stop everybody in town from talking. Lindsey's smile was a bit too "cat that ate the canary" for Maya's liking, but since Bear had one to match, everybody would be whispering by the end of the hour, no matter how she extricated herself from the situation.

"So, are you going to get something to drink?" Maya asked as she finally pulled away.

If Nick noticed that she was suddenly uncomfortable, he didn't show it. Instead, he waved off the question as if it was the most absurd thing he'd ever heard. "Yeah. I'm going to grab something. Do you want another drink?"

"Sure." Maya's grin was nearly wide enough to swallow her face.

"*Should* you have another drink?" Nick clarified.

"I've only had two. We also walked. I think I'll be okay with one more."

"I don't know. You've always been a lightweight."

Maya feigned mock outrage. "That is a damnable lie." She jabbed a finger at him.

He chuckled, the sound like a warm blanket wrapping her tightly during a blustery January day. "I guess you can handle one more. The good news is that since it's cold, you'll burn off the alcohol faster because it takes more energy to keep warm."

"Is that true?"

"It could be true."

She lightly slapped his arm. "I think one more is my limit. This is totally fun, though. I didn't know it could be this fun."

"No?" Nick's fingers were back in her hair, and they brushed against her skin when he tugged down her beanie. "Well, stick with me, Maya. I totally know how to have fun."

"That's the plan. I'm totally going to stick with you. No more being stupid."

"That would be nice, huh?" He winked. "I'll get your beer. Don't wander too far. I don't want you to get lost in the snow and have a *The Shining* moment."

"Oh, geez." Maya threw up her hands in mock frustration. "I said *one time* that I would be the one to die in a maze if we had one. I wasn't being serious."

He laughed and patted the top of her head. "Just don't wander away."

"I won't. I'm where I want to be."

Nick paused for a beat—as if he wanted to say something —but smiled. "I'll be back."

Maya nodded. It felt nice to know that was actually true for the first time in a long time. She entertained herself by shooting a series of exaggerated eye rolls toward Lindsey during his absence and was about to embark on another snarky expression tour when a familiar face at the bar caught her attention. When she focused, she found Camille standing with Nick. He had two beers in his hands and a wide smile on his face. Whatever Camille was telling him, he was enjoying the story and had seemingly forgotten that he was supposed to return to Maya.

"You're going to have to get on that," Lindsey intoned as she arrived at Maya's side.

"Get on what?"

"That." Lindsey gestured as she made a face. "That woman has 'crazy stalker' written all over her. You need to make sure she doesn't derail the Naya train."

If Maya thought she was confused before, she was well and truly lost. "The Naya train?"

"Do you prefer Mick?"

"I don't even know what you're talking about."

"It's your couple name," Lindsey replied. "When you put Maya and Nick together, you get either Naya or Mick. I went with Naya because Mick reminds me of Mick Salander. Do you remember him? He used to drive the bus. He was a true representation of what a mediocre man could do while still pretending he was great."

"And that's why you use Naya instead of Mick," Maya said. "I get it."

"I can switch to the other if you prefer it."

"I prefer neither. As for Camille, she's really not my concern. She and Nick are clearly friends, and since Nick and I are friends, I want him to be happy. Given the way he's smiling, he clearly is."

"Yes, he looks thrilled with life," Lindsey said dryly. "I mean, how could he not be thrilled, knowing he has a stalker?"

"Don't you think you're being a tad overdramatic with the stalker stuff?"

"Nope. She's a total stalker, and she's going to be trouble. You need to stake your claim on Nick so that she doesn't get a foothold and make things difficult for you. I'm still Team Naya for the win, but she could temporarily derail things, if you're not careful."

"Well, I'll keep that in mind." Maya told herself she was amused with Lindsey's take on the situation, but if she was being truthful—something she would only do with herself— she was concerned. Camille was the last thing she wanted to deal with. *If Camille's in Nick's life as a regular player, what does that mean for me?*

Nine

NICK

When talking to Camille after so many years removed from their relationship, Nick couldn't decide why he'd ever liked her in the first place. Camille hated sports and complained whenever he watched anything that didn't originate on the BBC. She was demanding, snotty, entitled, and spent more time looking down on people than she did playing nice. And while he didn't hate her, he certainly didn't like her.

"Do you want to sit over there?" Camille pointed toward one of the fires Maya wasn't sitting at. Nick had no doubt why.

"Actually, I'm hanging with Maya, Lindsey, and Bear tonight." Nick said it with a smile, but he hoped he'd put enough emphasis in his eyes to let Camille know he wasn't messing around.

"Oh, I'll come with you." Another thing Nick didn't like about her was she didn't ask for an invitation. She told him how it was going to be.

"I think we're just doing the high school crew tonight," he said as he moved away from her.

If she followed, he had no idea what he would do. He wasn't comfortable slicing her out of the group, but he didn't want her close. *Why?* The question bubbled up instantly. He was used to Camille and her machinations and never had any problem tuning her out. But that night was different, and although he didn't want to think about it too long, he recognized Maya was the reason.

Maybe it was because he knew Maya hated Camille. He would've liked to blame it on her, but that wasn't the sole reason. In truth, he didn't want Camille intruding on his time with Maya. Camille would make things uncomfortable, and what Nick wanted more than anything was to eradicate the small threads of discomfort that still permeated his relationship with Maya. He wanted things to go back to the way they used to be, even though that wasn't necessarily possible.

"Nick." Camille sounded exasperated when she called after him, but he didn't turn around.

When he returned to Maya and Lindsey, handing over Maya's drink, tension hung over them.

"What's wrong?" he asked, bracing himself.

"Nothing," Maya replied. The response was too fast to be truthful.

Lindsey, however, had never cared about being polite. "We hate Camille and wish she would fall into the fire."

Maya slapped her arm. "That's not what we were talking about." She turned to Nick. "Don't listen to her."

"It's too bad we don't have winter fire ants," Lindsey mused, refusing to back down. "I would totally strip her naked, stake her to the ground, and sit back and watch the show."

Nick barked out a laugh. He'd always found Lindsey amusing. In high school, Maya had often joined Lindsey, and the two of them were hard to contain. Maya wasn't piling on, though, and Nick knew why. "She's a bit much," he agreed, sending Maya an encouraging smile. "She's not happy unless she's making things difficult for others."

Maya smiled but worry lurked in her eyes. "She's not so bad. I mean, I didn't realize you guys were still hanging out, but she's got some good qualities."

Nick arched an eyebrow.

"What?"

Though it was dark, Nick was certain Maya's face was flushing. "Since when do you like Camille?" he asked.

"Yeah, since when do you like Camille?" Lindsey echoed.

Maya's shoulders drooped, and she averted her eyes. "I've always liked her."

"That is the biggest pile of crap I've ever heard," Nick said.

"Heaping piles of dinosaur crap is what that is," Lindsey agreed. "There's nothing to like about that woman."

"Fine," Maya said. "Maybe 'like' is a strong word. I don't hate her, though."

"I hate her." Lindsey obviously didn't care who heard her, because when two people about fifteen feet over snapped their heads in her direction, she nodded. "Yeah, I'm talking about you."

In a move Nick found adorable, Maya slapped her hand over her eyes. "I can't believe you just did that."

"Oh, please." Lindsey waved a hand. "That's Tilly Stinson. She adopted a dog for her son for Christmas last year, then gave it back after New Year's because, and I quote, 'It was too hairy.' I don't care what she thinks."

"I'm allergic!" one of the women, a willowy blonde, shrieked.

"You're not allergic. You're just toxic."

"Ah, all I have to do is follow the dulcet tones of my wife's voice to know all is right in the world." Bear joined the group, slinging an arm around Lindsey's shoulders, then dropped a kiss on top of her head. He towered over her. "I'm reminded of why I fell in love with you when you say things like that."

"Then you must be in love with me twenty-four hours a day."

"Seven days a week and twice on Sunday." Bear grinned. "Looks like the gang is back together again. It feels like old times."

"Yes, because Lindsey is going to get in a fight, and I'm going to have to jump in to make sure she doesn't get smacked around," Maya complained. "Who did you use for backup when I wasn't here, Linds?"

"I don't need backup. I'm just that good." Lindsey gave a smug smile, and she kept staring at Tilly until the woman looked away. "See? I'm a maestro."

"Yes, you're a maestro of meanness." Maya's gaze drifted back to Nick. "Did Camille want something?"

Nick couldn't be certain—they hadn't been in regular contact for years, after all—but Maya's voice was shriller than normal, and there seemed to be an edge to her tone.

"She was just doing her normal talking thing." He wasn't the type to cast aspersions on people, and no matter how annoying he found Camille, there was no reason to talk about her out of turn. "I'm sure she'll find someone to listen to her."

"She has," Lindsey confirmed, pointing with a devilish smile. "Eric Peterman. She probably thinks that will make you jealous."

"Why would it make me jealous?"

"I didn't say it would make you jealous. I said she was trying to make you jealous. There's a difference."

"And why would she be trying to make me jealous?"

"Oh, don't." Lindsey shook her head. "Let's not go there, huh? You know exactly why."

"No, I don't. We haven't been together for years."

"That doesn't mean she doesn't want to get back together. Why else would she move here?"

"I wasn't even here when she started her job at the high school," Nick pointed out. "She moved back to town a full six months before me."

"Your family was still here. While it's true she might not have been able to foresee your return, you can't argue with the fact that she jumped all over you like you were the only sweatshirt in the dryer, and she was the sock, just as soon as you got back."

Nick touched his top lip with his tongue, caught between amusement and annoyance. "I think you're seeing something that's not really there."

"And I think you're in denial," Lindsey fired back. "You'll figure it out sooner rather than later though."

"Oh yeah? What exactly am I going to figure out?"

"Oh, it would lose something in the telling." Lindsey gave a knowing smile to Nick and Maya. "This is one of those things you're going to have to figure out on your own."

The death glare Maya shot Lindsey had him curious, but he didn't press the issue. Instead, he sipped his drink and let out a sigh. "So, what are the odds someone falls into the fire tonight? I think it's been two weeks since we've had an incident."

"Brian Watros is here," Bear replied. "He's definitely going in."

"His eyebrows have just grown back after the last incident."

"That's why he's going in. He always forgets."

"Twenty bucks says he makes it another week before he forgets."

"You're on."

. . .

NICK THOUGHT HE MIGHT BE HUNGOVER the next morning, but he felt surprisingly good, enough that he put on his running clothes and headed for the downtown area. Bellaire wasn't the sort of town where people could run outdoors year-round, but since the snow wasn't sticking yet, he wanted to take advantage of the forty-five-degree morning while he still had an opening.

Nick didn't consider himself a fitness buff, but he liked to stay in shape. He lifted weights at the high school twice a week, and in the winter, he ran around the gym. Running outside allowed him to empty his mind, however, and just drift. Only he couldn't that morning.

Nick's mind refused to empty. It kept circling right back to Maya. She'd been at the forefront of his brain since he heard she was coming home. He'd been in the hardware store when the news broke. Another patron mentioned it in passing, as if he should've already known, which he probably would have if he weren't freezing his mother out. He'd stuttered a response, then fled without his new hammer. Nick had yet to go back and buy it.

The first emotion that had run through him was excitement, although he'd shuttered it quickly. He didn't want to acknowledge it or delve too deeply on why he'd felt that way. Instead, he jumped to the second emotion—anger. He'd asked, *Why is she coming back? Why did I have to find out from someone else that she's moving home? And why did I let out friendship lapse?*

He had some ideas, but he ruthlessly pushed them out of his head. He'd been angry with Maya for a long time, but when he thought long and hard about it, he knew that anger was misplaced. Sure, she'd been just as culpable as he was, but the friendship shouldn't have been severed over distance. More bubbled under the surface, and he was trying not to think about it too hard. He kept circling, however, and it wasn't something he could ignore.

"Hey."

Nick jolted at the voice, jerking his chin up. He was in front of the small deli, and Maya was in the lot, loading her car. He came to a stop and blinked several times. "Hey."

"Running?"

Nick took a moment to absorb the question then grinned. "Are you trying to find a conversation starter that couldn't possibly lead to trouble?"

Maya turned sheepish. "Yeah." She threw her bags into the trunk of her car, then closed it before moving toward him. "I feel a little ... off ... when it comes to you."

The admission caught Nick off guard. "And why is that?"

"Because part of me wants things to be exactly how they were before we stopped talking, and I know that's not reasonable. The other part is terrified that I'm going to say the wrong thing and lose you all over again."

Nick opened his mouth to reply, then closed it. He wasn't entirely certain what to say. Finally, he replied, "I feel the same way. I'm afraid to rock the boat."

"Maybe we should make a pact or something," she suggested. "Like ... we both agree that we can't get mad if we say something the other doesn't like."

"I'm not opposed to it, but emotions aren't always that easy. I don't think we can will ourselves not to get angry." *Or hurt.* "Maybe the pact should be that we have to talk about it if we do get angry."

"Oh, well, that's a good idea." Maya brightened. "Let's do that."

He laughed. "God, I missed you." He felt relieved to say it.

"I missed you too." Maya threw her arms around him. "I'm so sorry."

Holding her felt as natural as breathing. "Don't." Nick stroked his hand down the back of her head, silky strands slipping between his fingers. He remembered a hundred different times when he'd done the same thing, yet it still felt slightly different. *Why? Why aren't things exactly the same now that we've acknowledged we were wrong and agreed to put it behind us?*

Nick couldn't come up with an answer, so he forced himself to be in the moment instead of his head. Her body felt right against his, and he told himself it was for no reason other than he was glad to have her back in his life. Other reasons bubbled to the surface, but he refused to focus on that. He only wanted something good in his life.

Then the bad elbowed in and punched him in the stomach.

"Nick?"

He cringed. When he released Maya, who had turned to greet the newcomer, his entire body went rigid. "Melanie." Not calling her Mom was a point of pride with him. He didn't consider her his mother any longer, and he refused to treat her as anything other than a vague acquaintance.

Maya's eyes widened as she glanced between Melanie and Nick. She looked as if she was caught in a trap and ready to gnaw her own leg off to escape, something Nick couldn't blame her for. She clearly had no idea exactly how cold things had gotten between them.

Melanie's jaw worked, as if she wanted to pick a fight, but she focused on Maya. "It's good to see you again, dear. It's even better to see the two of you together."

To Nick, Maya looked as if she was trying to make herself smaller. Discomfort rolled off her in waves, and she held her hands together in front of her. It took him a moment to realize why.

"You can hug her," Nick said. "I'm not going to melt

down. Just because I don't want to know her doesn't mean you can't. I'm not going to be angry about it."

Relief fluttered across Maya's face, and she hugged Melanie quickly and tightly. Then she released her and took a step back. "It's nice to see you again," Maya said. "We didn't get to talk long at my mother's place the other night."

"Uh-huh." Melanie's smile didn't reach her eyes. "Don't worry about things being weird, dear. You're not the one making them that way."

"I guess that means you think I'm the one," Nick said gruffly.

"Yes."

Melanie had kowtowed to Nick when she first left Hank, but she'd stopped apologizing weeks ago. Nick wasn't certain whether he preferred her groveling or fighting back. Just being around her made his skin crawl.

"Maybe I should go," Maya said when the silence had stretched on for far too long. "I ... um ... have things to do at the shop."

"I look forward to seeing the finished product," Melanie replied. "I always knew you would do great things."

Maya appeared anxious when she glanced at Nick. "I don't know if I should go or stay, but this feels like a mother-and-son thing."

Nick nodded. He would've preferred to continue with their previous conversation—they still had the finer details to hammer out for their pact—but he didn't blame Maya for wanting to flee. If he hadn't been one of the direct participants in the conversation, he would've gladly taken off too.

"Um, I'll see you later." Maya squeezed his hand. Her fingers were warm as they wrapped around his. Then she moved to the front of the car. "It was nice seeing you again," she said to Melanie.

"It's always nice to see you," Melanie supplied. "I'm so

glad you're back. I'm even more glad that you guys are seemingly on the right track again. Maybe you can talk this one out of being so stubborn."

Nick's eyes narrowed to slits. "I think I'm good being me."

Maya wet her lips, then darted an "I'm sorry" look toward Nick. "I'll see you later."

"You will," Nick agreed.

He stepped out of the way when she pulled out of her spot, wishing he'd taken the opportunity to leave when Melanie was distracted. Instead, he remained rooted to the spot. When his mother finally shifted her gaze back to him, her expression was so bleak that guilt flooded Nick's senses. He didn't allow the emotion to take root in him and instead embraced the ever-bubbling rage he felt in his mother's proximity. "If that's all, I'll be going."

"That's not all," Melanie shot back. "We're not done here."

"No?"

Nick was ready to fight if she wanted to, but he knew that wasn't the tack she would take. She would ask him to be reasonable instead, and he was beyond being reasonable. "What would you like to talk about, Mother? How about Clark? How is the sex with Clark?"

Melanie's cheeks turned crimson. "Can you not be crude?" Her voice cracked. "I really want to get past this, Nick. Why can't you at least try?"

"Because I have nothing to say to you. You broke our family. You don't get to play the victim when I'm the one who has to put it back together. I'm not going to play that game with you."

"Nick." She sighed. "Is this really how you want this to go?"

"It's how it has to go. I have no room in my life for your

boyfriend, so I think I'm good with how things are. Have a nice day." With that, Nick resumed his run. He could feel his mother's eyes on his back as he moved down the sidewalk. He did not look back.

Ten

MAYA

All day long, Maya lambasted herself for not standing with Nick regarding his mother. She liked Melanie —a lot—but she knew Nick well enough to recognize that his mother's leaving his father would've devastated him. He'd always been proud that his parents were still together. They were one of the few couples in Bellaire who'd held strong for the long haul when they were growing up. Having them separate when he was an adult must have thrown him.

And you weren't there to help him.

Maya was still worried about it when she locked up the shop after a full day of preparations. *Why didn't I give him what he needed in that moment? Why did I get squirrelly and take off?* She was furious with herself, yet deep down, she knew it wasn't in her to be cruel to Melanie.

Yes, she'd had an affair. She'd cheated on Nick's father. Whether it had been an emotional or a physical affair, Maya had no idea. She didn't care to know. They were equally as bad. But Maya had trouble forming the same sort of anger Nick wielded like a sword. She'd known for years that

Melanie wasn't happy. Hank, though a nice man, was taciturn and difficult to deal with. He hated change, had never wanted to attend any of the town events, and basically lived like a shut-in when not working. Melanie was a social butterfly who thrived on those things. They'd never seemed like a good match to Maya. Nick, of course, didn't see that. He believed his parents had a happy marriage. The times he'd witnessed his parents fighting shook him. He couldn't see that Melanie was always yearning for more. That was likely why her leaving Hank had thrown Nick. He was angry, and Maya understood that. She just didn't know if she agreed with his determination to cut his mom out of his life.

Maya had believed she was going home when she left the coffee shop, but she ended up walking past the high school, which meant she was taking the long way. Nick was there, dribbling a ball in the lot and seemingly lost in thought, when she caught sight of the court.

Her heart soared, way higher than she would've thought possible. Just seeing his strong profile and the sculpted lines of his shoulders was enough to give her heart palpitations. She really had missed him.

That's not the reason your stomach is constricting, and your lady parts are singing.

Maya pushed the thought away. She had no idea where it had come from. Nick had always been her friend, even when they weren't together. Well, at least she wanted to believe that. Perhaps it was more apt that they were on a friend hiatus.

So why do you keep reacting the way you do when you see him?

Rather than dwell on the question, Maya opted to silence her inner voice and engage her outer one.

"It's not really winning if you're playing yourself," she called out.

Nick was already smiling when he looked up. "I thought maybe you would come here tonight."

"It's still in the forties," Maya said with a laugh. "We don't put basketball in the closet for the season until it's in the thirties. You know that."

"I *do* know that," he confirmed as she walked up to him. "I thought there was a chance you'd forgotten."

"Never." Maya shook her head. "I'm not some delicate flower." She reached for the ball.

Nick's reflexes were fast, and he held it away from her. His arms were longer, so it wasn't difficult. "What's wrong with being a delicate flower?"

Maya hesitated at the earnestness in his eyes, then shrugged. "I didn't say there was anything wrong with it," she said after a beat. "But growing up, when your best friend is a boy, looking delicate isn't a good thing."

Nick frowned. "Who says?"

"Um ... everybody."

"I don't understand. Could you not be yourself with me?"

He looked so pained at the prospect that it tugged at Maya's heartstrings. "I was always me. Never doubt that. I just couldn't be weak. I was afraid you wouldn't want to keep hanging out with me if I cried or anything, so I kept the crying to myself as much as possible."

"And why were you crying?"

Maya shrugged.

"Maya."

She gave a long, drawn-out sigh. "Geez. I forgot how intense you could be."

"I want to know why you were crying," he insisted.

"Why is it so important to you?"

"Don't deflect. It's important to me because you were important to me."

Maya gulped and tried to ignore the little pang in her heart when he said "were" instead of "are." She knew he didn't mean it that way, but she was still bothered. "Do you really want to know?"

"Yes. I would have wanted to know then, too, but I'll settle for hearing the reasons now."

"Fine. I cried because Denny died on *Grey's Anatomy*. And they couldn't get off the stupid island on *Lost*. And I might've cried once because I broke the lace on a shoe, and I had to wear the shoes that pinched."

Nick looked taken aback. "What now?"

Maya laughed. "Crying is not reserved for the big moments, Nick. Sometimes people cry just to cry. Well ... girls more than boys. It's cathartic. I cried for little things, but I didn't want to do it in front of you because I knew you would laugh."

"I wouldn't have laughed. Well, I wouldn't have laughed a lot."

Maya moved until she was directly in front of him, her eyes locked with his. "I didn't want you to see me as weak because I was afraid you would rethink your desire to be best friends with a girl and start hanging out with the boys more." She grabbed the ball from his hands before he could react. "It might be a dumb response—and in hindsight, it feels stupid—but that's how I felt. Teenagers are not known for being wise."

Nick made a face and tried to grab the ball back, but Maya anticipated the move and smoothly sidestepped him.

"Nothing in this world could've dragged me away from you. Friendship is not based on crying over *Lost*."

"Yes, well ... like I said, I was a moron."

"Ugh." Nick leaned forward and rested his forehead against hers. "You really are an idiot."

"Yeah." Maya stood there, basking in their proximity and shared warmth, then pulled back to start dribbling the ball. The night air was brisk. In the southern part of the state, people would balk at playing basketball on a forty-three-degree night, but Maya was made of tougher stuff than that and barely noticed the cold. "Do you want to play or just shoot around?"

Nick only hesitated for a moment before replying, "Shoot around."

Maya nodded. She was hoping he would say that. She dribbled to the top of the key and tossed up a jump shot. It banked in rather than swished, and she frowned. "I'm really rusty."

Nick chuckled. "You'll get back into the swing of things."

"Not before winter. It's just around the corner. We only have a week or two of this left, then we'll have to put the ball away until the spring." *Then what will happen?* Maya didn't want to think too much about it, but she couldn't stop herself. *If we don't have basketball as an excuse to meet, will we fall away from each other yet again?*

"Well, when that happens, we can go to the high school gym," Nick replied. "We open it three nights a week for shootarounds. It won't be just the two of us, but we can take one of the hoops to ourselves if you need to practice."

"You can just commandeer a hoop?"

"I'm the gym teacher in these parts, and I can do whatever I want."

Maya laughed at his exaggerated drawl. "I guess it's good to know people in positions of power."

"Totally." He held out his hand for the ball. "My turn."

Maya passed it over and watched him move beyond the three-point line.

"Do you want to talk about what happened earlier?" she asked.

When Nick froze before shooting, she thought it was a bad idea to go that route. He followed through on his shooting motion and missed the shot, and dread filled her stomach.

"Or not," she said when she raced over to retrieve the ball.

When he returned, she added, "I didn't mean to upset you."

Nick sighed. "It's okay."

"It doesn't sound okay."

"Well, it is." Nick forced a smile. "I don't want you walking around on eggshells because you think you can't talk to me about stuff. I've never wanted that. I just ... um ... I don't know." He dragged a hand through his hair and stared at the sky before redirecting his gaze to her. "I'm angry."

The statement was simple, Maya felt it in her bones. "Because your mother left?"

"Because my mother cheated on my father," Nick shot back. "And with Clark Mortensen to boot. I mean ... that guy is the town loser. His yard looks like a flea market exploded and nobody ever picked it up."

Maya wet her lips, uncertain what she should say. Fixating on Clark's lawn seemed like a waste of time—and something that was so superficial that it bordered on trivial—but she was afraid if she shut down the avenue of conversation, Nick would shut down too. "Does he still have that huge cement hippo in his side lot?" She smiled at the memory. "That was moved from that animal garden place by the putt-putt to his yard, right?"

Nick chuckled. "Yes, I remember that place. It was supposed to be for kids, but nobody ever went there."

"Hence why it closed."

"Clark took the hippo as a parting gift when he sold the land. It's still in his yard, although it's freaking frightening to look at. The paint is chipped, and two of the teeth are missing."

"I don't know." Maya considered. "I think a toothless

hippo is less terrifying than one that has teeth. That's just me, though."

"I guess you have a point."

Nick rolled his shoulders, then bent over to stretch, a delaying tactic Maya remembered well from when they were younger. She waited him out because she knew he wouldn't be able to stop himself from filling the silence. When he finally spoke again, his voice was so low that Maya had to strain to hear him.

"She made vows," he growled. "She promised to love and honor my father. Instead, she ran around with Clark Mortensen and made a fool of him. Clark Mortensen!"

Maya jolted at his vehemence but recovered quickly. "I'm not familiar with exactly how it played out. If you don't want to tell me, it's fine. I get it."

"I can tell you. It's not some big, convoluted story. Basically, my mother started volunteering her time at the senior center because she was bored. Clark volunteered there, too, because of his mother. They started hanging out. Then they started doing other stuff. Then my mother broke her promise to my father and moved out. She said she couldn't keep living a lie."

"Oh, Nick." Maya dropped the pretense of playing and moved closer to him, resting a hand on his shoulder. "I'm so sorry. That must have been terrible."

"My family was not a lie. We were real, and she ruined it because ... because ... she was bored or something. She said my father lost interest in living years ago, but that's not true. He's still here. He's still breathing. She crushed him."

"Is that why you came home?" That was the thing Maya had been struggling with most. "Was it for your father?"

Nick nodded, looking miserable. "He's not even the same man I grew up with. He's like a different person. He can't get past it."

Maya didn't know what to do to soothe him, so she moved closer and wrapped her arms around his waist. For a moment, she thought Nick might pull back. Instead, he leaned into the hug.

"He drinks all the time," Nick continued. "Like ... *all* the time. I've tried talking to him about it, but he doesn't listen. When he drinks, he fixates on Melanie. He keeps up on gossip about her and completely melts down when he hears stuff about her going to town events with Clark. It's ... too much."

Maya briefly pressed her eyes shut as she searched for the right words. "I'm sorry. I'm just ... so, so sorry."

"I'm sorry too." Nick rested his cheek on top of her head. "I don't know what to do. He's going to kill himself if he keeps it up, but there's nothing I can do to fix it. He's still in love with her, and he doesn't understand why she's not in love with him. It hurts to see him."

"Have you talked to your mother?"

Nick huffed a laugh. "I don't want to talk to her."

"Nick, she's still your mother."

"No, she's the woman who left my father. That's who she is to me, nothing more."

"Have you considered that maybe she really was unhappy, and that's why she left?" Maya felt uncomfortable bringing it up, but that didn't deter her. "I mean ... a person doesn't just seek out the company of another person unless there's something missing from their life."

Nick pulled back and eyed her with an unreadable expression.

"I'm not making excuses for her," Maya said hurriedly. "What she did was wrong. According to my mother—so take this with a grain of salt—Melanie knows that she did things the wrong way. She just wants to be happy though."

"What exactly did she have to be unhappy about? My father is a good man. Yes, he's going through a hard time right now, but she caused that. She's the reason he's so upset. This is on her. She's the one who's in the wrong."

Maya would step in it if she persisted, so she immediately backed off. Their renewed friendship was too tenuous to continue with the conversation. "It's just so weird. I mean... I never even thought about Clark as a dating option for anybody in town. The cement hippo ruled that out."

That time, when Nick smiled, there was softness to his eyes. "Right? What the hell?"

Maya shook her head. "Maybe there's some cement-hippo fetish we don't know about. That could be a thing."

"How could that be a thing?"

"Hey, there are people who take bird feathers, glue them to their bodies, dance under the full moon, then get it on. There's a fetish for everything."

Nick's jaw dropped. "Is that a real thing?"

"I have no idea. I'm betting you're going to check when you get home, though, aren't you?"

"Yes. I'm terrified about what I'll find, but I'll totally check."

Maya laughed. The immediate threat had dissipated. Hard conversations might be necessary in the future, but for the moment, they were good. "Just make sure you don't have your hand in your pants when you do. I don't want you to get caught up in that craze."

"I'll do my best." Nick slung his arm around her shoulders then brought her in close before rubbing his knuckles against her head. She struggled to pull away, but he held tight. "You earned it," he warned her as she sputtered. "I'm going to have chicken nightmares tonight, and it's all your fault."

Maya elbowed him and managed to dislodge his arm. "You did not just give me a noogie."

"I think I did."

"I'm an adult. You can't give an adult a noogie."

"Since when is that a rule?"

"Um, it's always been a rule."

"No, I think you're making that up."

"I'm going to find where that's a rule and show it to you, then you're going to be mortally embarrassed for giving me a noogie. I mean, come on." She threw up her hands.

Nick burst out laughing at her dramatic energy. "I can't believe I've missed out on this for so many years. Don't you ever leave me again, Maya. I need my best friend."

Maya's heart shuddered at the earnest devotion in his eyes. "I need my best friend too."

Nick pulled her in for a hug.

"I'm going to find a new one, if you ever give me a noogie again, though. You've been warned."

"Duly noted."

Eleven

NICK

Once Nick and Maya were back in each other's orbits, they were like magnets. Before they knew it, two weeks had passed, and all discomfort had disappeared. Routines they'd never had before became the norm within days, and they never went a day without seeing each other.

Mornings started with coffee and baked goods in the shop before Nick had to head off to work. He didn't mind getting up an hour early every day to spend time with Maya. It added an extra hop to his step when greeting his classes, something the students had begun teasing him about once word spread that a beautiful blonde had visited him during one particular class.

"You're going to make me fat, Maya," Nick complained and shoved half a cheese Danish into his mouth. "I'm the hottest teacher in the school, and I'm going to lose my standing if you keep filling me full of Danish pastries."

Maya snorted as she poured him a cup of fresh coffee. "That's the Colombian. And who else is teaching at that school who could be hotter than you?"

Nick shrugged. "Mr. Darling might give me a run for my money."

Maya choked on a laugh. "Mr. Darling is seventy."

"He's a young seventy, though."

"Does he still insist on wearing that bow tie?"

"Yup."

"Then I think your legacy is safe." Maya rested her elbows on the counter as she regarded him. "Do you like this Danish better than the one yesterday?"

Nick froze. It felt like he'd been trapped. "Um…"

Maya feigned patience as she waited.

"They're different?" he asked finally.

"Obviously, I'm not doing a good job, if you can't tell they're different." Maya's forehead creased in concentration. "Well, that sucks. Maybe I should try another recipe."

"Why do you have to try to improve on perfection? Does it look like I want my Danish changed?" He gestured at the front of his shirt, which was covered with flaky crumbs. "I mean, come on, Maya. You've been making me Danish since we were teenagers. I have zero complaints."

"You didn't even notice I changed the cheese. Who doesn't notice a cheese change? It's the central ingredient in a cheese Danish."

Nick popped his lips as he regarded her, then reached for the pastry container with exaggerated slowness.

"Are you playing that game where you think that if you move really slowly and don't say something, I'll forget I'm annoyed?" Maya demanded.

"I don't know. Will that work?" Nick grinned. "Maya, you're an amazing baker. You always have been. You're over-thinking this. People are going to love the cheese Danish."

Maya pursed her lips, then sighed as she slid onto the stool next to him. "I think I'm nervous."

"I think you are too." Nick broke his Danish in half and

115

handed her a piece. "Why do you think that is? You never used to be nervous about your baking."

"I don't know." Maya didn't make eye contact when responding, which was how Nick knew she was lying.

"I thought we agreed we wouldn't do that."

"Do what?"

"That." Nick moved his fingers around in a circular pattern. "We said we would be honest, then agreed nobody could stay mad more than twenty-four hours if there was a blow-up because of the honesty. That was part of the pact we made, right?"

Maya nodded, making a face. "Yes, but this is ... embarrassing."

"Oh, I saw you back in the day, when you had zit cream crusted all over your face and slept in Care Bear pajamas. Nothing you say can be as embarrassing as that."

Maya glared at him. "Did you have to bring up the zit cream?"

"Obviously. That's why I did it."

Maya rolled her eyes. "Do you promise not to laugh?"

"No."

Maya sent him an imploring look.

"I can't promise not to laugh, Maya," Nick replied. "You're a funny girl."

"Ugh." Maya rubbed her forehead. "I'm afraid. That's the big secret. I'm terrified I'm going to screw this up."

She was so solemn that Nick had no choice but to match her tone. "Of what, sweetheart?" He hadn't even realized the term of endearment had slipped out until a few beats later. By then, it was too late to take it back, so he ignored it.

"What if I can't do this?" Tears filled her eyes when they locked with his. "What if I can't fulfill my dream? I'll be a thirty-year-old failure with nowhere to go in my life."

"I don't think you can be a failure at thirty, Maya." Nick

brushed her hair away from her face to get a better look at her expression. "If this doesn't work, then you'll just try again."

She shot him an incredulous look. "Yeah, that's not really going to be possible. I used up every dime I have to launch this place. Like ... *every* dime. There's a reason I'm staying out at the old Sandusky cabins on the river."

Nick froze. He hadn't given much thought to where Maya was staying. They'd been spending their time in town as they eased back into things, and it hadn't come up. "*What?*" When he pictured the cabins out by the Cedar River, he shuddered. They'd been falling down when he was a teenager. Nobody had upgraded them since. "Maya, it's not safe for you to be in those cabins. The roof could cave in at any second."

"It's not so bad," Maya replied defensively. "In fact, they're kind of nice. They're surrounded by nature."

"They're surrounded by trees in the middle of nowhere. It's like you haven't even seen *Friday the 13th*." Nick felt irrationally angry. "You can't stay at the Sandusky cabins."

"I don't have a lot of options." Maya rested her hands on the counter. "I can't afford much. This place needs to turn a profit in three months, or all my savings will be gone. Forget launching a restaurant later."

Nick had had no idea her circumstances were so dire. But that still didn't mean he was okay with her staying at the Sandusky cabins. "Maya..." It wasn't his place to tell her how to live her life. Still, the idea of her being dragged into the woods by one of the fishermen who lived off the grid made his blood run cold. "You cannot live in the Sandusky cabins."

"They're all I can afford, and they're really not that bad. I bought mouse traps, and I cleaned really well before I moved in."

"That can't be right." Nick frowned. "There has to be someplace. What about with your parents?"

Maya cringed. "Um ... no."

Even though he considered it a serious conversation, Nick smirked. "Oh, come on. Moving back in with your parents in your late twenties is the dream."

"Don't go there." Maya vigorously shook her head.

Nick hesitated before making another suggestion, but it wasn't nearly as long of a pause as it should've been. "You can move in with me."

Maya's jaw dropped. "What now?"

"I'm not being a creeper," Nick said darkly, although why the idea of sharing a roof with Maya was so appealing, he couldn't say.

"I didn't say you were being a creeper," Maya replied shrilly.

"I have a spare bedroom," he said. "It's just a bed and a dresser, but you can stay in there until you get on your feet."

"I can't do that."

"Why?"

"Because... Because..." Maya looked helpless. "People will talk."

Nick hadn't expected that answer. "People have always talked about us. I want you safe. We just found each other again."

Maya looked as if she wanted to be stern, but she dissolved into softness in an instant. "Nick, I am safe. It's Bellaire. I guarantee I'm way safer up here than I was down in the city."

"That doesn't make me feel any better, Maya."

"Did I ever tell you about the time I had to work the closing shift at that first restaurant for a month straight?"

"No. You didn't tell me a lot of things back then."

"Yeah, well, I was an idiot." Maya leaned her head against his shoulder in apology.

Instead of dragging things out, Nick kissed the top of her head then rested his cheek there. Having her near him again felt so good. It felt as if she were filling his heart with the goodness he'd missed every day. Sooner or later, his heart would burst from the fullness. He wasn't there yet, though. Nick could take more of the fullness. He'd been missing it for so long that he was like an addict with her. Every touch or smile made him whole. He couldn't imagine how he'd managed for so many years without that feeling. It made him shudder if he thought about it too hard.

"I was an idiot too. Don't take it all on yourself."

"Do you want to hear the story?"

Nick hesitated. *Do I?* "Sure," he replied. Part of him didn't, but he was desperate to make sure there were no barriers between them.

"I worked in the Renaissance Center," she said. "You remember that part, right?"

He nodded as he linked his fingers with hers, never letting his cheek break contact with her head. She felt so right, and not just in a "friend" way. Though it was hard for him to admit, the second go-around with Maya felt different. Sure, the hallmarks of their earlier relationship were still there. Something new was bubbling beneath the surface, though. He couldn't put a name to it and was in no hurry to try.

"The building was nice, decadent even, especially for Detroit," Maya continued. "Because the restaurants inside were fancy, the beggars congregated in that area after dark."

Nick kept his breathing even, but his heart rate picked up. He was going to hate the story.

"I didn't think much of it after a few months. I was so afraid and hypervigilant about the area when I first started there, but it didn't last very long. I was always so tired after my shifts and just wanted to get to my car so that I could go home and sleep. I stopped being as aware of my surroundings."

Nick gripped Maya's hand tighter. "Honey, are you about to tell me something awful?" If something had happened to his Maya when they weren't talking—something so terrible he couldn't even use the word—he would never get over it. *Did she go through the worst thing imaginable without me?*

"It wasn't that," Maya reassured him.

Nick sighed with relief.

"It might've turned into that, though."

"Maya." It hurt to breathe, and Nick didn't want to continue. "This isn't making me feel better about the Sandusky cabins."

Maya studied his features with a curious expression. "Is something wrong? Your face is beet red, and you look as if you're about to pass out."

Her observation wasn't entirely wrong. "It's possible. I can't hear a story where you were hurt because I failed you." He swallowed the lump in his throat. "I just can't."

"Failed me? How do you feel as if you failed me?"

"You were clearly attacked."

"I was sexually harassed by some panhandlers and turned the fire hose—which wasn't secured properly—on them. I wasn't strong enough to hold the hose and lost my grip, and it flopped around the parking lot like a huge snake. It scared the panhandlers away, and I ran to my car and never told anyone I was the one who turned on the hose."

"Oh."

"Oh." She managed a smile. "It's a much better story when I can do the proper build-up, but I didn't think you would be able to sit through that version. It's kind of sad, too, because it's one of my better stories. There's a part where I hold on to the hose, and it's so strong that I actually ride it for a few seconds."

Nick barked out a laugh. He was still smiling when he gripped her shoulder, although an intensity he wasn't prepared for filled the air. "I'm sorry I ruined your story. My head went to a bad place."

"I guess I can see that. I wanted to call and tell you the

story back then, but it was four in the morning when I got home, and I knew you had to be up at six."

"I wish you had. I wish we hadn't been such dumbasses."

"Yeah, well, we can't go back." She patted his hand. "We can go forward, though."

"I want that." He beamed at her. "I want to hear all the stories now."

"Okay."

"You still can't stay at the Sandusky cabins. They're gross, and you're not safe there."

"Well, they're my only option, and I don't believe we're ready to move in together. I think I'll survive."

"You always survive." Nick stared into her eyes. "Geez, Maya, how did I make it without you?"

Suddenly, the shop's front door opened, and Blaine entered.

Nick, who had been feeling so open and happy moments before, froze. He'd never been good with identifying his emotions, but the one he was currently feeling could easily be described thanks to the flash of green that momentarily blinded him.

"Maya, I got your trim," Blaine said, his attention focused on a box he was carrying. "I also got your electrical outlets, and the delivery service called to confirm the booths are coming tomorrow. That's a big job, so it's going to take three days. Prepare yourself for a lot of hammering and nailing."

Maya moved toward Blaine. "I don't care how long it takes, as long as it gets done. I want those booths more than I want coffee in the morning, at this point."

"Yes, you've been a little intense," Blaine agreed as Maya hugged him. His arms were full, so he didn't return the hug, but adoration lurked in his eyes as he regarded her. "I'll get them installed as soon as possible."

As Nick watched their interaction, coldness moved

through his chest. He'd always hated Blaine. Maya had hooked up with him shortly after they arrived at Central Michigan University. They'd barely gotten settled, and she was already raving about a guy she'd met on campus. Nick had been frustrated then, and he was even more frustrated to see him again.

"Blaine," Nick said when he finally shifted from Maya.

"Hey, man. It's good to see you."

"You too," Nick lied. It was not good to see Blaine and most certainly not with Maya. *Why are they hugging? Are they back together? Are they considering getting back together?* Nick was thrown by the sheer breadth of the questions running through his head. "I didn't realize you were still working on the shop. I thought you were done." He tried to keep his expression neutral, but he wasn't entirely successful.

"Oh, Maya tapped me to help when she was looking at this building," Blaine replied. He sounded uber casual, which just irritated Nick more. "She wanted to make sure there was nothing structurally wrong with it and didn't entirely trust the inspector she hired. I came in as a favor, and things just sort of spiraled. I'm here until the bitter end now."

"Blaine has been invaluable," Maya gushed. "I thought I had everything figured out, but he always knows a better way to look at things. I don't know what I would've done without him." She shot Blaine an adoring gaze. "He's my hero." She grabbed his cheek and gave it a good jiggle, which was enough to have Nick shooting to his feet.

"I should go," he blurted. "Um ... the Danish are great, Maya." He gave her a wide berth as he started for the door.

Surprise covered Maya's face as she turned away from Blaine. "You're leaving?" She checked the clock on the wall. "You still have fifteen minutes."

"I have stuff I need to get done today," Nick replied, refusing to make eye contact. "You know ... balls to inflate. That sort of thing. I'll see you later."

"Balls to inflate?" Blaine called.

Nick cursed himself for saying it, but it was too late to take it back. "I'll see you around. Have a nice day."

Nick wasn't certain why he'd responded the way he had, and though he had an inkling about why he'd gotten so uncomfortable—and so fast—he didn't want to delve too deeply.

No, he wasn't ready for that, not by a long shot.

Twelve

MAYA

Nick's abrupt exit threw Maya. She had no idea what to make of it. Since people were flitting in and out of the shop, she kept her concerns to herself until Blaine was working in the kitchen, and Lindsey had made an appearance. She immediately told Lindsey what happened because she needed her friend's expertise.

"So, that was weird, huh?"

Lindsey arched an eyebrow. "What was weird? I thought I was quiet."

Confused, Maya asked, "What are you talking about?"

"What are *you* talking about?"

"The way Nick took off as if he couldn't get out of here fast enough. I thought things were going well between us. What were you talking about?"

"Oh, I farted. It was silent, though. I thought I got away clean, then when you said that, I figured you were going to call me on it. It's all good."

Laughing, Maya shook her head. "Well, thanks for that, I guess."

"Hey, when you have kids, things like that happen."

Lindsey rested her elbows on the counter as she regarded Maya. "As for Nick, how are you so confused? He left because of Blaine."

"Why would he care about Blaine?"

"Are you being serious?"

"Why wouldn't I be?"

"I just can't tell sometimes. You're sweetly naive, something you've held on to since we were kids. It's very weird."

"Um, I don't know what you're saying. Maybe you should just spell it out for me."

"Oh, I've been spelling it out for you. It's not my fault you refuse to listen."

"Lindsey." Maya groaned

"Maya, Nick is in love with you. He's always been in love with you. When we were kids. When you headed off to college. Now, I wasn't around when you guys were trying to make a go of it at your new jobs, but I'm willing to bet he was in love with you then, too, which makes the fact that you fell out of touch all the more difficult for him."

Maya blinked several times. "What?"

"It's not as if this is the first time I've brought it up. Come on, Maya. How can you not see this?"

"Because it's not true."

"No? Tell me why it's not true."

"Because ... we were always friends. I know you've been teasing me about the possibility since I got back, but I didn't think you were being serious. I figured you were just trying to bug me."

"I do enjoy bugging you. It's so easy." Lindsey grinned. "I'm being serious, though, Maya. The man loves you. He always has."

"I don't know." Troubled, Maya turned to stare out the window. "I think that's something only you see."

"Oh, get real. Everybody in this town has seen it at one

time or another. I wasn't joking about the pool. We were convinced you guys would somehow magically get over your crap and realize you loved each other. It didn't happen before you left. Then we assumed it would happen when you went to college. I mean, it was just the two of you."

"But he never acted like he felt that way about me." Emotions Maya couldn't identify flooded her. Part of her didn't want to identify them. "That's just not the way things were between us."

"How was he supposed to act?" Lindsey asked, using her most reasonable tone. "Like, should he have gotten down on one knee and begged you to love him back? Honestly, I'm not sure he understands what he's feeling. He's a man. These things need to be spelled out in crayon for them. Heck, sometimes I write the shopping list in crayon for Bear just because I think he comprehends it better. It's not like you were alone in being an idiot. He was right there with you."

"But that's not right." Maya shook her head. "There would've been signs."

"You mean like when Todd Gilliam said you looked like you were going to grow up to be a high-class hooker, and Nick beat the crap out of him? Or how about when Shane Wildfong backed you into a corner at homecoming that one year and tried to grope you under your dress?"

Maya shuddered at the memory. "What happened to him?"

"He works construction in Traverse City. He's been charged twice with sexual misconduct. Everyone agrees that he's a rape waiting to happen, and we're all holding our breath that he'll run his car into the bay when he's drunk driving one of these times. Like, we don't want anybody else to get hurt, but if he were to disappear from the face of the earth, nobody would mind."

Maya popped her lips then shook her head. Focusing her

attention on Shane would cause nightmares. She didn't want that. "Nick was just being a friend when he did that stuff. He didn't want anything bad to happen to me and would've done that for anybody."

"While it's true he would've jumped in to help others in that situation, did you miss the part where he was practically foaming at the mouth when he went after Shane? I thought there was going to be a *Dateline* special about men who kill to protect the women they love by the time he was finished."

"Oh, you're exaggerating." Even as she said it, Maya felt the doubt creeping in.

"Are you saying you don't love him?" All traces of mirth were missing from Lindsey's features. "Can you really look me in the eye and tell me you don't love him?"

"He's my oldest friend. Of course I love him. There are different types of love, though."

"Fine." Lindsey held up her hands in supplication. "I acknowledge there are different types of love. You're in love with Nick, though. You always have been."

"I…" Maya's breath came out in short bursts. "I don't think I want to talk about this any longer." A hodgepodge of emotions filled her, and she couldn't focus on one long enough to register exactly what she was feeling. The only thing she knew for certain was that she was panicking.

"We don't have to talk about it. But you do need to think about it, because this is your shot. You and Nick are in the same place. It feels like fate to me. You guys have worked through your initial issues. Now you just need to tackle the big one."

"I still think you're seeing things that aren't there." Maya avoided making eye contact. "Nick only looks at me as a friend."

"I'm only going to say one more thing on this topic, because it's obvious you're having trouble digesting it."

Lindsey angled herself so that Maya had no choice but to look her in the eye. "I get it. I really do. You're afraid."

"I'm not afraid," Maya said with more bravado than she felt.

"You're terrified," Lindsey pressed. "You can't imagine your life without Nick, especially now that you've gotten him back. You don't want to rock the boat and trying to date him might ruin a great friendship. Well, at least that's what you're thinking. The thing is your fears aren't unfounded. If things go badly with the relationship part, you could lose the friendship. You could also get everything you've ever wanted, but you're too afraid to allow yourself to embrace the truth."

Maya pressed her lips together and returned to staring out the window. *Is Lindsey right? Have I been burying my feelings for Nick my entire life?*

Yes.

Maya shivered when the word echoed in her head. Then she forced herself to lob a "You're so silly" smile at Lindsey. "You're really getting good at bugging me. It's like you were out of practice when I first got back, and now you're perfecting your skills. I almost fell for that."

Clearly exasperated, Lindsey sighed. "You're not fooling me. I know you're thinking about what I said. You might not be ready to admit it, but I laid the groundwork. You're not going to be able to ignore those feelings going forward."

Maya's greatest fear—and it was something she couldn't admit out loud—was that Lindsey was right. *What if I do have feelings for Nick? What am I supposed to do about that?*

MAYA SPENT THE BETTER PART OF THE afternoon working alone. Blaine left after handling the trim, promising he would be back the following day. Once total silence descended over the shop, Maya's thoughts became a relentless stalker, and no matter which corner she tried to hide in, they followed her.

Then she made a decision.

Her father owned a lumberyard on the outskirts of town, the biggest one in the area, and even though he'd largely handed over the day-to-day operations to her cousins, who served as managers, he still spent time in his office five days a week. He handled most of the books and left the actual fulfillment services to others. Maya had a theory that he liked being the boss but was ready to skirt the work so that he could be partially retired, but she kept it to herself.

"Hey, Dad." She knocked lightly on his open door and popped her head inside to survey the room. If he was busy, she would leave, although since she'd committed to the plan, there was no going back. Daniel Markham was the most honest man she knew. He would tell her the truth. "Do you have a minute?"

Daniel glanced up from the ledger he was balancing and nodded, despite the confusion that registered in the depths of his eyes. "This is a surprise." He closed the ledger book. "You haven't been out here since you got back."

Sheepish, Maya replied, "I meant to come sooner. I've just been busy."

"Running your own business is a big deal," Daniel agreed as he swept a hand through his thinning brown hair and indicated one of the chairs across from his desk. "I should know. I started this business thirty-five years ago. It's still a success."

"It's great," Maya agreed. "I always liked hanging out here when I was a kid."

"It's such a success that one might think a new business owner would ask the person who started it for some tips when opening her business."

"Dad, a lumberyard is different from a coffee shop. And I want to do this myself. I already told you that."

"Hm." Daniel didn't look impressed with her response. "What's up with you? Do you need me to fix something that moron you used to date messed up when renovating? I saw that coming."

"Blaine is doing a great job," Maya replied. "I'm happy with his work. He's also doing it for me at a steep discount."

"Is that because there are sexual favors involved?" Daniel looked horrified at the thought. "I will break his neck if he's taking sexual favors in trade."

Maya did her best to push the insult out of her head. *What does it say about me if my own father is willing to believe that's a possibility?* "There are no sexual favors, Dad. I'm not here to talk about Blaine. He's doing a good job, and things are on schedule. Everything is good at the shop."

"Oh." Daniel looked taken aback. "Is it your mother? If she's sticking her nose in your business, I can't get involved. She'll stick her nose in my business, if I'm not careful. It's better when she has you to focus on. I still remember when she was bored two summers ago and decided the lumberyard needed 'rearranging.' Who rearranges piles of wood? Your mother. That's who."

Maya laughed. Her father had ranted and raved over the phone during the rearranging process to the point that she started dodging his calls, something she wasn't exactly proud of. "I'm still kind of sorry I missed that."

"Then I'm telling the story wrong." Daniel steepled his fingers and gave Maya a firm looking over. "Something's bothering you. What is it?"

He was right, and she was at the point that she was about to explode if she didn't talk about it with someone. "Do you think I'm in love with Nick?" she blurted.

"Wow, you really do have something on your mind, huh?" To Maya's surprise, her father looked more amused than bothered. "Do *you* think you're in love with Nick?"

"No."

"No?"

"No. Lindsey just put it in my head. It's not possible, right?"

"Ah, Lindsey." The corners of Daniel's mouth curved up. "There's a reason she's one of my favorite people. She just throws it all out there like a bomb and leaves the mess for everybody else to pick up."

"She's wrong, right? I haven't always been in love with Nick."

Daniel hesitated then let out a sigh. "Kid, I don't know if we should be having this discussion."

Because she'd expected her father to wave off the notion, Maya's anxiety increased. "You *do* think that."

"I think that you and Nick have a complicated relationship," he hedged. "You've always been great friends—and his loyalty knows no bounds—but things were never as easy as you two seemed to think they were."

Stumped, Maya said, "That wasn't really an answer."

"And you want an answer."

"I need one. I thought Lindsey was just messing with me when she said everybody in town was taking bets as to when Nick and I would jump in bed together. It turns out she wasn't. Apparently, this is something everybody believes."

"Yes, and I have two weeks from Thursday in the pool, so if you could hold off until then, that would be great. Your mother wants new curtains."

Maya's jaw dropped. "You're taking bets as to who I'm going to sleep with?"

"Oh, well, don't say it like that." Daniel made a face. "We're not betting on when you guys are going to do ... *that*. Also, for the record, I don't want to know when it happens. We're betting on when you guys admit you have grown-up feelings for each other."

That didn't make things better. "I don't understand any of this," she lamented. "We're just friends."

"No, kid, you're not." Daniel almost looked sad. "You were just friends when you were ten ... and even thirteen. By the time you were sixteen, the truth was right there for the taking. You were both too afraid to take it, though.

"If you want to know the truth, I was glad you weren't ready to admit what you were feeling," he continued. "I wasn't ready for you to find true love as a teenager, because I wanted you to stay my little girl a bit longer. You and Nick were terrified to see what was in front of you, so that made things easier, for a few years, at least."

Maya worked her jaw, her heart rate picking up. "You're saying that I'm in love with Nick."

"I'm saying that you've always been in love with Nick and vice versa. Maya, it's not a bad thing. Nick is a good man. Actually, I always knew he was going to be a good man. I just didn't want him to be the right man for you before you could live a little."

Helplessness flooded Maya. "I don't know what you mean by that."

Daniel touched his tongue to his top lip, obviously debating, then barreled forward. "When you were about eighteen, I was afraid Nick was going to derail your life. I believed that if you two admitted how you felt, you were going to screw everything up and ruin your bright futures to stay here together. That didn't happen, though."

Maya didn't respond.

"Instead, you both screwed up your lives on your own and still ended up back here," he continued. "The difference is now you're supposed to be here. You've lived the part of your lives that were supposed to be away from this place, and fate brought you back together."

"Meaning?" Maya's voice was raspy, as if she'd gone days without water.

"Now I think Nick is the key to getting your life back on track. I think you're the key for him too. It's something you need to do together."

"But I didn't know any of this." Maya flapped her hands, distraught. "I'm not ready for any of this. And I'm not even sure it's true."

"Oh, you know it's true. That's why you're so upset. By the way, that hand thing you're doing, you inherited it from your mother. It's a little freaky."

To Maya, the offhand comment was like a slap to the face. "That's the meanest thing you've ever said to me."

"It's the truth, though. All of it is. You might not be ready to hear it, but that doesn't change that it's happening. For better or worse, you and Nick are on a collision course. You just need to decide how you're going to handle the inevitable crash when it happens."

Thirteen

NICK

Nick's mood could only be described as surly as he struggled through the day. He paid very little attention to the kids as they played basketball in the gym—which wasn't his way—then proceeded to pout in his office during his off hour. By the time practice for the basketball team rolled around after school, he felt numb. He had no idea why he was reacting the way he was.

You know, his inner voice argued.

Nick ruthlessly shoved it away and caught the ball underneath the rim to signify it was time to wrap up practice.

"Free throws," he announced. "You need to make twenty before you can hit the shower. Try not to make fifty attempts, if you can." He managed a smirk for Jake Sherman, his prize center, who didn't believe free-throw skills were necessary for the big man on the court. "Concentrate."

"Nobody gets million-dollar endorsements for making free throws," Jake complained. "The honeys love the rebounds and blocks. They don't love the free throws."

Nick didn't bother to hide his eye roll. "The honeys—which is a terrible way to refer to our female friends—like a hero on the court. Imagine, if you will, that our team is three points behind, and you manage to put up a bank shot in the paint as time expires, and you're fouled in the process. You could be the difference between overtime and losing. Doesn't that sound exciting?"

"Not as exciting as not having to make twenty free throws."

Nick tried not to let his exasperation show. "Just do it. You're giving me a headache."

"I think you have a headache because you screwed up with that honey who visited you last week."

Nick's forehead creased. "I don't know who you're talking about."

"The blonde. The hot, hot blonde." Jake pressed his fingers to his lips for a chef's kiss. "She was smoking. I'm hoping she's still available when I'm legal in a year."

Nick scowled. "Don't call her a honey. Show her some respect. Her name is Maya. Ms. Markham to you."

"Woot-woot!" Several of the players started catcalling.

He graced each of them with a dirty look. "Knock it off. Maya is my childhood friend. I know you guys like to see things that aren't there ... and exaggerate other things ... but we've been best friends for more than half our lives. It's not the sort of relationship you're trying to make it out to be."

"If she was always your best friend, how come we haven't seen her until now?" Chris Morton demanded. He was normally one of the quieter ones, yet he seemed invested in the answer.

"She was down in Detroit, working," Nick replied. "She came home to open her own coffee shop. Yes, that's right. You guys will have a new place to hang out in a few weeks, although I'm not sure any of you need more caffeine to hype yourselves up."

"My mom says that you and 'your friend' used to be

famous in town," Steve Corman interjected with air quotes. He had dark hair, and his green eyes were keen. "She said that everybody in town used to watch you guys because they were certain you were going to start reenacting scenes from romance movies."

"Your mother said that, did she?" Nick crossed his arms.

"She also said she used to babysit you guys when she was a teenager, and she could tell you were hot for each other even when you were eight," Steve added.

"No offense, but your mother was a terrible babysitter," Nick fired back. "She spent all her time on the phone with boys and paid zero attention to Maya and me."

"That doesn't mean she's wrong. My dad says she's always right ... even when she's wrong. I trust her on this."

"We want to know about the pretty lady," Jake insisted. "All the girls in school are in love with you. They think you're hot, and they go out of their way to walk past the gym when you're in it. Heck, before you showed up, most of the girls didn't want anything to do with gym class. Now they're all about it."

"I think we've gotten off track." Nick shifted from one foot to the other, uncomfortable. "You need to do your free throws."

"We'll do our free throws," Chris promised. "If you answer a question about Pretty Maya for each one we make."

Nick frowned. "I'm not agreeing to that. You guys are going to do your free throws regardless."

"But we'll try harder," Jake offered. "Like, we'll put effort in. If you answer our questions."

Nick recognized it was a bad precedent to set, yet he nodded. "Fine. If you all make a free throw, I'll answer a question." He figured it was impossible for each of them to make one. Somebody would have to miss.

But he was wrong. Every player nailed their first shot.

"What are the odds of that?" he grumbled.

"I'll ask the first question," Chris said. "Were you ever with Maya?"

"No. Maya and I were always friends."

"See, I don't believe that," Steve shot back. "My mom says you were in love with her way back when, and somehow, you lost her. Nobody saw it coming."

"Have you considered that your mother is simply wrong?"

"No. My dad says she's always right."

Steve's father was a famously docile man who adored his wife. As for Steve's mother, the aforementioned babysitter, she'd always been a terrible gossip. In truth, Nick liked her, at least for the most part. He would've preferred she not share old gossip with her son in an attempt to entertain the next generation, however.

"I don't know what to tell you guys." Nick shrugged, holding out his hands. "There's no sordid tale. Maya was my best friend growing up. We played basketball together in the parking lot all the time."

"My mom said you left for college together," Steve insisted.

"Your mother clearly has a lot of time on her hands." Nick did his best to keep his agitation from coming out. "We did go to college together. We also graduated together."

"Yet you came back here without her," Jake pressed. "Why?"

"Because ... sometimes life doesn't work out how you think it's going to." Nick was talking more about himself than anybody else. "We got jobs in different parts of the state, and we worked different hours. So we lost track of each other for a bit."

"But now you're together," Jake said. "You're going to be together now, right?"

Nick studied Jake's face with confusion. The boy seemed

intense, more so than the rest of them. "We're friends again," Nick replied. "We're going to be friends."

A whistle of disappointment rippled through the crowd. All Nick could do was shake his head.

"Free throws. Do them," he ordered. "Now. Question time is over."

The boys made grumbling sounds but did as they were told. Nick could make out a few of them complaining, but he refused to listen to their musings. It seemed everybody was interested in what the future held for him and Maya ... except for Maya. She was much more interested in hanging around with Blaine. *What is that guy even doing helping her anyway?*

Nick had never liked Blaine. He'd always felt as if the guy was putting on a show. He'd never mistreated Maya or anything—Nick wouldn't have put up with that—but there was always something inauthentic about the way Blaine interacted with Maya. It seemed as if the things he was supposed to feel for her were fake.

Nick had been relieved when Maya and Blaine broke up after Blaine's graduation. For the first time since they'd hooked up, Nick had been able to breathe again, although he couldn't figure out why he felt that way. Maya hadn't seemed all that brokenhearted at the time. She said she liked Blaine but didn't feel he was a "forever" sort of love. That had also been a relief.

So why is he back now? Did Maya change her mind? More importantly, why didn't Maya mention that Blaine's back in her life?

Maybe she was worried, Nick mused as he picked up a few balls that had skidded to the corners of the gym as the boys finished. Since their renewed friendship still felt tenuous to both of them, maybe Maya was waiting to drop the bomb on him that she was involved with Blaine again. Perhaps she wanted their friendship to be on firmer footing before she did that.

The idea of Maya sneaking around with Blaine and not telling him about it was enough to light the fuse on Nick's fury. Without realizing what he was going to do, he heaved one of the balls he was holding toward the wall and watched with impassioned disinterest as it bounced against the bricks and careened toward the bleachers.

"Somebody is having a bad day," a woman said from behind Nick, causing him to jolt.

When he turned, he found Camille watching him with amusement.

"It's just been a long day," Nick replied, shaking off the dregs of his annoyance.

"You should have a beer."

"If it weren't frowned upon to drink on school grounds, I would already have one." Nick attempted a smile ... and failed. "I'm just tired. I'm sure tomorrow will be better."

"Was it your team?" Camille gave a forced smile as she eased into the gym.

Nick marveled at how uncomfortable she looked when in his natural habitat. He hadn't noticed when he was younger, yet he recognized it had always been there. Camille was the type of woman who wanted to mold herself to fit another person. She was never comfortable being herself and finding someone who fit her life.

"They were fine," Nick replied, his eyes drifting to the doorway that led to the locker room. "They're showering."

"If it's not them, then what is it?" Camille acted as if she were truly concerned, but Nick detected an edge about the way she carried herself. *What's that about?*

"I already told you," Nick replied. "I'm just tired. It's been a long day."

"Did you start it at Maya's little coffee shop again?"

Nick recognized Camille's tone and had to bite back a sigh. "I did. She's been peppering me with caffeine and baked goods in the morning. Actually, she's been providing both to anybody who wants to stop in. She's doing daily tastings right now."

"All that refined sugar and butter is bad for you. It will clog your arteries and kill you."

That was such a Camille thing to say, and it took everything Nick had not to roll his eyes. "What a way to go, though. I mean, Maya's cheese Danish is the stuff of legends. I used to dream about it after ... well, after."

The corners of Camille's mouth tipped down. "You mean after she blew you off like you didn't matter."

"No, that's not what I mean." Irritation clawed through Nick's chest. "Not that it's any of your business, but Maya and I both made mistakes. We didn't value our friendship in the right way, and we drifted apart. Things are better now."

"Yet you're in a foul mood," Camille mused. "That's interesting to me."

Nick opened his mouth to snap something not so nice but caught himself just as Jake exited the locker room. Because the boy was eyeing him curiously—and darting suspicious looks toward Camille—Nick switched tacks. "All finished?"

Jake nodded. "That's not the hot blonde."

For some reason, the simple statement—and Camille's distressed eye-narrowing—had Nick frantically trying to swallow a laugh. If he reacted, Camille wouldn't take it well. Worse, she might cause a scene, and the last thing he needed was his players witnessing it.

"I happen to think I'm very hot," Camille replied primly. "Perhaps you're too young to grasp my attributes. I'm sure everybody over the age of twenty-five seems ancient to you."

"The hot blonde doesn't," Jake replied.

"Who is the hot blonde?" Camille demanded.

"Maya," Nick replied. For some reason—and he would have to think about exactly why later—he relished saying it to

Camille. He knew it would bother her, and since she was intent on bothering him, he didn't feel a lot of sympathy for her. "She stopped in here the other day, and my players are fascinated with her."

"Because they think she's hot?" Camille looked as if she were ready to breathe fire.

"Because everybody says they belong together," Jake replied.

"Who is everybody?"

Nick didn't like Camille's tone and moved to interrupt her. "They're just being kids, Camille. Don't let it get to you."

"Everybody is everybody in this town," Jake replied, unruffled by Camille's death glare. "Lots of people are talking about it. The old-timers in the diner are taking bets."

"Well, bully for them." Camille turned her back on Jake, essentially telling him he no longer existed, and focused on Nick. "I have something I want to talk to you about."

"Hold up." Nick was in no mood for whatever Camille wanted to discuss, but he didn't want to be rude ... to either of them. Instead, he flashed a smile at Jake. "Ignore the old-timers in the diner. I know you wash dishes there and can't help but overhear some of the things they say. Sometimes they just talk to talk, though."

"I want them to be right about you." Jake's expression was impossible for Nick to read.

"And why is that?"

"Because if you guys are meant to be together like they say, maybe things will work out for other people."

"Like who?" Nick couldn't figure out whether the boy was referring to himself or his parents. Rumors had circulated that his parents were separated and living in different houses, but Nick knew that wasn't his business and didn't question Jake on it.

"It doesn't matter." Jake shook his head. "All that matters

is that you guys work out. If you do, it's proof that others can."

Nick wet his lips. "Jake—"

"I have to go." Jake abruptly turned and headed for the exit. "See you tomorrow, Coach."

"You most definitely will." Nick was thoughtful as he watched the teen disappear, and when he finally turned, he was disappointed to find that Camille was still there, watching him. "What were we talking about again?"

"You need a beer," Camille replied brightly.

"I'm thinking I might need six beers," Nick readily agreed.

"Good. You can have them with me, over dinner. I'll drive so that you don't have to worry about it and can drink to your heart's content."

"Um ... what?" Nick's face flushed as he panicked. Part of him knew that Camille was going to broach the subject of trying their relationship again at some point, but he'd thought he had more time. *Why did she pick today to full-court-press me?*

"Dinner," Camille repeated. "There are some things I want to talk about with you, and I think the conversation will be more comfortable for both of us if we have dinner while we're talking."

"Oh, well, that's a nice offer." *How do I brush her off without hurting her feelings?* If Camille felt slighted or embarrassed, she might do something to repay the favor. Nick wasn't in the mood for more drama. "I can't go to dinner tonight, though. I have to spend some time with my father."

News regarding Hank Griffith's mental state had spread through a town the size of Bellaire relatively quickly. Everybody knew he was drinking his dinner ... and his breakfast and lunch as well. They also knew Nick was trying to hold it together.

Rather than give Nick a hard time because of his response,

Camille unleashed an angelic smile. "Of course. You're stopping in multiple times a week now, right? That makes sense."

"I have to stop in regularly," Nick gritted out.

"Then we'll just make dinner plans for tomorrow. I'll pick a place and text you. How does that sound?"

"Well..." Nick had no idea how he was going to get out of it. The sound of footsteps made him snap his head to the open door behind Camille, and when he saw Maya standing there watching them, he forgot what he was even trying to do. "Maya," he rasped.

"Nick."

"And Camille," Camille added with a laugh, apparently not finding it weird to talk about herself in the third person. "We're all here. Nick and I were just making a date for tomorrow night. It really is like old times."

"A date, huh?" Maya's eyes glittered when they locked with Nick's. "Well, that sounds fun."

Nick didn't know what to say.

"Once Nick and I are back on track, we should do lunch," Camille suggested. "Since you guys are friends again, and we're going to be something more again, that only makes sense."

"Sure," Maya said. "That sounds ... interesting."

Interesting? That wasn't the word Nick would've chosen. It sounded like a trap for all of them.

Fourteen

MAYA

Maya stood rooted to the spot and briefly wondered if she was dreaming. She'd always disliked Camille, from the moment she'd met her. Since she'd returned to Bellaire, that dislike had grown into outright hatred, which was impressive, since they'd only interacted a grand total of two times.

"Nothing is decided," Nick blurted, jolting Maya out of her reverie. "We were just talking."

Camille's eyes narrowed as she focused on him. "We're having dinner, aren't we?"

Nick merely shrugged and kept his eyes on Maya. "I don't know. Maybe." He forced a smile he didn't feel. "Did you need something?"

Maya's mind was going a mile a minute. *Did she need something? Why did I come to the school in the first place?* Her thoughts were jumbled.

Well, that wasn't entirely true. She'd planned to invite Nick out for a meal so that they could talk. Camille's presence —and declaration—had thrown her. "I just ... um ... was in the area." *Such a lame lie. Come up with something better.*

"Do you need something?" Nick looked as if he was going through some sort of ordeal.

"No." Maya shook her head and straightened her shoulders. If another romantic interlude with Camille was what Nick wanted, then as his friend, she had to encourage him. "It's great that you guys are going out again."

Nick narrowed his eyes. "It's weird you would think that."

"I'm your friend, right?" Maya's voice was unnaturally shrill. "I want what's best for you. Obviously, you think that's this. I should go." She barely took a breath between sentences and turned on her heel to leave.

"Let's talk about logistics," Camille said to Nick before Maya had even made it to the door.

Maya couldn't hear his reply, but before she could fully escape, his fingers snaked around her wrist to stop her.

"Hey," he said softly.

Maya tried to smile as she turned, though it must have come out as a grimace.

"Geez." Nick dropped her wrist. "That's a creepy ... whatever it is."

Maya refused to acknowledge the statement. "Do you need something?" she asked in a flat voice.

"I don't know." Nick studied her face for what felt like a really long time. "Maya, are you okay?"

"Of course I'm okay. Why wouldn't I be okay?" Her voice came out shrill again, so she forced herself to adjust her tone. "Why wouldn't I be fine?"

"I don't know. You seem weird, though."

"Kind of like you when you ran out of my coffee shop this morning for no good reason?" She told herself she shouldn't be flinging accusations, but she couldn't help it.

He drew up to his full height. "I was ... late for work."

Maya shot him a "Yeah, right" look.

"I was." The slope of Nick's shoulders telegraphed exactly

how defensive he was feeling. "What does that have to do with anything anyway?"

"I was just curious," Maya replied. "I mean, we're friends, right?" She searched his face for hints that he wanted to be something more. Perhaps Lindsey and her father were right. Maybe the signs were there, but she was simply blind to them.

"We're friends," Nick confirmed. "We've always been friends, even when we weren't friends."

"How does that work?" Maya demanded. She felt agitated, although if pressed on the issue, she wouldn't be able to explain why.

"All you had to do was call," he replied simply. "I would've dropped everything and come. If you'd needed me..."

I always needed you, Maya wanted to scream. "I would've come for you too," she said finally.

He nodded. "I know."

"This is weird, and I don't know what to do," she admitted.

"We'll figure it out." He sighed and glanced at the gym. Camille must still be in there. "Will you be at the court tonight?"

Maya wasn't expecting the question. "Oh, um, probably. I hadn't really thought about it."

"We won't be able to hang out at the court much longer. Probably days instead of weeks before the weather forces us inside. We're going to run out of time."

Maya couldn't help but wonder if he was talking about basketball or something else. "We'll figure it out." That time, she gave a legitimate smile. "I should get back to the shop. I have to make my final decision on the trim for the bathroom hallway today."

"With Blaine?"

Taken aback, Maya replied, "He's been helping me."

"Oh, I'm sure."

"Do you have a problem with Blaine?"

"Do you have a problem with Camille?" Nick shot back, his eyes flashing with annoyance.

They stared into each other's eyes for several seconds, the questions—and the things they refused to say—hanging over them.

"I think we're both off our games today," Maya said finally as she picked at an invisible piece of lint on her shirt. "Maybe we should take a breath, then regroup later."

"Maybe," Nick agreed. "Does that mean you'll be at the basketball court?"

Nick was acting strange about the basketball court, Maya realized. He was almost fixated on it. She didn't want to know what would happen if she declared she wasn't going. "I'll be there."

"Okay." Relief seemed to fuel his smile. "That's good."

"I'll bring a thermos of hot chocolate and some snacks too," she offered.

That made him grin. "Cheese Danish?"

"No." She shook her head. "I'm trying a new recipe this afternoon. It's a maple-glazed bear claw."

"That doesn't sound as good as a cheese Danish."

"You'll live."

Nick's grin spread across his face. "I'm sure it will be delicious. Everything you bake is."

"Yes, I'm a yummy treat," she agreed, not realizing until she'd said it that the words could be construed in multiple ways. Her cheeks burned as she tried to regain control of the conversation. "I should go."

"Yeah. I have to finish cleaning the gym."

"And make plans for your date with Camille," Maya added. She hoped she sounded encouraging, although she doubted she'd managed to pull it off.

"I'm not sure..."

"I need to go." Maya didn't want to talk about his potential date with Camille for one more second. "I'll see you later?"

"Yeah. I'm looking forward to it."

MAYA WAS STILL IN A FUNK WHEN SHE made her way back to the shop. The sound of hammering in the kitchen drew her attention, and she headed in that direction.

Blaine, wearing jeans and a simple gray T-shirt, was on the floor, focused on the baseboards behind the grill. He seemed intent on his project.

"Is something wrong?" Maya asked, suddenly fearful. "Is it bad? How much is it going to cost me?"

Slowly, Blaine raised his eyes to her, amusement curving his lips. "You're like ... the chillest person ever," he teased, laughing.

Maya frowned. "I don't have a lot of extra money," she hedged. "I can't help being nervous. This is my dream. Or rather, the start of my dream."

"I'm well aware." Blaine rolled to a sitting position, giving his crooked smile, something she remembered well from their dating days. "Do you want to talk about what's bothering you?"

"What makes you think anything is bothering me?" Maya asked, trying to be evasive. "I'm great. I'm ... as right as rain, although I've never understood that expression. I'm totally fine, though. There's nothing to worry about."

"Did you chase Nick down to talk? I'm guessing that's where you were, right?"

The question made Maya distinctly uncomfortable. "What do you mean?" She likely sounded defensive, but she couldn't stop herself. "Why would I chase Nick?"

"Because he was upset when he saw me here today."

Maya had always liked that Blaine wasn't the type to drag

things out. But his insistence on tackling a problem head-on was more annoying since they were adults.

"Why would he be upset about that?" Maya demanded. "That's a stupid thing for him to be upset about."

"Maybe," Blaine replied. "But I believe he's upset because he thinks there's a chance we might get back together. Have you considered telling him that's not going to happen?"

"How is it any of his business?" Maya crossed her arms. "I mean, he doesn't get a say in who I date." She paused to inhale. "Just like I don't get a say in who he dates," she muttered.

Blaine's eyes narrowed as he studied her. "I can't help but feel as if I'm missing part of the story," he said finally. "Who is Nick going to date?"

"Apparently, he's going to date Camille again. That's what she says anyway."

"Is Camille some girl from high school?"

"No. He dated her in college. She even moved with him after graduation, although they broke up somewhere in there. Conveniently, she ended up teaching at the high school, and she's pressing him to go out to dinner with her so that they can pick back up where they left off."

"Huh." Blaine scratched his cheek. "And Nick said he was going out with her?"

"Yup."

"He actually said that?"

Maya cocked her head and ran through the conversation. *Did he say that?* Everything that happened at the high school was a jumble in her mind. "I'm not sure." She made a popping sound with her lips as she tried to remember exactly what was said.

"That's what I thought." Blaine pushed himself up from the floor and dusted his hands on his jeans. "Have you considered telling him how you feel?" he asked in a low voice.

"I don't feel anything," Maya snapped. "Why does everyone keep saying I feel something when I very obviously don't?"

"Oh, I don't know," Blaine drawled. "Perhaps it has something to do with the fact that you're bordering on a full-on meltdown because he might go to dinner with an ex-girlfriend. That's just a guess, though."

Maya narrowed her eyes. "I don't think I like your tone."

He laughed, which hadn't been her intention, then he slung his arm around her shoulders. "Come on." He led her into the front of the shop and didn't stop until they were at one of the booths. Then he motioned for her to slide in. "Have you ever asked yourself why we didn't work out when we were younger?" he asked as he sat in the seat opposite her.

"Not really." Maya gave a rueful smile. "I mean, I always liked you. We were compatible. I think I always knew we weren't built for forever, though. I was sad when we broke up but not all that surprised."

"Yet we were together for two years."

"Yeah, well... I don't know what you want me to say." Maya leaned forward. "This isn't going to take a weird turn, is it? Like ... you're not going to ask me out, are you?"

"I'm gay," Blaine said. "You know this because I told you I thought I might be when we broke up. You were extremely understanding about it."

"I didn't want to presume," Maya replied. "I mean, you could've adjusted your thinking since college. That's allowed. I thought maybe you were bisexual or something. It's really none of my business."

"You're my friend, so I'm making it your business. And I'm gay. I mostly knew it back then, although I didn't want to admit it. I was afraid it would change people's perception of me, but ultimately, I wanted to live my truth. Most people are open to it, even up here. But that doesn't change the fact that I loved you back then."

"You loved me?" Maya asked, surprised.

"I did, but it wasn't the sort of love that could sustain a relationship. I loved you as a friend, and I just didn't realize it. Hindsight makes that stuff a lot easier to swallow."

Maya nodded thoughtfully. "I wasn't surprised when you told me. That's not a dig or anything. I think part of me knew. I was more confused about why I was okay staying in a relationship when I knew there was no future than I was hurt by what went down. We're good." She patted his hand. "We've always been good. You treated me like a queen, even if you wanted a king instead."

Blaine barked out a laugh. "You're so funny. You've always been. That's why I was so comfortable with you. There was never some big push to declare my emotions or intentions."

"I don't see the point in that."

"I've done a lot of thinking since college too," he continued, his expression serious. "It took me time to figure out my emotions. Your emotions were tied to them, and it took me longer to figure out your motivations than it did my own."

"Now I'm confused."

"Honey, you dated me because I was safe. You wanted Nick but didn't feel you could have him. I think you were afraid of ruining the friendship. Dating me kept Nick in his box, but it also allowed you to protect your heart because there was no danger of falling in love with me."

Maya balked. "I loved you."

Blaine shot her a withering look. "Are you going to sit there and tell me that with a straight face?"

Anxiety shot through Maya. "I did love you," she growled. "I just didn't realize it was friendship love instead of romantic love until after. There was no malice involved."

"I know." His expression softened. "Maya, I don't blame

you for anything. Things worked out back then, and we managed to extricate ourselves from the relationship without hurting each other. The only reason that was possible is because you were hiding your true feelings for Nick."

"Oh, geez." Maya shook her head and groaned. "Here we go. Do you have any idea how many people have told me that I've been hiding my feelings for Nick since I returned to this stupid town? It's ludicrous."

"Lindsey?" A small smile played at the corners of Blaine's mouth.

"She would be one of the people I'm referring to."

"Lindsey's blunt to the point of being rude, which makes her one of my favorite people in the world these days. She also loves you and wants what's best for you. That's what I want too."

Helplessness made Maya want to scream. "Nick is my friend. And in case you missed it when I mentioned it the first time, he's going to be dating Camille."

"He didn't say that."

"She did, and he didn't correct her."

"Maybe because he's a good guy who doesn't want to embarrass her in front of people. That's neither here nor there, though. Nick is not going to date this Camille person."

"How can you be sure?"

"Because he's got wisdom on his side now. He may not be the smartest man in the world, but he understands his feelings. You guys didn't lose touch because you couldn't maintain the friendship. You lost touch because you both wanted more and didn't know how to get it, so you were afraid. Now you're back in the same spot, and even though the fear might still be real, the magnetic draw you feel toward each other won't allow you to keep running. You're going to have to figure things out this time."

"And what if we decide we're better off as friends?" Maya

demanded. "Everybody in this town apparently thinks they know better than us, but they're not the ones who have to figure things out."

Blaine held out his hands and shrugged. "If you guys decide you're better off as friends, then the town will have to accept that."

Maya felt mildly placated.

"You guys aren't going to decide that, though. Some things are inevitable, Maya, and your relationship is one of them. You can keep running, but eventually, you and Nick are going to catch each other. When that happens, your thinking is going to shift ... and fast."

"How can you be so sure?"

"Because when you're with the one person who fits you completely right, there's no running from it. You guys are like a puzzle, and you have one piece in the wrong place, but you don't realize it yet. When you do, and you move that one piece, the whole picture is going to become clear."

"That sounds a little too easy."

"Yet I believe it." Blaine winked. "Your puzzle is almost finished, Maya. You just need to find that one misplaced piece."

Fifteen

NICK

Nick was at the court before Maya and tried a few practice shots. All of them were bad misses because his nerves were jangling. He had no idea why he was so worked up, yet all afternoon, he hadn't been able to shake the feeling that he was missing something important.

Getting rid of Camille had been difficult—she was never one to take a hint—but he'd finally managed to beg off making plans for their "date." *Am I opposed to dating her for a specific reason?* He didn't have many fond memories of their time together, but it hadn't been terrible—not exactly a rousing endorsement.

Camille should've been an important part of his life. She was his first—and only, if he was being truthful—*real* girlfriend. When they'd broken up, he hadn't been devastated, though. It had felt inevitable, so when it happened, he shrugged it off. He'd been more upset about losing contact with Maya at the time, something he would never admit to Camille because he knew it would cause an epic meltdown.

So why didn't I shut her down right away when she proposed

154

starting up again? He only had one answer, and it was one that left him feeling distinctly uncomfortable. It all came down to Maya. Camille could serve as a shield if need be. *If Maya gets too close...*

He refused to finish that thought. They'd barely rekindled their friendship. *What am I even thinking?*

"It's cold," Maya announced from behind him, causing him to jolt.

Nick stopped dribbling the ball—*how long have I been doing that?*—and turned to face her. "Yeah." The sight of her took his breath away. She wore those stupid yoga pants she insisted on wearing even though they molded to every curve, causing his heart to skip a beat. Her hair was pulled back in a ponytail, and she wore no makeup, yet she did things to his pulmonary system that he couldn't put a name to. "You're here."

Maya raised an eyebrow. "I said I would be."

"Yeah, well, I wasn't sure. Today was ... weird."

Maya huffed a laugh. "That's one way to describe it."

"I don't like it when things are weird between us."

"I don't either." She sidled toward him. "I get fearful when we're not clicking," she admitted. "I don't want what happened before to happen again."

"I don't want that either." He squared his shoulders. "We need to come up with a rule or something that says we can't stop talking."

"I thought we already agreed to that."

"I know, but it doesn't feel like enough."

"Do you want a blood pact?" Her eyes lit up with amusement. "Do you want to cut our palms and become blood ... friends?"

"If I thought that would work—and not be gross—I might agree. All I can think about is a potential infection from a rusty knife, though."

"Nobody would use a rusty knife." Maya plucked the ball from his hands. She was close enough that he could see her breath in the limited illumination from the lone streetlight. "How about we just agree that even if things feel weird, we can't hide from each other? That seems like something we can both follow through on."

"Yeah." His fingers itched to brush away the stray wisp of hair that had escaped from her ponytail, but he managed to refrain. The air was thick between them, as if a cloud of the things they should be saying was hanging heavily in the atmosphere.

Maya was the first to break under the weight of the moment. "So, um, are we playing one-on-one tonight?"

"Sure." Nick bobbed his head. "We can do that or..." Whatever he was going to say died on his lips. Even he wasn't certain what he was about to suggest.

The sound of footsteps snapped his attention away from her, though, and he narrowed his eyes as he made out a lone figure approaching them.

It took him a moment to recognize who it was, and when he did, his heart dropped to his shoes. "Dad?"

Maya followed his gaze, frowning when she caught sight of Hank Griffith. She seemed surprised by his appearance, but she gave a warm smile when Hank moved to stand beneath the streetlight. "Hey."

"Well, hello." Hank's voice was low and raspy. Nick recognized why without having to get close enough to get a whiff. He'd been dealing with the drinking for months and knew exactly what state his father was in.

"What are you doing wandering around?" Nick demanded.

Maya's eyes slid to Nick, but she didn't speak. Instead, she let father and son converse, watching the interaction without interfering.

"Oh, don't take that tone with me," Hank growled. "I don't need any crap from you tonight." He lifted his right hand, displaying what looked to be a bottle in a paper bag. "I had to run to the store."

"Whiskey?" Nick grimaced.

"So what if it is?" Hank always acted defensive lately, as Nick knew all too well. "I ran out and wanted a cocktail. There's no law against that." He shifted in exaggerated fashion, telling Nick that he was already multiple cocktails deep.

"Geez." Nick pressed his eyes shut to rearrange his thoughts. His goal had been to talk to Maya and maybe sort out some of their issues, but he had another problem he couldn't ignore. "You shouldn't be out here. It's cold, and you tend to pass out fast. You'll freeze to death if you do that out here."

"Oh, nobody is going to pass out," Hank shot back. "It's one cocktail."

Hank wasn't slurring, but he had a high tolerance—mostly from practice—and the word-slurring didn't come into play until it was time to pass out.

"Just ... give me that." Nick strode toward his father, but Hank proved he was still on top of things enough to read his son and smoothly tucked the bottle inside his jacket.

"You're not the boss of me," Hank snapped. "Good grief. What makes you think you get to decide anything? You get more and more like your mother with each passing day."

Nick reacted as if his father had slapped him. He was close to exploding.

Then he felt Maya's warm presence at his side.

"How about we all go for a walk together," she suggested in a soothing tone. "I haven't gotten a chance to spend nearly enough time with you since I got back." She directed the words toward Hank, but her gaze was on Nick.

Emotion nearly overcame Nick, but he held it together.

Maya was providing him with an opportunity to walk his father home. She would serve as a buffer for the walk, too, even if it wasn't her responsibility to broker peace. She'd offered because that was simply who she was.

"Yeah, let's go for a walk," Nick agreed, letting out a sigh. "It's a nice night for it."

Hank blinked several times, as if debating whether he was being set up, then turned and started marching in the direction of his house. Nick fell into step behind him and tried not to react with surprise when Maya slipped her hand into his. He didn't pull away. Her small hand was warm, and she was providing him with an emotional anchor to hold on to as his father's ship listed in the channel and threatened to go down.

Hank's house was only four blocks away, and Maya chatted with him the whole time. Nick remained silent, his focus on the way her hand fit perfectly in his. It felt right, even though the moment seemed altogether wrong, thanks to his father's drunken presence.

Maya didn't release his hand until they arrived at the house. Then in her quick and efficient way, she ushered Hank inside and started fussing over him.

"Your hands are cold," she noted as she helped Hank out of his coat. "You need to warm up."

"I know one way." Hank let loose an evil cackle and held up the whiskey bottle.

Maya grabbed it from him, taking everybody by surprise. "How about I make some tea to go with this," she suggested. "Everybody loves a hot toddy, right?"

Hank worked his jaw. "I don't need tea," he said finally, making a grab for the bottle. "I can drink straight from the source."

Maya smoothly deposited the bottle on the counter then placed herself between Hank and his prize. "You need to warm up first. You'll get sick otherwise. Do you want to get the flu?"

Hank snorted. "That's not how you get the flu, young lady."

"Get in your chair." Maya's tone brooked no nonsense, and when she crossed her arms, Nick saw hints of Catherine Markham in her. He had to bite back a laugh. The only thing Maya had ever said with regularity when they were growing up was that she didn't want to grow up to be like her mother.

It seemed she'd failed on that, although Nick didn't think it was so bad. He'd always loved Catherine.

"You're very bossy," Hank groused as he kicked off his shoes and sat in the chair. His eyes widened when Maya shoved the lever on the side, tossing him back in a supine position with his feet up before he could even get comfortable. "Hey!"

Maya smirked. "If you don't want to be treated like a child, you need to stop acting like one." She grabbed a blanket from the couch. "It's cold outside. You could have frostbite and not even realize it. You have to warm up before I give you another cocktail."

Hank's brow furrowed. "You're not the boss of me," he growled.

"Well, it seems to me that you need someone to be the boss of you," Maya replied. "When left to your own devices, you tend to make bad decisions."

Hank's eyes flew to Nick. "Are you listening to her? All women think the same thing. They believe they get to make all the choices, even if they're not making them for themselves. It's a sickness."

"Shut up," Nick replied, shocking even himself. "She's trying to help. Do what she says."

"You stay here for fifteen minutes," Maya ordered as she tucked Hank in. "I'll come back when those fifteen minutes are up, and if I'm satisfied you're not going to get sick—and that you need another cocktail—I'll provide one. Until then, sit there, and look pretty."

Hank was bordering on apoplectic. "What happened to you?" he demanded. "You used to be such a sweet girl. Now you're a bossy know-it-all. How did that happen?"

"I guess my mother's genes are impossible to avoid," Maya replied. "It is what it is." She left Hank stewing and grabbed Nick by the wrist to lead him into the kitchen. Her eyes widened when she saw the mess, but that didn't stop her from grabbing the garbage bags from under the kitchen sink and starting to clean.

"Are you going to help?" she asked when Nick just stood there, watching her.

"It's a waste of time," he said when he found his voice. "He's a mess. He likes living in a mess."

"Well, maybe tomorrow will be different," Maya suggested. "Perhaps tomorrow he'll wake up and see the clean kitchen and decide he doesn't want to be a mess any longer."

Though that was the most preposterous thing Nick had ever heard, he couldn't help yearning for that outcome. "He's going to kill himself, Maya," he admitted, his voice cracking. "He's going to drink himself to death, and I don't know what to do."

Maya's glassy eyes locked with Nick's. "I know. I'd heard he was drinking, but this is worse than I imagined. We'll figure it out."

"Just like that? We'll figure it out?"

Maya shrugged. "I'm playing it by ear right now, Nick. I need to think. There has to be something we can do for him."

"This is all my mother's fault," Nick complained as he started throwing garbage into one of the bags she'd provided him with. "If she hadn't left him, none of this would've happened."

"I'm not going to get into a fight with you," Maya said,

"but this is not your mother's fault. She might've made some mistakes when abandoning the marriage, but she didn't cause this. Your father is a grown man. He made the decision to react this way. Your mother is not here every night, shoving that bottle into his hand. He's doing that." She moved to the liquor collection on the counter and cocked her head. "What happens if you throw the bottles away?"

Nick remained rooted to his spot on the other side of the counter, debating whether he wanted to continue railing against his mother. The change of subject had thrown him. "He goes and buys more the next day."

"Does he buy eight bottles or just one?"

"Why does that matter?"

Maya shrugged. "I don't know. I was just thinking that maybe he would be forced to slow down, due to circumstances if nothing else, if we tossed the bottles."

"I've tried. He doesn't care."

Maya pursed her lips, then grabbed one of the vodka bottles and dumped it down the sink without hesitation. Then, to Nick's utter surprise, she filled the bottle with water.

"He's going to know that's not vodka," Nick said. "He's a drunk, not stupid."

"I don't care. I'm still doing it."

Her adamant growl drew a laugh from Nick. "I forgot how stubborn you are," he said as he moved closer to her. "I missed it."

When Maya turned, Nick stood right beside her. "I missed it all." She searched his face. "I missed all of it ... even this." She rested her hand on his arm. "We're going to figure this out. I don't know how, but we will."

"How can you be sure?"

"Because I've always believed that we can do anything when we put our minds together."

Nick blinked repeatedly. The house was a mess, with

liquor bottles and food wrappers strewn everywhere. The smell was atrocious. Despite all that, in the moment, he'd never seen anyone more beautiful or wondrous than she was.

"Maya." He choked out her name and went in for a hug. He needed it.

She responded without hesitation, wrapping her arms around his neck and pressing herself against him. Her hand moved down the back of his head as she held tight. "You're not going to be doing this alone. Not any longer. I'm here, and while I'm not perfect or an expert, I refuse to let this be the end of your father's story."

Nick let out a guttural sob as he moved his forehead to rest it against hers. She felt so right there, against him, that all he could think was *I'm not letting her go. Not ever.*

The emotion surprised him, but he wasn't done. He was so lost in the moment that he did the unthinkable and let his mouth wander toward hers.

The kiss felt like a million years in the making. Her plump lips were like welcoming pillows against his. What should've been a friendly moment turned hot in an instant, and to Nick's surprise, her hand moved from the back of his head to the front of his shirt as she dragged him closer.

Nick lost all sense of control and tugged her so that she was plastered against his body. He was so intent on her that he couldn't breathe, until he realized he might pass out from lack of oxygen.

He only pulled back far enough to study her face. Her eyes were so cloudy that she looked almost drugged. Then he went in for another round, letting his tongue take a little walk in her mouth. She responded in kind, and they were breathless again in an instant, their hearts pounding against each other through layers of clothing, demanding to be heard.

What are you doing? Nick thought. Nick didn't care to

provide answers, however. He had no idea what he was doing. But he couldn't stop. He would die if he did.

If the mewling sounds Maya was making while trying to climb him were any indication, she felt the same way. Without thinking, Nick grabbed her around the waist and hoisted her onto the counter so that he would have better access to her mouth. They were both sweating, and they'd barely moved a muscle.

Maya's backside collided with the bottle of whiskey Hank had brought back to the house, causing it to fall over with a bang in a death knell of the moment, only Nick didn't realize it until his father stirred in the next room.

"Where's my cocktail?" Hank demanded.

Like a spell ending out of nowhere, Nick and Maya reared back from each other. Their eyes wide, they blinked and fought to catch their breath.

"I... You..." Nick had no idea what he was supposed to say. *Should we talk about it? Pretend it didn't happen?*

Maya made the decision before he could think things through. "We need to finish cleaning," she said, avoiding his probing gaze as she hopped down from the counter. "It's going to take us an hour at this rate."

Nick couldn't think of anything he wanted to do less than to clean his father's house. But he needed time to regain his senses. "Yeah. Um ... let's get it done."

They set about cleaning, avoiding each other at every turn around the kitchen island. There was no eye contact and no inadvertent touching. They were essentially two strangers working toward the same goal.

What just happened? Nick was at a loss. All he knew with any degree of certainty was that he wanted it to happen again. *How did we get to this place?*

Sixteen

MAYA

Maya dreamed of tangled tongues, and she woke up sweating and out of breath, with her hair snarled, indicating she'd tossed and turned all night. Despite the fact that she could feel the chill in the air throughout her cabin—the insulation was terrible, and it would be a long winter—she only allowed herself a lukewarm shower because she was afraid to indulge in a hot one. She was already hot enough, and since her best friend—he *was* still her best friend, no matter what her traitorous heart was suddenly telling her—was the cause of it, she needed to calm down. But it wasn't as easy as she'd hoped.

She was dragging by the time she got to the coffee shop. Lindsey was already inside, which should've struck Maya as odd, but since Maya had given her a key to help with deliveries, she barely blinked.

"Are you hungover?" Lindsey asked when Maya went straight to the coffeemaker without saying a word.

Maya had given the kiss a great deal of thought while getting ready for work, and she'd decided it was a fluke. Emotions had been heightened, thanks to Hank's drunken shenanigans, and her need to comfort Nick had forced the train off the rails. It made sense, and she refused to listen to that inner voice that told her she was deluding herself. Instead, she was prepared to put the kiss behind her. That meant she couldn't mention it to anybody. It wouldn't be real if nobody knew about it.

"I just had a long night," Maya replied as she left the coffee machine to warm up and moved to the cooler to grab some almond milk. "Do you want a latte?"

"Sure." Lindsey narrowed her eyes. "What did you do last night?"

Lindsey was digging for gossip. She was a master at it, but there was no way Maya was going to crack under pressure.

"You know, the usual," she said breezily. If she allowed the tension to show in front of Lindsey, it would be a disaster.

"The usual, huh?" Lindsey didn't look convinced in the least. "Well, if it's just the usual, then you won't mind if I call Nick to confirm." She reached across the counter to snag Maya's phone.

Because her reflexes were dulled from an exhausting night of dirty dreams, Maya wasn't quick enough to stop her. Sputtering, Maya tried to grab Lindsey's wrist, but it was already too late.

"No texts." Lindsey's brow knit with disappointment as she went through the messages on Maya's phone. "Not a single one in at least forty-eight hours. What's up with that?"

"What are you talking about?" Maya was at the end of her rope. She was grateful for Lindsey's friendship, but she didn't need the constant interference.

"Did you see Nick last night? Bear said the two of you were supposed to play basketball, even though it was freezing. For the record, Bear and I cuddled in front of the fire with beer and talked about how much better sex is when we don't have to worry about adding another kid to the mix."

Maya's cheeks heated. "Well, that's great for you, I guess. I'm not sure what that has to do with me, though."

"Oh, please. You're not fooling anybody." Lindsey stared at Maya's phone a beat longer, then pursed her lips. "How much tongue did you guys use?"

"What?" Maya was convinced her cheeks were going to catch on fire and considered shoving her face into the cooler to cover her embarrassment. Since she had no way to explain that action, she froze in place instead.

"How much tongue was there when you and Nick finally kissed last night?" Lindsey asked.

Despite her best intentions to hold strong, Maya couldn't stop from crumbling under the pressure. "How did you know?" she wailed.

"You just told me." Lindsey's lips spread into a grin. "I want every filthy detail."

Maya blinked rapidly. "You didn't know?"

"You're horrible when it comes to keeping your mouth shut," Lindsey replied. "Like ... horrible. I knew something was up because you weren't your usual chirpy self. Also, Nick has walked past the window three times since I've been here. He looks in but keeps going. It's all very odd."

Maya straightened, her gaze immediately going to the window. Most of them were still shrouded until the grand opening, but she'd uncovered one to allow some natural light to filter in. "He's been by?"

"Oh, he hasn't come inside. He just walks by, tries to be nonchalant when looking in the window, then keeps going. I'm sure he thinks he's acting natural, but I know both of you too well to fall for that."

Sheepish, Maya replied, "There might have been a thing between us last night." She couldn't maintain eye contact, and it frustrated her to no end.

"Might?"

"Might."

"Uh-huh." Lindsey tapped her fingers on the countertop. "I'm going to need more than that."

Maya finally cracked. "It didn't happen at the basketball court."

"Did you take him home?" Lindsey was practically salivating.

"No. His father stopped by." Maya frowned at the memory.

"Hank?" Lindsey's nose wrinkled. "He probably shouldn't be walking around after dark, with it getting colder and all. He's going to pass out in a snowbank and freeze to death one of these days. He drinks too much."

Maya's stomach constricted. "Yeah. I don't remember him being like this when I was a kid."

"People change." Lindsey held out her hands and shrugged. "Ever since Melanie left him, he's become a different person. The rumor is he started drinking toward the end of their marriage, and that helped propel Melanie to make the break. Nick never talks about it, though—well, other than to call his mother names—so I've learned not to ask too many questions."

"I've seen Melanie a few times since I've been back," Maya replied. "Once, she was having cocktails with my mother and seemed happy. I didn't ask questions because I felt uncomfortable about it. I ran into her again, though. Actually, I ran into Nick outside the grocery store, and she happened to run into us. It was ugly."

"Yeah, Nick isn't hiding his disdain for his mother," Lindsey agreed. "If you ask me, his anger is misplaced. It's not as if Hank was an easy guy to live with, even back before he was a drunk. The drinking has just exacerbated things to the point of no return. Nick enables him, though."

Maya bristled. "That's not a nice thing to say. Hank is his father."

Lindsey snorted. "I get that. But Nick has to realize he can't just sit back and do nothing if he wants Hank to get better. Hank is too far gone, and by doing nothing, Nick is telling him it's okay to fall apart. Something has to give in that situation, or Nick is going to be hosting a funeral, then there will be no coming back for Melanie and Nick."

Though the statement was jarring, it was chock-full of truth. "I want to help, but I don't know what to do."

"There's nothing you can do. Listen, you can love Nick and stand with him, but in the end, he is the one who has to handle Hank. He's also the one who needs to make up with his mother.

"I give Melanie credit," she continued, barely taking a breath as Maya started frothing milk. "She could've buckled under Nick's petulant-baby act, but she didn't. She knew her mental health was important, so she didn't give in to Nick's whims. If you ask me, she stayed with Hank a lot longer than anybody else would have simply because she knew it would upset Nick if she left. She's sacrificed enough, though. It's time for Nick to get over it."

Maya's jaw dropped. "Tell me how you really feel."

"That is how I really feel. And before you get worked up, I've told Nick all this to his face. He just doesn't want to listen to me. He might, however, listen to you."

"I sincerely doubt it." Maya pumped four squirts of pumpkin-spice syrup into a cup for Lindsey's latte and four squirts of vanilla into another for hers. "Nick has no reason to listen to me. I mean, I'm barely back in his life."

"Oh, geez." Lindsey rolled her eyes and moved her lips, as if silently praying for patience. When she focused on Maya again, determination filled her eyes. "Tell me about the kiss."

The embarrassment Maya was convinced she'd managed

to bury roared back with a vengeance. "It wasn't a big deal." She began averting her eyes again. "It was just an accident."

"Don't make me hurt you." Lindsey crossed her arms. "I've been waiting for this to happen for weeks. Well, check that." She lifted a finger. "I've been waiting for this to happen since we were fifteen. You guys suck at managing expectations. Spill."

Maya didn't know whether Lindsey had managed to wear her down, or she simply needed someone to talk to. It was likely a mixture of both. "It just happened," she said as she passed Lindsey her latte. "We were in the kitchen, cleaning up —Hank lives like an absolute pig—and we were talking. The next thing I knew, our lips were glued to each other, and there was no prying them apart."

"Now we're getting somewhere." Lindsey bobbed her head and sipped her latte. "There was tongue, right?"

Maya felt distinctly uncomfortable with the line of questioning. "Does that matter?"

"Yes."

"Why?"

"Because if it was just a peck, then you guys have a long way to go before you start climbing each other and swinging from the branches. If there was tongue, you're sticking to my schedule ... and you know how much I like a schedule."

"You're unbelievable," Maya grumbled and turned her back to Lindsey.

"Talk," Lindsey snapped. "My mother is only watching the little ones for two hours this morning. She has an appointment to get her chin hairs lasered—and that's totally something I'm going to have to do before I'm forty, by the way—and she can't stay late. That means you have to get it together if you want me to help you break things down."

Maya narrowed her eyes as she turned back. "Why do you always have to be so difficult?"

"Because I'm good at it." Lindsey sipped her latte again. "Talk."

"I don't know what to tell you," Maya replied, frustrated. "We were talking. He was upset. I didn't know what to say. The next thing I knew, we were kissing."

"And there was tongue, right?"

"I will hurt you," Maya gritted out.

Lindsey's smirk said she wasn't worried. "How long were you kissing?"

"I don't know." Maya raised one shoulder. "I lost track of time."

"That's a good sign." Lindsey perked up. "Was there groping?"

"Why are you focused on that stuff?"

"Because I want a clear picture of what happened."

"There was no groping." Maya rolled her neck and glanced at the window. Nick hadn't passed since she'd arrived at the cafe. Perhaps he'd decided it wasn't worth his time to keep circling the building.

"None?" Lindsey's disappointment was palpable. "Well, that sucks. He's going to have to let his fingers start doing the walking sooner rather than later if I'm going to win the bet."

Maya shot her a withering look. "Can we not go there?"

Lindsey snickered. "I'll think about it. What did you guys say to each other after the kiss? Did you make a date? Oh, better, did he ask you to come over to his place so that he could grope you there? I mean, maybe he was worried his father would walk into the kitchen and witness the groping. That sort of makes sense."

It took everything Maya had to keep from exploding. "Nothing happened afterward. We didn't talk about it. I didn't even stay long enough to help him finish cleaning the kitchen. I took off."

"You ... took ... off." Lindsey pressed her eyes shut. "Lord, give me strength." When she focused on Maya again, she had calmed. "You guys are going to totally blow past my window. I know it. I could use that extra money too."

"My love life isn't contingent on your winning a bet."

"Well, at least you admit Nick is part of your love life," Lindsey mused. "That's something. As for my winning the bet, I admit that my needs are not tantamount in this situation. Yours are important. Mine are secondary."

"Well, at least you admit it."

Lindsey ignored Maya's sarcastic smile. "How did you guys leave things?"

"I just told you. I ran like a coward, and he let me."

"And you haven't spoken since?" Lindsey flicked her eyes to the window just as a familiar figure appeared.

Nick, decked out in his running gear, took a moment to peer through the window. He almost looked as if he was going to enter the cafe. Then he met Maya's curious gaze and froze in place.

"He's got his statue routine down," Lindsey noted. "He's kind of like a cat. He thinks if he's really still, no one will see him or react."

"Shut up," Maya barked. Her heart was pounding, and she didn't know what to do about it.

Nick stared through the window for a beat longer then pulled away to resume his run.

"What a coward," Lindsey complained. "I'm seriously going to have to send Bear to him for a talk. I mean, what the hell? He needs to get it together."

Slowly, Maya turned to Lindsey. "You're driving me insane. You know that, right?"

"I'm fine with it. If I were a superhero, that would be my superpower. My name would be the Agitator, and I would spread frustration and anger throughout the land."

Maya had to force herself not to laugh by reminding

herself she was in a pickle. "At least you recognize your strengths," she said finally.

"And you don't recognize yours." Lindsey's shoulders drooped with resignation. "What are you going to do to fix things with Nick?"

"I thought I would hide for the rest of winter. He'll probably forget the kiss by spring, don't you think?"

"Will you forget the kiss by spring?"

Maya hesitated, then shook her head. She could've lied and said it wasn't a big deal, but Lindsey would see right through her. "I'll never forget that kiss. It was ... magical. I swear it felt like I was under a spell."

"Oh, so cute." Lindsey rubbed her hands together. "This is good. You're finally starting to wrap your head around things. We can get ahead of this."

Maya wasn't certain that was possible. Even if it was, her head was a jumbled mess, and she didn't know if she wanted to get ahead of things. "He's going to go out with Camille," she reminded her. "I heard them talking."

Lindsey gave a dismissive wave. "Don't worry about that. It's not going to happen."

"Of course it is. Camille isn't simply going to let it go."

"You let me worry about Camille."

Maya's spine went ramrod straight. "What is that supposed to mean?"

"It means that I'm going to handle Camille. You don't need to worry about it. Just worry about Nick and how you're going to broach the subject of another kiss with him."

"We are not going to kiss again." Even as she said the words, Maya knew they were nonsense.

"Uh-huh." Lindsey chuckled. "I'll bet you free lattes for a year that you and Nick have your mouths glued together again by the end of the day."

Maya's competitive spirit reared its ugly head. "You're on."

"I don't want you to cry too hard when you lose, okay? Even when you technically lose the bet, you'll be winning Nick. It's a good trade-off."

"Oh, stuff it."

"Don't be bitter because you know I'm right."

"I can't take the sound of your voice for another minute."

"I love you too."

Seventeen

NICK

Nick should go in and smooth things over with Maya, yet his courage was in the toilet. The kiss—that explosive, ridiculous kiss—had thrown his life into turmoil. He wasn't the sort of guy who needed a routine to get through the day, but nothing felt solid in his life lately as it was, and the kiss hadn't helped.

If Maya had been alone, he might've risked entering the cafe and pretending nothing out of the ordinary had happened. If they both pretended, they could forget. Lindsey's presence frightened him, however. He couldn't act normal in front of Lindsey. She was like a shark. If she smelled fear, she would strike and chew until there was nothing left but a masticated husk. He couldn't risk that.

Frustration coursed through him as he turned away to continue his run. Obviously, he wouldn't get a chance to fix the problem before he had to go to work. It would have to wait, which meant he was doomed to a day of overthinking the kiss, and no good could come of that. His dreams had been bad enough.

His sweaty, heart-pounding dreams had resulted in him waking flustered and horny.

Ugh. How did this even happen? How did I let it happen?

Morose, he returned to his house. Even though the morning air was brisk, and he shouldn't be warm, he had no choice but to take a cold shower. That would snap him out of it, cool the hot blood coursing through him, and force him back to rational thinking. He was sure of it.

An hour later, he was at the school and setting up for the day. His first period was a prep hour, and he felt grateful for the empty gym. Once at the school, he changed into his normal shorts and T-shirt then proceeded to start practicing his free throws, a mindless activity he could enjoy while trying to push Maya out of his head.

It didn't work.

"There he is." Bear walked into the gym with Garrett Stone, another high school friend who happened to work at the high school. "How's life, man?"

Nick narrowed his eyes. They never visited him so early. His antenna was up and broadcasting shrill SOS warnings. "Why are you here?"

"I was helping Garrett fix the lift in the auto shop," Bear replied. "It was sticking, and Larry over at the garage couldn't spare any time to take a look until later in the week. Turned out to be the chain. We've got it running again."

"Awesome." Nick flashed a smile he didn't feel. "At least you're being productive." He threw up another shot and frowned when it bounced off the rim.

Bear easily caught the ball and secured it at his side rather than returning it. "So, I hear you and Maya kissed last night."

Nick's jaw dropped. "Who...?" That was a stupid question. Obviously, Lindsey had told her husband, and she'd clearly gleaned the news from Maya.

"Everybody in town is placing bets for when it's officially 'game on,'" Garrett offered. He didn't look bothered in the least by Nick's glare. "I have two weeks from Sunday. I don't suppose you could drag it out that long, could you?" He stared Nick down. "No, that's obviously not happening."

"It's not happening," Bear agreed. He dribbled the ball, his eyes never leaving Nick's face. "So, do you want to talk about it?"

"Do I look like I want to talk about it?" Nick shot back.

"Yes," Garrett and Bear replied in unison.

"Well, then you both need glasses." Nick turned back to the hoop and frowned when he remembered he didn't have a ball. "Give me that." He held out his hands and waited.

"Let's play Horse," Bear suggested, dribbling the ball to the paint, then threw up an easy basket. He grinned when it swooshed. "I'll obviously go first."

"Geez." Nick grabbed the ball and threw up a shot from the spot where Bear had been standing. It made a clanking sound when hitting the rim.

"Well, that was a brick, huh?" Garrett grabbed the rebound. "It seems like your game might be off today."

"Are you guys here for a specific reason?" Nick gritted out.

"We already told you why we're here. It's time you opened up, buddy. You need support, and we're here to be your support system."

"Let me guess. This was your wife's idea."

"My wife has quite a few poor ideas," Bear replied. "I happen to agree with her on this one, though. She says Maya is worked up."

Nick stilled. "How worked up?" Even he was surprised when the question escaped.

"Are you asking if she's having palpitations?" Garrett asked with a grin. "If so, I don't know that Lindsey went into specifics. It's possible, though."

"She just said Maya was agitated," Bear replied. "It appears you're agitated too. Do you want to give me some specifics, because Lindsey was light on them?"

"I don't believe I do." Nick inclined his chin toward Garrett. "Are you going to shoot that thing or just stand there gawking?"

"I can do both." Garrett threw the ball from where he was standing but didn't move his eyes from Nick's face. He smirked when the ball swooshed through the net. "It appears only one of us is off his game today. Fancy that."

"I can't stand either one of you right now," Nick growled. "I just ... hate you both."

"You love us, and you know it." Bear ignored the ball as it rolled past his feet and moved closer to Nick. "You'll feel better when you talk about it."

"Says you. I don't think I want to talk about it."

"Because you're sorry it happened?"

Nick hesitated. He hadn't asked himself that. "I don't ... know."

"I don't think he's sorry it happened," Garrett supplied. "He's confused by his man feelings and needs some direction."

"How are you even part of this conversation?" Nick snapped. "You haven't had a girlfriend for more than a month straight in years."

"That's by design." If Garrett was bothered by the statement, he didn't show it. "I don't happen to think I'm in a place to settle down right now."

"And I'm an expert," Bear added.

Nick shot him a look. "Since when are you considered a relationship expert?"

"Since I married the love of my life not long after high school, and we've made it work," Bear replied.

"Just because you've had four kids doesn't mean your relationship is perfect," Nick argued. "You're just good at the physical stuff. I'm dealing with emotional stuff."

"Oh, please." Bear waved off the statement as if Nick had just declared his favorite color was blue. "Lindsey is in the pros when it comes to relationship drama. She likes to argue ... then make up. If you think it's all smooth sailing for us, you're wrong. We have our issues. The thing is we work through them together."

"Except now she's sticking her nose in my business."

"Yeah, that's one of her issues. She's a busybody. She owns it, though." Bear stepped closer. "She's also a good friend, and right now, she thinks you and Maya need some help. That's why I'm here."

"I thought you were here to help with the equipment in the auto-shop class."

"I can multitask." Bear planted his hands on his hips. "Talk. You're not doing yourself any good sitting here wallowing in ... whatever this is." He waved his fingers around. "You'll feel better if you tell us what you're thinking."

"Maybe I don't know what I'm thinking," Nick groused. "Maybe I'm confused."

"That's okay too," Garrett reassured him. "Nobody expects you to kiss Maya for the first time after how close you've been and not be confused. We're here to help with all that."

"Oh, you're here to help," Nick said sharply, but he sighed and sank to the gym floor. "I don't know how it happened. I keep thinking about it. We were cleaning my father's kitchen for crying out loud, and I can't get past the initial ... you know."

"Exchange of saliva," Bear said. "We know how kisses work."

"You're a total tool," Nick replied, laughing. "One minute we were talking about what a mess my father is, and the next minute we were all over each other." He pressed the heel of his hand to his forehead. "It makes no sense."

"No?" Bear pursed his lips. "I hate to break it to you, but it makes sense to those of us who have been watching you for years. It's not hard for us to figure out how it happened."

"It's called chemistry," Garrett added helpfully. "You and Maya have always had chemistry out the hoo-ha."

"Is that a technical term?" Nick asked.

"It's just the truth." Garrett crouched in front of him. "I know we've been joking about the pool—and everybody wants to win it. I would be lying if I said otherwise—but there are more important things. How do you feel about what happened?"

"Lost."

"Do you not want it to happen again?"

"I don't know." Nick couldn't make eye contact. His heart was too fragile for that.

"You do too know," Bear argued. "Just be honest with yourself, even if you can't be honest with us. How did you feel when you kissed her?"

Nick took several moments to consider the question. He'd been so busy telling himself it *shouldn't* happen again that he hadn't bothered to ask himself if he *wanted* it to. "I felt like things were better," he said finally. "It was like all the bad things in my life went away for ten minutes."

"Your kiss lasted ten minutes?" Garrett looked impressed. "Wow. Maybe I do need to open myself up to a long-term relationship."

"I don't know how long it lasted. I lost track of time. It felt like forever yet not long enough."

Bear smirked. "Ah, progress." He sat on the floor across from Nick, crossing his legs. "I know you don't want to hear it..."

"But you're still going to say it," Nick surmised.

Bear pretended he hadn't spoken. "You've always wanted this, man. We can see it." He gestured between Garrett and himself. "Your parents could see it. Heck, Maya's father used to swear up and down he was going to shoot you if you developed a case of wandering hands. Did you think he was joking?"

Nick bobbed his head without hesitation. "Kind of."

"Well, he wasn't. Dude, you've been in love with Maya since we were teenagers. You just never let yourself see it. I mean, why do you think you took it so hard when your friendship fell apart?"

"Because she was my best friend. Nobody wants to lose a best friend."

"Why didn't you call her yourself?" Garrett interjected. "When you guys fell out of touch, why didn't you take the necessary steps to mend the friendship?"

Frustration churned in the pit of Nick's stomach. "She could've called!"

"She could have, but she didn't call for the same reason you didn't," Garrett said. "She was afraid that she loved you more than you loved her. You felt it from the other side. Just admit it."

"I ... can't. I don't know what I'm feeling. Everything is a mess. That's the only thing I know with any certainty. I don't like this feeling."

"Did you like the feeling when you were kissing her?" Bear challenged him.

"Yeah." Though it was hard for Nick to admit, lying wasn't really an option. Bear and Garrett would see right through him. "I liked it, okay? It felt right."

"Then what are you afraid of?" Garrett asked softly. "If it felt right, why don't you want to chase that feeling?"

Nick shrugged. "I don't want to lose her again."

"So, basically you're saying that you're willing to settle for a friendship when you want more simply because you don't want to risk her leaving for good," Bear surmised.

"Maybe." Nick focused on his shoelaces because it was easier than looking at their faces. "So what if that's true? Maybe friendship is better for us."

"But that's not what you want," Bear insisted. "You want Maya in every facet of your life."

"I can't lose her again."

"Have you considered that you won't lose her?" Garrett asked. "Have you thought about what it would be like to get everything you've ever wanted?"

"No, because all I can see happening is the worst thing possible." He steeled himself for potential ridicule. "I don't want us ending up like my parents. I don't want to love her so much that I fall apart when she leaves."

"Who says she's going to leave?" Bear demanded.

"Isn't that how it works?"

"No." Bear shook his head. "That's not how it works. Yes, your mother left your father, but you're kidding yourself that they had a happy marriage before it happened. They were struggling. You were just blind to it because you didn't want to see it."

"On top of that, Maya isn't your mother," Garrett added. "And you're not your father."

"Most definitely," Bear agreed.

"You and Maya are going to have your own story," Garrett continued. "You just have to open yourself to it."

Before Nick could respond, the sound of high heels on wood drew his gaze to the gym door. He wasn't surprised when Camille appeared in the opening. She was dressed in one of her smart suits and had a smile at the ready.

"Ugh," Bear muttered. "She just couldn't stay away, could she?"

"She's like the spider to Nick's fly," Garrett agreed in a low voice before plastering a fake smile onto his face and waving. "Hey, Camille."

"Hello, boys," she drawled. "What's going on here?"

"Just some reminiscing about old times," Bear lied smoothly as he stood. "What are you doing here? Don't you have a class to teach?"

"I had to stop by the office and heard voices when passing by."

"The office is that way." Garrett pointed to his left for emphasis. "You wouldn't walk past the gym to get to the office."

"Thanks for the geography lesson," Camille shot back. "I'm actually here for Nick. I won't interrupt for too long." She turned to him. "I got us a reservation at the French restaurant out on the lake for seven o'clock tonight."

"What?"

"For our date," Camille replied, laughing lightly. "You act like you forgot. What a silly goose."

"Yes, he's a total silly goose," Bear replied.

"Anyway, I thought we could just meet there so that there are no expectations for after the date. That should take the pressure off."

Nick opened his mouth to tell her he hadn't agreed to a date in the first place, but she kept talking and didn't give him an opening.

"I'll see you there at seven o'clock. I'm really looking forward to it." Camille waved at Garrett and Bear before disappearing from the gym.

"That woman was clearly a killer clown in a previous life," Bear growled. "I mean, seriously. How does she think this is going to work? She's well aware that Maya is back in town."

"She's delusional," Garrett agreed, flicking his eyes to Nick. "You're not going out with her, are you?"

"I had no intention of going out with her," Nick admitted. "She's kind of backed me into a corner, though."

"You could just not show up," Bear pointed out. "It's not as if you actually gave her an answer."

"But then she'll show up at the restaurant and be alone."

"So what? She did it to herself."

"No." Slowly, Nick shook his head. "I'll go, if only to let her down easily."

"I don't think she wants to be let down easily," Garrett argued. "She's going to be difficult regardless."

"Well, I still can't stand her up. We have history."

"You have more history with Maya," Bear reminded him.

"This has nothing to do with Maya. Even if there were no Maya, I wouldn't be happy with Camille." Nick had known it almost from the start, yet he still hadn't cut Camille out of his life. She'd served as a safety buffer, something he finally recognized. "I'm going to let her down easily, tell her it's never going to happen, and let her find someone else to fall in love with."

"Oh, well, that sounds like a fairy tale," Bear said. "She's not just going to accept it."

"She's not going to have a choice. I don't want to be with her."

"And what about Maya?" Garrett asked. "Once you've cut off Camille at the knees, what are you going to do about her?"

"I don't know." Nick exhaled heavily and dragged a hand through his hair. "I need time to think about it. All I know right now is that Camille isn't the one for me."

"I guess that's a start," Bear said, his disappointment obvious. "Don't leave Maya hanging for too long. It will just make things more difficult when you finally get your head out of your ass."

"I'm not rushing anything." Nick refused to even consider what they were suggesting. "I need to think. That's not the worst thing in the world, is it?"

Dubious, Bear replied, "If you say so."

"I *know* so. I'll handle Camille, then give myself some time to think about the Maya situation. That's the smart thing to do."

He was almost positive that was true.

Eighteen

MAYA

Maya worked all day, made decisions on a few decorative plans, and tried to focus on finalizing her menu. She couldn't get the previous evening's events out of her mind, however, and eventually, she stopped trying. That ridiculous, never-ending kiss would likely be the one thing she could never fully shove out of her mind, even on her deathbed. But she also couldn't stop thinking about the situation with Hank.

What is going on with him? How did things get this bad? She remembered him as a taciturn fellow who liked a beer or two while watching the game at night, but that had been the extent of it. Occasionally, he came outside and shot baskets with her and Nick. He'd always laugh at their banter but was one of the few people who never asked the most annoying question in the world. *When are you two going to start dating?*

Everybody in town asked that question and on a regular basis. It had driven Maya and Nick insane when they were teenagers, although they'd eventually come to terms with it and started laughing it off. But Maya had to wonder whether they'd reacted that way because they weren't interested, or they were too frightened to actually embrace the idea. *What if we screwed up back then and somehow derailed our own train?* The notion sobered Maya and made her stomach churn.

On a whim, she ran to the grocery store. She'd noticed when cleaning Hank's kitchen that he had very few groceries. She decided she could fix that, so she stocked up on some basics—lunch meat, bread, chicken, et cetera—then headed over to the house. Nick would still be at the school, so she wasn't worried about running into him. Her decision wasn't about Nick, at least not on the face of it, and she was focused on helping Hank.

Well, if it's even possible at this point.

Hank was still in the same clothes he'd worn the previous evening when he opened the door. His eyes widened when he saw the groceries Maya had brought with her, and he wordlessly moved aside, studying her as she carried her offerings inside.

"What are you doing here?" he asked dumbly as she started putting the groceries away.

"You have nothing to eat here," Maya replied. "Like ... absolutely nothing. I figured I would pick up a few things for you."

"Got any whiskey in there?"

"Nope." She cast him a serious look. "You don't need any more whiskey."

Hank rested his hands on the counter. "I'm pretty sure that's not for you to say."

"I disagree." Maya wondered if she was overstepping her bounds, but there was no turning back now. She wanted to help Hank, but she was doing it for Nick too. He needed help, and she wanted to be the one to give it. "You've been drinking too much whiskey."

"Says who? Did Nick tell you that?"

"No." Maya shook her head. "Nick is on your side."

"He doesn't act like it. He's always over here giving me a hard time, telling me I need to stop being a pig and find something to do with my time now that I'm retired. He's turned into a real nag."

Maya narrowed her eyes. "You might want to step carefully when talking about your only son," she warned him. "The last time I checked, he was the only one in this town taking the time to make sure you don't die in a ditch somewhere."

"Oh, wow." Hank laughed. "I forgot how dramatic you can be. Just for the record, Maya, I don't need your drama. I've got my own."

"You mean Melanie." Maya had already decided she wasn't going to hold anything back and planned to stand by that. "It's okay if you're upset about what happened."

"Thanks for your permission."

"I get why it threw you," Maya continued as if he hadn't spoken. "Melanie was your wife, and you didn't see it coming."

"She's a harlot."

Maya made a face. "Who uses that word? Come on." She had to laugh. Her jocularity actually drew a smile out of Hank, too, although it didn't last. When she sobered, she held up her hands in a placating manner. "Just because you didn't see it coming, Hank, doesn't mean you shouldn't have."

"Excuse me?" His voice was so raspy that it sounded as if the words were being dragged over rocks in a river. "How can you say that to me?"

"Because it's the truth. I love you, Hank. I always have. You're a good man."

"Yet my wife still left me for the town loser."

"I'm guessing that's because the town loser paid attention to her."

Hank worked his jaw. "I don't... You..."

Maya waited. When he didn't continue, she crossed her arms. "Has nobody mentioned that possibility to you before?"

"I don't need your grief. I was a good husband to Melanie. I provided everything she could've possibly needed. I didn't abuse her. I didn't demand she not go out with her friends. What more could I have done?"

"You could've loved her."

Hank made a protesting sound. "I married her."

Maya waited.

"I married her, so that means I loved her," Hank growled when the silence had stretched on too long.

"Did you ever tell her that? I mean, did you ever look her in the eye and say, 'I love you' just because you were feeling it?"

"I..." Hank worked his mouth as if he were chewing on something hard. "This is none of your business," he said after a few seconds, turning his back on her. "You can go, and you can take that crap with you. I don't need it."

"Well, I'm not doing that." Maya finished putting the groceries away. None of the food in the refrigerator wasn't past its expiration date, which was almost sadder than having a refrigerator full of garbage, so she surveyed the kitchen when she closed the door. The room was basically clean, thanks to her efforts the previous evening. Nick must've finished after she left. "Maybe we should clean the living room, huh?"

Since she was familiar with where things were in the house, she didn't hesitate when opening the cupboard under the sink and pulling out a garbage bag. Her smile was at the ready when she turned and found a glowering Hank.

"Do you want to help or just sit there fuming?" she asked.

"Will my response stop you from sticking your nose where it doesn't belong?" Hank growled.

"Nope." Maya brushed past him and strode into the living room. The scent was bad, and she immediately started tossing fast food wrappers and anything else she stumbled across that even remotely reminded her of garbage, not bothering to sort through it. If she threw away anything important, Hank would start yelling at her.

"Why are you even here?" Hank demanded, crossing his arms as he leaned against the doorjamb. "Shouldn't you be out doing ... whatever it is you do?"

"I'm opening a small cafe," Maya replied. "It's going to have mostly coffee and pastries, but it'll have some sandwiches too. Eventually, I hope to open my own restaurant ... but that's a long way off. The cafe is my stepping stone."

"Do you want me to applaud or something? You're going to be serving coffee. Bully for you."

Maya shot him a pointed stare. "You used to love it when I made coffee for you when I was a teenager. You said it was the best coffee ever and always made a big deal over it."

Hank's expression softened but only marginally. "You're not a teenager any longer, young lady. You also don't belong in this house. Don't you have a home of your own?"

"Technically. I'm living out at the Sandusky cabins for the next couple of months."

Hank replied with a look of horror, "That's not safe."

Maya chuckled. "Nick said the exact same thing."

"Well, he's smart." Hank sighed. "I can't believe your father is letting you live there. That's the place drug dealers go to clock in at work, Maya. You're a single woman. Something bad could happen to you."

"My parents wanted me to move back in with them." Maya had already filled half the garbage bag but had barely made a dent in the trash. "I politely declined. I'm too old to live with my parents. Besides, this isn't a permanent thing. I just didn't want to waste money on rent when I was opening a new business."

Hank grabbed a McDonald's bag and shoved it into the garbage bag. "It's still not safe. What does Nick say about it?"

"He's not happy."

"Of course not."

"He's also not in charge."

For some reason, that struck Hank as funny, because he started laughing. "I'm betting he feels otherwise. I happen to know he's a bossy cuss when he wants to be. He stops in here three times a week to boss me around and doesn't seem to think there's anything wrong with it."

"Are you sure he's bossing you around? It seems to me he's probably taking care of you."

"No, he's bossing me around."

Maya laughed and sat on the coffee table. "Nick loves you. He always has. I have too."

Hank made a face. "I wish you wouldn't say things like that. I want to be mad at you for invading my space."

"I know, but I want to take care of Nick. I don't think anybody has been taking care of him for a really long time."

"He's an adult."

"Yet he's still your child, and I see such sadness in his eyes sometimes." Maya blinked back tears. "I know I caused some of that sadness, back when we fell out of touch. I want to make it better, though."

"Oh, kid, you can't take all the blame." Hank plopped down on the couch. "You and Nick managed to screw up your relationship together. It wasn't just one of you."

"He seems to feel that I'm the one who made the mistake first."

"That didn't stop him from continuing it, did it? Come on, Maya. All he had to do was call you, and things would've been fixed. But neither one of you picked up the phone. Do you have any idea why that is?"

Maya pressed her lips together and debated how to answer. In the end, she opted for the truth. "I didn't have a clue why it happened until I came back home. It seems everybody else has an opinion about it, and most of them overlap."

"Is that a fact?" Hank gave a sly smile. His eyes were mostly clear but rimmed with red. If he'd been drinking that morning, it wasn't much, which Maya was gratified to see.

Maya nodded. "I've been hanging around Lindsey a lot since I got back."

"Lindsey Torkelson?"

"Yeah."

Hank made a derisive sound in his throat. "You might want to be careful there. That woman has never met an opinion she didn't want to share with the world."

"I like it when she shares her opinions about other people, just not when she shares her opinions about me with me."

"Because she's right?"

"I don't know. I can't decide whether she is or not."

"Uh-huh." Hank absently scratched his cheek. "How are things with you and Nick otherwise?"

Maya wasn't expecting the question, at least not phrased as it was, so she took a moment to consider it. "We've been playing basketball in the parking lot of the high school."

"That's a pretty vague answer."

"It's all I've got. Things are weird between us right now." Maya didn't mention the kiss. It seemed like a bad idea on top of everything else.

"It's going to be too cold to play basketball outside after dark in about a week, young lady," Hank replied, turning stern. "You need to come up with another plan if you want to continue to play this game."

"And what game is that?"

"The 'we don't love each other' game." Hank gave a sly grin when Maya's jaw dropped. "Oh, don't even," he chided her. "I might not have pushed you guys when you were younger, but I wasn't blind. Everybody saw it, Maya."

"I don't know what you're talking about." She averted her gaze and stood. "We should finish collecting this trash."

"Oh, don't start lying to me now, kid. You guys were always hot for each other. You just couldn't admit it because you were afraid of losing the friendship. The thing is if you'd actually tried to make it work, you would've strengthened the friendship along the way."

"And what would've happened if we'd ruined our friendship?"

Hank arched an eyebrow. "You did ruin the friendship, kid. Both of you ended up with broken hearts anyway. Guess what? You survived."

He had a point, as loath as Maya was to admit it. "I don't know how I feel about any of this," she said. "Part of me is angry because I feel as if I've spent the better part of my life being blind. The other part is afraid."

"Are you frozen in fear? Do you not know whether you should go left or right?"

"That's exactly how I feel."

"It's how I was when Melanie left me."

"Do you wish you'd made a different choice?"

"Every single day of my life. It's too late, though."

"It's not too late. You can still pick up the pieces. You might not be able to get Melanie back, but that doesn't mean your life is over. Nick needs you to be the parent he remembers. He needs you to hold on to."

"Are you sure it's not you who needs me?" Hank challenged her. "I mean, if you're going to make a move on my son, you need to know where his head is. If he believes like I do that love is a waste of time and people aren't worth investing in, then you've already lost."

Maya gulped. "Is that what you believe?"

"Yes," Hank replied without hesitation "Love is a waste of time."

"What about Nick? Do you regret being his father?"

"How can you even ask that?" Hank's face flushed with anger. "He's my son. I love him. I could never regret him."

"Yet to get him, you had to fall in love with his mother and build a life with her," Maya pointed out. "Nick is who he is because you guys gave him a strong foundation. How can you reconcile your belief that love is a waste of time when you've got him as a son?"

Hank opened his mouth to respond, but nothing came out. After a few seconds, he snapped it shut.

"I'm going to take advantage of your being speechless," Maya said as she moved to stand directly in front of Hank. "I have no idea how things are going to work out. I've made so many mistakes that I've lost count. Sometimes, I think I might be an idiot. But one thing, I know for certain."

Slowly, Hank lifted his chin, and stared into her eyes.

"Nick is one of the best people I know," she said, her voice barely above a whisper. "He's so good ... and kind ... and loyal. Right now, he's estranged from his mother because he's fighting your battles.

"I get it," she continued, raising her hand before Hank could speak. "I know she betrayed you. I don't think she did things the right way. I'm willing to bet she would acknowledge that. None of it matters, though, except for Nick.

"You're his father, and he took your side in all this. He loves you beyond reason, but you're killing yourself. You need to let him help or at the very least get help for yourself. It's important, because he's never going to be happy unless you get it together."

"It's not his job to take care of me," Hank gritted out.

"It's not," Maya agreed. "That's who he is, though. I know you don't believe in love right now or in me. But deep down, you don't want your son to be unhappy. You need to do what's right for him to make sure he's not miserable his whole life."

Hank blinked several times, then nodded. His hands shook when he snagged the garbage bag from Maya. "I can finish this. You don't have to stay."

"I want to."

"I don't want you to. I need to do this myself."

Maya hesitated—*will he really try to clean up his life without a chaperone?*—then nodded. "Okay. I'll be around if you need me."

"Don't worry about me," Hank replied in a gravelly voice. "Worry about my son. He should be your focus."

"He is, but like I said, he can't be happy without you."

"I said I would think about it. Don't push me. I don't need a mountain of guilt weighing me down. I just want to ... be me."

"Then be you." Maya pressed a kiss to his forehead. "I'll be around if you need help. Don't hesitate to call."

Hank stood quietly until she reached the front door. "You really shouldn't be living at the Sandusky cabins," he called to her back. "It's dangerous out there, and you're far too important to my son to die before you hit thirty."

"I'll think about it."

Maya smiled all the way through the door. Hank wouldn't suddenly revert to form—that would be far too easy—but if he was willing to consider getting better, that was a good first step.

She just had to figure out which direction her first step would be in, though she was way less certain about how all of that would go. Maya had to make a choice, and it was one she wasn't ready to make.

Nineteen

NICK

Nick didn't feel nervous when it came time to meet Camille for dinner. No, he'd had the entire day to stew. He was annoyed, and that didn't bode well for his ex-girlfriend when he sat down across from her at the fancy French restaurant.

She'd dressed up in a black cocktail dress with sheer accents showing off her body, but Nick had opted for simple khakis and a blue polo shirt. He wanted to be comfortable when he tracked down Maya later ... because that was the plan. After a full day of stressing and wondering whether he'd missed the obvious signs over the course of his life, Nick was ready to tackle the problem head-on, even if he had no idea how things were going to play out.

"Isn't this place beautiful?" Camille asked. She'd pulled her hair into a fancy bun and had a sheer shawl draped over her shoulders. "You can see the whole lake from here."

"I've seen the lake before," Nick replied. He didn't bother looking through the window, as he wasn't interested in focusing on something he could see from multiple places in town. "We need to talk."

Camille's delicate ski-slope nose wrinkled with confusion. "About what?"

"About ... this." Nick gestured between them. When he was younger, he'd been afraid of confrontation ... but only with women. He never wanted to argue with Maya, at least about anything big. He argued with males on his various teams, but that somehow felt different. By the time he embarked on a relationship with Camille, keeping the peace had been ingrained in his soul. As a couple, they'd never argued.

He had a feeling that was going to change.

"About ... the table?" Camille looked confused.

"No, about us." Nick refused to let her redirect. He was well aware of how her mind worked, and he wouldn't let her control the conversation. "You and me."

"Oh, what about us?" Camille straightened and grinned. "Are you as happy as I am that we ended up in the same place?"

"Actually, I'm not." The answer escaped before Nick had a chance to think better of it. He didn't want to hurt her feelings, but she needed to understand that there was no future for them.

"You're not happy that I'm here?" Camille cocked her head. "I don't understand."

"See, I think it's more that you *won't* understand." Nick chose his words carefully. "I don't want to upset you, Camille. Honestly, that's the last thing I want. I don't want to be with you either."

Shock reverberated across Camille's dolled-up features. She'd gone all out with the makeup. "Are you saying you don't want to be with me? How can that be? We're at dinner together."

Frustration filled Nick. "A dinner you set up. I never wanted to be part of this dinner."

"Of course you did."

"No, I didn't." Nick rolled his neck, prepared to drop the hammer on her, but had to force a smile when the server showed up to take their drink orders.

"I was thinking we would have hors d'oeuvres," Camille supplied, her attention on the menu. "They have smoked salmon canapés, a yummy-sounding cheese tart, an onion tart, and cheese puffs. We can get a combination plate. How does that sound?"

All Nick wanted was to talk to Maya, and if she happened to have a cheese Danish in her hand during the conversation, all the better. "I'm not going to eat." He wasn't sure he was going to say it until it was already out of his mouth. When the words escaped, he felt a sense of relief, even as dread threatened to take over.

"What do you mean, you're 'not going to eat'?" Camille demanded. "We're here on a dinner date. Normally, food is part of that process."

"I get it, but I'm not staying for the date." He shot an apologetic look toward the server. "I'm going to tip you regardless—don't worry about that—but can you give us a few minutes? I just need to speak to my ... *companion* ... about a few things. Then we'll give you the table back, and you can make double the tips."

The server was young, maybe twenty-one, and seemed intrigued by the scene playing out at the table, but she didn't pressure him to explain. "Sure. Take as long as you need." She flashed a smile at him then a pitying look at Camille before sliding over to check on a nearby table.

"I don't understand what's happening here," Camille snapped. "Are you playing a game? Is this some sort of bit I don't understand?"

"It's not a bit." Nick had to force himself to breathe in and out at regular intervals so that he wouldn't risk passing out. "It's just how I feel."

"And how do you feel?"

"Like I don't want to be here." Nick girded himself for an explosion. When it didn't happen, he rushed forward. "I enjoyed our time together when we were younger, Camille. We had some good times, like when we went to that culinary event at the student center on campus. That was a riot. Or that time we went to the horror-movie festival, and that guy spilled all that fake blood down the front of your shirt, and somebody mistakenly called 911. That was hilarious too."

Camille didn't respond and only narrowed her eyes.

"It's just ... we were never meant to be more than a good time," Nick continued. He'd practiced what he was going to say in the mirror for an hour before he left his house, but he'd already gone off script, something that didn't bode well for either of them. "Sometimes, it's okay to have a good time then move on."

"And that's what you think is best for us, huh?" Camille crossed her arms and rested her elbows on the table. "You think I should be grateful we had a good time however many years ago and let it go."

Nick shrank under her hateful glare. "That would be my preference, yes."

"I see." A muscle worked in Camille's jaw. "Well, that is just ... so stupid." Her eyes flashed with venom. "This is about Maya, isn't it?"

Nick felt as if he were performing a circus act without a net, and his feet were too big for the tiny wire he was supposed to be balancing on. "This has nothing to do with Maya." It actually had everything to do with Maya, but it also had to do with him and the things he was starting to figure out. Camille didn't need to know that, though. "This is about us."

"Uh-huh." Camille looked as if she were ready to lay waste

to Metropolis with her deadly laser eyes. "Do you really expect me to believe that you're ready to call me a good time and walk away right on the heels of her return and have those things not be related?"

"I ... don't ... know." Nick felt as if he were caught in a trap and began wondering at what point he would have to start gnawing off his leg to escape. "I just need you to know that we can't be together. I'm really doing this for your own good."

"My own good?" Camille's icy tone could freeze fire. "Are you really going to sit there and pretend this is for my own good?"

"It is. I can't give you what you want."

"You don't know that. You haven't even tried."

"But I don't want to try." Though it was hard for him to get out the words, he pushed himself to finish. "I care about you, Camille, but not in the way you want. I don't love you, and quite frankly, I'm incapable of ever loving you. We're not a good match.

"It's important that you understand that so you can find someone who is a good match," he continued. "I've been worried since you showed up here that it was somehow strategic, and I feel bad if that's the case. But that doesn't change the fact that I need to follow my instincts, and they don't lead me to you."

Calmly, he pushed himself to a standing position and fished in his wallet for some cash to leave as a tip. Since he'd inconvenienced the server, and he was feeling guilty, he dropped everything he had on the table.

"I'm sorry that I did this here," he offered as he stepped away from the table. "It's not what I wanted, but you don't listen. I tried to nicely back away multiple times when you approached me. You bulldozed your way over my feelings. I just couldn't let you bulldoze me again."

He turned to leave, but her voice, soft and thick with tears, stopped him.

"I'm sorry if I backed you into a corner," she said. "That wasn't my intention. You were always so indecisive. I thought you needed someone to help you make up your mind."

"I did make up my mind. Just not the way you seem to think it should be done."

"So you're going to her?"

"I ... um... That doesn't matter." *Don't let her drag you off course. Don't let her turn this into a circus.*

"I guess it doesn't, at least from where I'm sitting. But from where you're sitting, it does." She leaned in and caught Nick's eye before he could make a break for it. "Just one more thing."

"What?"

"We didn't go to a culinary festival when we were in school. We most certainly didn't go to a horror-movie festival. You did those things with Maya."

Nick gulped. "I... Are you sure? I could've sworn we went to the horror-movie festival together."

"Well, we didn't. I distinctly remember you guys coming back from it covered in fake blood, though. You were laughing like loons, and I yelled about the mess you were making."

"Oh." The guilt Nick thought he'd tamped down flared to life. "I'm sorry about that."

"Yes, I'm sure you are." Camille wasn't the type to break down and cry, and she was stoic as she stood. "I'm leaving now. I would appreciate it if you didn't mention our ... date ... to anybody. It doesn't really matter, going forward."

If she wanted to save face, Nick figured that was the least he could give her. "I can do that."

"Great. Go get your girl."

"I don't know that anything is going to happen," Nick hedged.

"Of course it is. It was never not going to."

MAYA WASN'T IN HER ROOM AT THE SANDUSKY CABINS, and after cruising through the parking lot, Nick was ready to pick a fight about her living arrangements despite the other things he wanted to talk to her about. But he had to find her first.

Since she wasn't home or at her mother's house, he took a chance and drove past the coffee shop. A light was on inside, which told him somebody was present. Since it was late—well after business hours—he figured it had to be her.

"Maya?" He let himself in without knocking, scanning the gloom. Only the back row of lights had been turned on. "You need to start locking the door when you're here after dark," he growled when a shadowy figure moved out from the kitchen. "It's not safe for you to be here."

"Thanks for the warning, Dad," came a male voice. "I'll take that under consideration."

Nick scowled. "Blaine."

"Oh, you got it in one guess." Blaine flipped the switch on the wall and flooded the room with light. "Isn't it a little late for you to make a doughnut run?"

"I'm looking for Maya." All the hope he'd been feeling, all the energy, drained in the face of Maya's ex-boyfriend. *Why is he here? Why can't he just leave us alone? Is something more going on between him and Maya? Have I been wrong all along?* "Is she here?"

"No. I'm handling the bathroom trim. It just arrived today, and I had an appointment this afternoon. I figured I would come back and install it so that Maya could be surprised tomorrow. She's a bit of a geek about trim."

"Right." Nick shoved his hands into his pockets. "Do you know where she is?"

"No. I'm not her keeper." Blaine cocked his head. "You're all dressed up. Did you guys have a date?"

"No. I had a date with someone else, although it wasn't really a date."

"Uh-huh." Blaine flicked his eyes toward the clock on the wall. "So, you had a date with someone else, yet you're here at seven thirty, looking for Maya. I'm guessing the date went poorly."

"It could've gone better."

"Did Maya know you had a date?"

"Not to my knowledge."

"Because she was distracted all day," Blaine pressed. "Like ... really, really distracted."

Nick thought back to the kiss. "I just need to talk to her. She's not at home. She's not at her parents' house. I thought she would be here."

"She's not. I'm sorry." Blaine crossed his arms. "Are you finally going to get your head out of your ass?"

Nick had no idea what to make of the question. "I don't believe my head is in my ass. But I do have a question for you."

"Okay."

"Are you working for Maya because you're interested in getting her back?"

Blaine's lips curved up. "Is that what you think?"

"I'm just asking a question." Nick knew he was coming across as snippy, but he couldn't seem to help it.

"Is that why you took off the way you did the other day? It is, isn't it? Oh, that makes sense. Maya and Lindsey were confused about why you reacted the way you did. I was only half listening, but they spent a good hour dissecting your behavior."

"Lindsey and Maya can spend an hour talking about peanuts, if that's the mood they're in," Nick fired back. "I really just want to know what your intentions are toward Maya."

"Because she's your best friend?"

Nick swallowed hard. "Because I don't want her to get hurt."

"And you think I'll hurt her?"

"Just answer my question!" Nick exploded.

Blaine choked on a laugh then sighed. "Dude, I'm gay."

"What now?"

"You heard me. I'm gay. I'm pretty sure that means you don't have to worry about my getting between you and Maya."

"But ... no." Nick shook his head. "You and Maya were a couple for two years. I happen to know you did ... you know. You weren't gay back then."

"Actually, I was." Blaine looked caught between annoyance and amusement. "I just wasn't sure what I was feeling. I didn't want to be gay and thought my life would be easier if I was straight. I wanted to be straight for my parents because ... well, just because. I knew they couldn't accept the truth."

Nick felt as if he were in the movie of somebody else's life. "You're really gay?"

"I am. I figured it out fairly soon after Maya and I stopped dating. My partner's name is Daniel, and he works as a lawyer in Kalkaska. We live together and are trying to adopt a baby."

"Oh." Nick had thought nothing could make him feel worse than the way he'd spoken to Camille. Apparently, he was wrong. "Does Maya know you're gay?"

"Yes. She likes to pretend she was so much woman that she turned me gay, even though that's not how it works. I let her say whatever she wants because she gets such a charge out of it, and it also serves as a distraction from her own messy feelings."

"What messy feelings? Who does she have messy feelings for?"

"You, dumbass," Blaine snapped. "She's always had feelings for you. Tell me you don't know that."

"I..." Nick had no idea what to say. It should've been just another instance of other people recognizing something he was blind to, but it felt different.

"I knew back then," Blaine offered.

"You knew what?" Nick's mouth was suddenly dry.

"I knew that the two of you belonged together, and you would end up together. Heck, I knew you were hopelessly in love with each other."

"But—"

"Don't." Blaine shook his head. "I was confused. So was Maya. You weren't ready for her yet. Nobody got hurt. We were dumb kids doing dumb things. Thankfully, they weren't the sorts of things that could derail a life."

Nick couldn't find the words necessary to respond.

"We're not dumb kids any longer," Blaine said pointedly. "We're adults. You and Maya are in places in your life where you can finally be everything to each other, and it's not only expected but encouraged."

Nick blinked back tears, his heart pounding.

"You and Maya are supposed to be together," Blaine insisted. "You realize that now. I can tell by the expression on your face that you recognize that. It's time."

"Time for what?" Nick rasped.

"To man up. She's your heart and soul." Blaine leaned closer and unleashed a devastating grin. "Go get her. She's been waiting for you her whole life."

"What if it doesn't work?"

"It was always going to work."

Nick searched his heart to see if he had another argument, but he didn't. Deep down, he knew Blaine was right. "I don't know where she is."

"You know her better than anybody," Blaine shot back. "You do know where she is. Think!"

The answer came almost immediately. Nick *did* know where Maya was, and she wasn't far away. "Thank you." He started for the door then paused, his cheeks heating with embarrassment. "About the gay thing..."

"Oh, geez." Blaine threw up his hands. "What?"

"I'm glad you found someone to love."

Blaine grinned. "I'm glad you finally realized exactly who you've always loved. Now ... get a move on. It's getting late, and believe it or not, my idea of a good time is not hanging out, talking to you."

"Right back at you."

"Somehow, I knew we would be in agreement there."

Twenty

MAYA

Somebody had left a basketball in the lot. Maya picked it up, dribbled it, and debated how to fix her life. The only thing she knew with absolute certainty was that she felt an ache, as if something inside her was empty and needed filling. Food wasn't the answer, but she wasn't opposed to trying when she got home and could dig into her freshly baked cookies. Maya just hated feeling like she needed to keep searching for fulfillment elsewhere. She wanted to be the one to fulfill herself.

Do I love Nick? Coming up with an answer wasn't as easy as she'd thought it would be. Of course she loved him—she always had. *But is the love romantic or platonic?* Before the kiss, she would've said it was platonic and died on that hill. But everything had been thrown into disarray, and she doubted herself. No, she was feeling something more for Nick. The question was: *how is he feeling?*

She didn't have to wait long for an answer, because when she threw up a shot, and the ball ricocheted away from the rim, it never hit the ground. Confused, she turned and found

Nick holding the ball about fifteen feet away. He looked as unsure as she felt.

"Hey."

"Hey." His voice was low and raspy.

"You're dressed up," she blurted because she was afraid she would say something else she couldn't come back from.

"Yeah. I went out to dinner with Camille."

Maya's spine stiffened. "Oh, well ... good for you." *I guess that answers that question.* "I take it you two are getting back together."

"No, we're not."

"You're not? Why would you go out with her if you're not getting back together?"

"She kind of backed me into a corner." Nick took a tentative step forward, then stilled. "Camille's a master at getting what she wants and has been for as long as I've known her. She makes demands, and I'm the type of person who isn't good with disappointment."

"As in you don't like disappointing others," Maya surmised.

"Pretty much." He sighed. "The thing is, I don't want to be with Camille. She might want to be with me, although I don't think she actually does. It's more like she convinced herself we belong together and admitting we don't is akin to a loss for her. I don't know how to explain it."

"She's bossy and territorial," Maya replied. "She's always been that way."

"Yeah." Nick nodded and dragged a hand through his hair. He seemed to be having trouble meeting her gaze. "I went looking for you earlier. I thought you might be at the shop."

"No. Blaine is there, working on a few things. I saw his truck when I walked by."

"I know. I talked to him." Nick finally raised his eyes. "Why didn't you tell me he was gay?"

Maya made a face. "No offense, but that's none of your business. It's not really mine either. I mean, it is because we're friends. He doesn't owe me anything, though."

"I know, but ... I thought you guys were considering getting back together," Nick said, showing his frustration. "I'm mad, Maya. If you'd told me he was gay, you might've saved both of us some heartache."

"How?"

"I always hated that guy," Nick growled as he dropped the ball and used his foot to nudge it toward one of the grassy areas surrounding the court. His breath billowed in the chilly air under the streetlamp. "Do you have any idea how much I hated him back when we were in college?"

"You never mentioned it." Maya crossed her arms, hiding her frigid fingers under them. The conversation felt like it was going somewhere important but somehow off the rails at the same time. Her heart pounded, and all she wanted was to feel warm again. But nothing could drag her away from that parking lot at the moment. She was far too invested, even as a niggling voice in the back of her head warned that things were about to change forever, and she should run.

"I wasn't nice to him," Nick argued. "Whenever we all hung out in college, I was rude to him."

"I remember." Maya smiled at the memory. "You guys had that testosterone thing going. I couldn't understand it, so I stayed out of it."

Nick made an exaggerated face. "We had that testosterone thing going because we were competing over you."

Maya froze. "What? I'm not sure I understand."

"Oh, you understand." Nick threw his hands in the air, then paced back and forth. "I had feelings for you back then. I know you had feelings for me too. That's why you started dating him in the first place."

Maya was convinced her throat had suddenly turned into a

desert when she tried to swallow. "I liked him," she said finally. "I mean, he was fun."

"I know. I get it. I'm not talking about him specifically." Nick fidgeted, moving his hands to his hips then dropping them, as if he couldn't get comfortable. Maya understood the feeling. "It wasn't about Blaine back then, but I was too much of an idiot to see it. It was about us.

"We were spending a lot of time together," he continued. "We were sleeping in the same bed. Sure, we were doing it just as friends, but I think we both felt things were going in a different direction. We just didn't want to admit it."

Maya couldn't form words, so she just stood there like an idiot.

"Or maybe I was the only one who felt things," Nick said after a beat.

"It wasn't just you." Maya felt sick to her stomach. She'd never thought she would have such a conversation with her best friend. Yet there they were. They had to either talk or walk away from each other, and neither one of them could survive walking away a second time. "I felt things but... I couldn't... I wouldn't... I just couldn't wrap my head around any of it. It felt like too much."

"I know." Nick took another step toward her. It seemed as if he was taking advantage of spurts of bravery then pooling his energy before taking another step. "You were afraid that if you acted on what you were feeling, I would laugh at you and things would get weird between us."

Maya nodded. "You knew that?"

"Baby, I was feeling the same way too."

Maya didn't jolt at the endearment. She briefly wondered why—he'd never called her anything other than *babe* when making jokes—but she didn't dwell on it too long. "So you were afraid."

"I've been afraid for a very long time where you're

concerned," Nick confirmed. "You have no idea how afraid." He took another step. A good eight feet still separated them. "Maya, you've always been my best friend. We bonded at an age when we couldn't look at each other and love for any other reason than friendship. As we grew older, though, well, those feelings started to shift. At least I know they did for me."

Maya licked her lips and pressed the heel of her hand to her forehead. "Lindsey has been telling me that I had feelings for you since we were teenagers for days, and I refused to listen to her. I think I was just being stubborn, though, because when I looked back, I recognized it was there."

"I know." Nick looked morose. "It's the same for me."

"I didn't want her to be right, because if she was ... well..."

"Then there would be no choice but to start acting like adults," Nick surmised. "You can't decide whether we're ready to be adults."

Maya gave a hollow laugh. "It's as if you're reading my mind."

"We're both afraid of the same thing. That's why we drifted apart. I was so angry with you when you stopped calling, but I didn't call you to express that anger. I didn't realize why at the time, but I do now."

"Oh yeah?" Maya cocked her head. "Why?"

"Because I recognized we were at a point where we would have no choice but to acknowledge we had feelings for each other. We weren't ready for that. Heck, we were living on opposite sides of the state. Can you imagine if we'd tried to put a relationship together when we were that far apart?"

Maya blew on her hands and considered the statement. "One of us would've sacrificed everything for the other," she said finally. "I would've left the restaurant to go to you because it would've been easier for me to make the move."

"And you would've resented me for it eventually. It happened because it had to happen. We just didn't realize it at the time, which makes us morons ... but morons who did the smartest thing they could in the moment."

"It doesn't feel smart. It feels stupid. We went years without talking to each other, and look at us now. We're standing in the middle of a basketball court, risking frostbite, and for what? What are we going to do?"

Nick closed the remaining distance and caught Maya's hands in his before she could shove them back under her arms. He brought them to his lips and breathed on them, causing her heart to stutter.

"We're going to figure it out, Maya. We're not backing away again. We're just ... going to figure it out."

"How?"

"How do you think?" He smiled ruefully. His emotions shone in his eyes. He'd opened himself to her by design. "I knew before I went to dinner with Camille that I had to act. She was the one who made the plans—and I could've been a coward and run—but I decided that I couldn't be a man with you if I couldn't do the same with her."

"What did you tell her?"

"I told her I was sorry if I'd ever led her on and expressed sincere belief that she would find someone who could give her what she wanted, but it wasn't going to be me. Then I stuck my foot in my mouth when reminding her of two instances when we had a good time and said we would always have those memories."

"How was that sticking your foot in your mouth?"

"It turns out I was with you for both of them. I didn't remember. I just knew I had fun. She remembered, though."

"Oh." Maya pressed her lips together in an effort to keep from giggling. Then she took them both by surprise when she bent over and let the laughter wash over her.

"What's so funny?" he demanded. "It was an accident, and I'm pretty certain she didn't find it even remotely funny."

"I'm not laughing at her. Well, mostly." Maya straightened and got control of her giggles. "I would be lying if I said I hadn't wanted to punch her in the face at least a hundred times when you guys were together. I assumed it was because she was a terrible person. Now I think I was jealous, and I never considered myself the type of person who would be."

"I get it." Nick matched her smile. "I was jealous of Blaine, although I didn't want to admit that either. I was still mad at him tonight when I saw him. He then took it upon himself to set me straight on a few things."

"Like what?"

"He said he knew we had feelings for each other back then and explained that he had been confused about his own, and it took him a bit to sort things out. He's obviously still fond of you, but the romance angle is dead, and the only one holding on to that possibility is me."

"And how do you feel about that?"

"Stupid."

"Stupid?"

"I stormed out the other day because he showed up, and it totally wasn't necessary."

"That's why?" Maya laughed again. "Oh geez. You could've just asked."

"And you didn't storm out of the gym because of Camille?"

Maya lowered her gaze. "Um... I don't think I want to answer that."

"And you don't have to, because I already know."

Tentatively, Nick slid his arm around her waist and lightly tugged her until her chest was pressed against his. She had nowhere to look but his face, and when they locked gazes, their mouths only inches apart, it felt as if all the barriers between them had been eradicated.

"I need us to try. I need you to try," he said.

"I need you to try too. I'm afraid, though. It's not just us figuring things out. Everybody in town is watching us. They're taking bets on when we're going to get together."

"It's going to be like dating in a fishbowl," Nick acknowledged. "I don't care about that. I can't not be with you. It hurts too much."

Maya's breath clogged in her throat at his earnest expression. "Yeah. I... Yeah."

"Such a way with words," he murmured as he leaned in.

His lips hovered over hers, and he breathed into her mouth. She did the same with him.

"Maya." His voice was strangled.

"You can kiss me. It's fine. You have my permission."

"That's great," he said after a beat, shaking his head. "I want to kiss you. I just need you to tell me that this is what you want too. I *need* to hear it."

"I'm terrified of losing you ... and for good this time, if this doesn't work out. But I'm going to be tortured if we don't try. I'm going to fall apart in spectacular fashion and turn into a neurotic mess."

"Baby, you're already a neurotic mess. It's one of the reasons we're perfect for each other. I'm a neurotic mess too." He cupped the back of her head and searched her face. "I'm afraid just like you are. Everything hurts when I think of losing you. I am terrified that I'm somehow going to screw this up and lose you as a friend on top of everything else. I'm more afraid not to try, though."

Maya nodded. "Maybe we can make a pact to go back to being friends if it doesn't work." She knew how ridiculous that sounded.

"Or maybe we'll just take our time, promise to talk things out, and ignore all the busybodies in town. We're going to make mistakes. Let's just accept them and promise to do better next time, huh?"

"Okay."

"Okay." He rested his forehead against hers and shut his eyes, breathing her in. "I need to kiss you now."

"Is it going to be like last night? Because I think my lips are still numb. I've been haunted by that kiss all day."

"I think that was a hundred kisses."

"I'm fine with that."

"Me too." His mouth covered hers before she could respond again, something Maya was thankful for. She would've kept talking out of nervous energy if he hadn't put a stop to it.

The second their lips met, they gasped into each other's mouths. Maya gripped the front of his shirt and practically climbed him in an effort to get inside him. Nick met her need with explosive desire of his own. Then he moved his lips to her neck and pulled her as tight against him as he could, his teeth grazing her as she shuddered in his arms. Breathless, he roamed back to her mouth.

"We should go somewhere," Maya said as she slipped her freezing hands under his shirt, brushing her fingers against his stacked muscles and causing him to hiss. "We shouldn't stay here."

"Where do you want to go?"

"We could go to my place."

Nick made a face. "You live in a hole. We're still going to talk about that, by the way. Let's go to my place. At least there, we're certain a drug deal won't go awry outside the bedroom window."

Maya's lips curved up. "Will we be spending time in the bedroom?"

He matched her smile. "We can talk about it once we're warm. Odds are good, though."

"Are we really doing this?" She thought she might burst

into tears. Though she told herself it was because of the cold, she knew better.

"Yeah. I don't have a choice but to. I think I might die if I don't get to keep touching you."

Because she felt the same way, Maya nodded. "Maybe we're finally ready."

"We'd better be, because there's no turning back now."

Twenty-One

NICK

Nick had had every intention of ushering Maya into his house, pouring her a glass of wine, and creeping toward romance in a slow fashion. It didn't work out that way.

They were barely through the front door before they were on each other, both of them rabid to the point of practically frothing at the mouth. They left a trail of clothes throughout the house on the way to his bedroom.

If he'd had time to think about it, he might've been worried about his performance. They hadn't waited for so long for him to fall short, after all. The need was so great, however, that he didn't even think about it. Emotions and hormones took over, so the first round was behind them before he had a chance to think about it. They were softer during the second round, romantic and dreamy. By the third round, it seemed as if they'd always been doing it. Sure, Nick was still learning what Maya liked, but nothing felt awkward about the way they came together, and when they finally drifted off to sleep, Maya's head lay on his chest, and he wondered how he'd ever made it without holding her when surrendering to sleep.

Nick was the first to wake the next morning, and he stopped himself from stretching when he felt an unfamiliar weight on his chest. A smile came to his lips when he saw the fan of her hair, and he closed his eyes again, wondering if he was dreaming, because the moment was so perfect. If it was a dream, he didn't want to ever wake up again.

Maya was angelic in sleep. All she was missing was a halo. She made soft sighing noises and drooled a bit, but that only added to her appeal, as far as Nick was concerned. When her eyes finally opened, calm blue after a turbulent night at sea, he smiled as she got her bearings.

"Hey," she said softly.

Nick hadn't been certain how she would react in the bright light of day. He was prepared to have a long conversation, if it became necessary, but it seemed she hadn't changed her mind. "Hey." He lightly brushed her hair away from her face. "How are you?"

Maya's face screwed up in concentration. Nick didn't think it was the sort of question that required a lot of thought, but she obviously felt otherwise.

"Should I take that long stretch of silence as a warning that you're going to pull away?" he asked, his stomach constricting. He didn't blame her for being afraid—they both were—but he didn't want space between them, and if she put some there, it would break his heart.

"No." Maya pinched his flank, causing him to squirm. "Don't be a moron."

"Hey!" He grabbed her fingers and laughed when he saw the merriment in her eyes. "It was just a question. You seemed ... doubtful ... when you first woke up."

"Not doubtful. I was just getting my bearings. You know

it takes me at least twenty minutes to wake up. Double that if there's no coffee."

Nick *did* know that. He grinned when he remembered the times they'd shared a bed in college. "You were always a grumpy thing, weren't you?"

"Not all of us think mornings are good." Maya stretched her arms over her head, only remembering she was naked when the blanket started to slip, and she grabbed it quickly before he could get a peek.

He found her reaction utterly adorable. "You know I've already seen you naked, right?"

She shot him a withering glare. "Yes, but now I'm feeling self-conscious. You'll have to give me a minute. It's weird to think you've seen me naked."

"I hate to break it to you, but I saw you naked back then too."

"You did not! Don't go telling people you saw me naked. They'll think I was trying to seduce you or something."

"Oh, you were." He moved his hand to her back and marveled at how smooth her skin felt. He had calluses from playing basketball and hoped he wouldn't accidentally scratch her skin. "I remember the day clearly."

"It doesn't count if we were five," Maya growled.

"Oh, I'm not talking about that phase you went through in elementary school when you were constantly going around flipping up your skirt."

"You're the one who told me to do that! You said my mother would stop trying to make me wear dresses if I kept flashing my underwear."

Nick laughed. "I forgot that part. Your mother was determined to make you a proper lady for a good two months. She got over it, though."

"I hated wearing dresses back then."

"What about now?"

She pursed her lips, considering, and leaned her head back on his shoulder. "They're fine for special occasions, like dinner or something. For work or Bellaire winters, I think jeans are more practical."

"I guess it's good I like you in whatever you wear."

"I suppose so." Maya angled her head so that her face was buried in the crook of his neck, nuzzling close. "I thought it would feel weirder," she admitted quietly.

Nick tightened his grip on her. "Yeah, I did too. I figured there would be an adjustment period."

"But I don't feel weird. I feel ... good."

He smiled against her forehead. "I do too. More than that, this feels right."

"We still have to deal with the people in town," Maya pointed out. "They're going to come out of the woodwork when they realize we're together." She froze suddenly. "Wait ... are we together officially? Are we going to date, then decide whether we want to be in an actual relationship? How is this going to work?"

Nick felt torn between amusement and annoyance. "Do you really not know the answer to those questions?"

"I know how *I* feel, but I don't know how *you* feel."

"Fair enough. How do you feel?"

Maya pulled back far enough to stare into his eyes. "I don't want to answer first."

"Why?"

"Because if I say I want us to be in a relationship, and you say you want to casually date, then I'm going to be upset, and there's no protecting myself from looking like an idiot."

Nick wanted to argue with her, but he understood. They were in uncharted waters, at a point in which they felt the most vulnerable. "Then I'll go first." He didn't even know he was going to say it until it was already out of his mouth. "I want the whole enchilada."

Maya's brow furrowed. "Meaning?"

"Well, that I want Mexican, of course." He grinned at her scowl and poked her. "I didn't bare my soul to you last night because I want to casually date," he said as he sobered. "I want it all, Maya. That's all of you, all of me, and all that we can offer each other. I know it won't be easy, especially right out of the gate, but things feel right."

Maya nodded, her expression thoughtful. "What are you going to tell Bear when he starts digging for information on us?"

"That I was awesome and not nervous at all."

She giggled, as he'd intended. "Well, that goes without saying. You were amazing. I'm kind of sad I missed out on all those fireworks when we were in college. I might've stayed in more and done some actual studying if I had that to look forward to at bedtime."

"Yeah." He traced his thumb over her bare shoulder. "I'm torn on that."

"On what? On our being together?"

"No." He shook his head. "I meant everything I said. I want to be with you more than anything. Back then, though... I'm not sure we could've held a relationship together, Maya. I know everybody has been giving us grief because they expected us to get together a long time ago, but I can't help but feel as if fate stepped in and handled that decision for us."

"You mean the fear," Maya mused. "I've been wondering about that too."

"We wouldn't have been mature enough back then. I would've gotten jealous when the frat boys hit on you. I mean, I was already jealous. But I had to hide it. That kept my emotions in check."

"And I would've been forced to yank Camille's hair out of her head with tongs if we'd been together back then." Maya smiled at the prospect. "I still remember the day you introduced me to her. You said she was your 'study partner,' but I knew." She used air quotes. "The only thing she wanted to study was your anatomy."

"It is a superior subject," he agreed, wiggling and giggling when Maya went in for another pinch.

"I'm being serious." Maya levered herself so that she was on one elbow and could look down at him. "Everybody is going to give us grief. They're going to say, 'It's about time' and ask for details. But I think it was meant to happen now."

Nick caught her face in his hands and put his mouth on hers in a split second. The kiss started hot then eased into sweet. They both sighed when he pulled back. "There's nothing casual about this," he said.

"No." Maya's eyes were glazed, and she blinked repeatedly. "You know our parents are going to be all over us about this, right?"

Nick hadn't given it much thought. "My old man doesn't care about anything but his booze these days. He won't know until we tell him. Your parents, on the other hand, will be mad. Good luck with that." He laughed and dodged the pillow she threw at his face.

"I saw your dad yesterday," she said when he'd stopped laughing.

"You did? Where did you see him? Was he at the grocery store, buying whiskey?"

"No. I went to the store and took him some food options. There was no whiskey involved. We even cleaned up the living room together."

Taken aback, Nick said, "You didn't have to do that."

"I didn't *have* to. I wanted to."

"But ... was he mean to you?"

"He was fine," Maya reassured him. "We had a nice chat."

"About what?"

"Him. Your mother. You."

"I can guess what he had to say on all three of those topics."

"Yes, well, he's a work in progress. I told him he was being unreasonable."

"He has a right to be upset over what my mother did."

"Not about that, although he's taking it to the extreme. He's a grown man and needs to let it go. I told him he was being unreasonable about you. He treats you poorly, and he needs to remember that he's the father, and you're the son."

"He just can't seem to get a grip on himself. I don't know how to fix it." Nick darted his eyes to the window. The day was gloomy and threatening snow. None had been in the forecast, but he wasn't opposed to some flurries, especially if they allowed him to stay in bed with Maya all day. Since it was Saturday, he didn't have to go to work. He had no idea what her schedule entailed, but he was open to the idea of enticing her to hide with him for the duration of the weekend. They could deal with the town on Monday. For the moment, he just wanted to bask in what he was feeling and enjoy her.

"We can work on him together," Maya said. "But I don't want to ruin our day with talk of your father ... or my mother, for that matter. She's going to melt down if we don't tell her that we're together before other people find out."

"See, I happen to believe that's your problem," Nick countered. "I mean, she is your mother. Besides, you're going to get it from both sides. Either Lindsey will melt down about not being first, or your mother will. I guess you could sit them down and tell them about it together, but that sounds like a nightmare of a meeting."

"You're not wrong." Maya rolled so that she was on top of Nick. They both made groaning noises when their naked bodies rubbed together.

She fits me, Nick mused. Everywhere that mattered, she

just fit him. It seemed as if they were made to be together. He didn't even care how schmaltzy that sounded.

"We're going to have to deal with the outside world, and it's going to be a pain. The thing is we don't have to deal with the outside world today ... or even tomorrow, for that matter. I was thinking we could hide here for the whole weekend. We can shut out the entire world. We can even get food delivered."

"What about coffee?"

"I have coffee."

"Do you have my coffee or your coffee? Because I have to be honest here, old-school black coffee like you drink isn't going to cut it. I need something fancier."

"Of course you do." Nick smiled. "Believe it or not, I bought one of those fancy Keurigs with a milk frother three months ago."

"You did?" Maya's forehead creased. "Why? You don't need a frother. Unless... Were you dating someone who liked fancy coffee at the time?"

"I haven't seriously dated anyone since I got back home," he replied. "And before you ask, I haven't casually dated anybody since I've been back either. I've been a monk."

"I've always wondered what monks wear under those robes," Maya teased. "Maybe you can show me later."

"I'm showing you right now." He rubbed himself against her, enjoying the way her body melted against his. Yes, a weekend in bed sounded exactly like what they needed. He would convince her of that, one way or another. "As for the fancy coffee maker, I bought it the day after I heard you were moving back to town."

Maya froze, and when she raised her eyes to his—after what felt like a really long time—stunned disbelief waited for him there.

"Ah, I know what you're thinking." He tapped a finger against her nose. "Was I planning this all along? Did I know this would happen? The answer is no. I had no idea. I think my heart wanted it to happen, though, because I am not an impulse shopper. I don't just buy three-hundred-dollar coffee makers on a whim."

"But you did that day," Maya mused.

"I did. I also bought pumpkin-spice syrup."

"You hate pumpkin spice."

"No, I said it's taking over the world for no good reason. I don't hate it. I just don't want to like it."

Maya laughed, falling off him and landing on the mattress. Nick rolled over her smoothly, pinning her beneath him.

"I'm all in, Maya," he said quietly. "I want all of you. The town will make things difficult, but they'll move on to something else after a week. Carly Cunningham will get a new wig ... or Dylan Brewster will OD on Viagra, strip naked, and run through the downtown area again."

Maya's eyes widened. "Did that really happen?"

"Yes, everybody thought we were under a missile attack." Nick chuckled when she jabbed his side. Then he sobered after a few seconds and lowered himself so that they were chest to chest, pressing his forehead against hers. "We're going to make this work. It might be a slight adjustment, but after last night, I'm starting to think it's not going to be quite as much as we were anticipating."

Maya nodded. "I've come to the same conclusion." She ran a finger over his cheek. "I think a weekend in hiding sounds good. I have no clothes, though. We're going to have to run to my place to get some."

"Here's the thing, baby." He pulled back far enough for her to see his impish grin. "You're not going to need clothes. If you need jogging pants or a T-shirt to be comfortable, I can provide those. We're going to have food delivered and shut out the world for the entire weekend. It's just going to be you and me. Even the clothes aren't invited."

Maya started to laugh, then sighed when he rubbed his lips against hers. "I can deal with that."

"Good." He went in for a kiss, but she was already sliding out from under him. "Where do you think you're going?" he demanded when she paused naked in the doorway.

"To the bathroom, then to check out that fancy coffee machine. You don't think I'm going to just ignore that you said you have flavored coffee syrups, are you?"

"What about me?"

"Oh, I'm going to shower you with attention. Don't you worry. But I need coffee first."

"That doesn't seem fair."

"You'll live. Of course, you could help me make the coffee."

"Are you going to be naked the whole time?"

"You know it."

"Sold." He tossed off the covers and moved to follow the sound of her giggles. "You'd better be quick. I've got plans for you, and they don't involve pumpkin-spice syrup."

"They could, though."

"I guess they could. Good point."

Nick couldn't stop smiling as he followed her. Yes, things were exactly how they were supposed to be. He'd been afraid, but it turned out to be for nothing. He had what he wanted and wouldn't let it go.

Twenty-Two

NICK

Nick and Maya had thought it would be difficult for the town to accept they were together, but it turned out they were wrong. Sure, the first time they hit East Cayuga Street holding hands, they got people honking horns, rolling down windows, and yelling, "It's about time!" But it was hardly the end of the world. They laughed it off and expected way worse, but it never came. Everybody had not only expected them together but also accepted it without blinking. All the worrying they'd done was for nothing, because the relationship felt right for everybody involved ... and a bunch of people who weren't involved.

So they had two weeks of utter bliss to build the foundation of their relationship. Then reality hit them in the face. Maya's fear regarding the cafe, which was due to open in less than twenty-four hours, was at an all-time high.

"Eat it." She shoved a blueberry Danish into Lindsey's face and glared. "I need to know if it's better or worse than the cherry Danish."

Lindsey's eyes narrowed. "I've already eaten three of them and had four cups of coffee, and I've been here exactly thirty minutes. I'm going to be bouncing off the walls." She turned her attention to Nick and Blaine, who were sitting on adjacent stools, eating pastries and drinking coffee. "Are you going to stand up for me here or not?" she demanded.

Nick slowly turned to her. "Um ... did you say something?"

"I forgot she was even here," Blaine said teasingly. "She has such dulcet tones that they fade into the woodwork."

"I'll make both of you cry if you don't stop it," Lindsey warned them. "I have a voice like a flute."

"A flute, huh?" Nick took another bite of his Danish. "Did you decide that yourself, or did someone else mention it to you?"

"I know things." Lindsey tapped the side of her head. "And I'm not eating another ounce of sugar," she snapped at Maya, shoving the pastry back at her. "I've eaten so much that I feel like I'm about to give birth to twins—and that's a feeling I unfortunately know well."

Maya chewed on her bottom lip as she stared at the rejected pastry. "Maybe cherry and blueberry are both bad. Maybe I should try strawberry."

Nick sighed and climbed off his stool. He had been talking Maya down from multiple ledges for days. The closer they got to the cafe opening, the more freaked out she became. He swooped in to smooth her frazzled nerves whenever she had an incident, which helped for a time, but Maya was one bad pastry away from spinning out.

"All the pastries are amazing," Nick assured her as he slid his arm around her back and anchored her to his side. "Stop freaking out. I swear everything is going to be okay."

"That's easy for you to say. You're not the one who finally has everything she wants. I just know everything is going to fall apart now. Things are going too well. I can feel it."

"Oh, that wasn't dramatic or anything." Nick moved to

stand behind her, pressed his broad chest against her back, and held his arms tight around her waist as he rested his chin on top of her head.

Lindsey's and Blaine's faces looked both worried and amused.

"You don't understand." Maya's voice cracked. "I just don't want to ruin everything when it's going so well."

"You're not going to ruin anything." Nick kissed the top of her head and debated the best way to deal with the issue. "Come on," he said finally, dragging her from behind the counter, then situated her on the stool he'd just vacated. "Sit there."

Maya glared at him as he moved behind the counter again and studied the huge coffee maker. "What are you doing?" she demanded.

"I'm going to make something for you for a change, and you're going to shut up and like it."

"Oh, how sweet," Blaine drawled. "Has anybody ever told you that women don't like being bossed around? I think we've hit on the reason you were still single when Maya returned to town."

"He was still single because he was pining for Maya," Lindsey countered. "There's a difference. I guarantee multiple women in this town would've been perfectly happy to be bossed around by him. Not me, of course—I do the bossing around in my house—but other people. I had to listen to their grand plans about how they were going to snag Nick for months, even though I knew it would never happen."

"How did you know that?" Maya asked as Nick slipped one of the blueberry Danish in front of her.

"Eat that. You've been shoving food on everybody else all morning. I need you to take a breath and eat something yourself." He glanced at the clock on the wall. "I have to head to work in thirty minutes, and I do not want to leave you in this state when I go."

Maya made a face. "I happen to think I'm in a great place mentally."

"Oh, you're so cute." Nick leaned in and gave her a kiss, then shoved the Danish into her mouth when she opened it to say something. "Eat that while I make your coffee."

"She's going to hurt you if you're not careful," Blaine said with a laugh as he took in Maya's glare. "She's already plotting exactly how she's going to do it."

"Well, that's something to look forward to." Nick beamed at Maya before starting some almond milk frothing and moving to the syrup display. "Do you want maple sugar or pumpkin spice?" He glanced at Maya and found her methodically chewing, all the while murdering him with a glare. "I'll surprise you," he said after a beat. "Baby, you need to calm down. The cafe is going to be a big success. Your streak of good luck is going to continue. I promise."

"I have a question." Lindsey's hand shot into the air.

Nick pinned her with a dubious look. He loved Lindsey, but she had mischief written all over her face. "No, you don't."

"Yes, I do. I already got hosed when you two got together and didn't tell anybody for days. Don't think I've forgotten that, by the way. I know it was all you." She jabbed her finger in Nick's chest. "I'm still working out your payback for that."

"And I'm terrified about whatever you're going to come up with," Nick drawled.

"You should be." Lindsey barreled forward as if she didn't recognize the sarcasm. "Did Maya's streak of luck start when she decided to move back to town, or did it start when you guys finally got your heads out of your asses and decided to touch tongues—and other parts—on a nightly basis?"

Nick glared. "Why do you always have to go there?"

"It's what I do." Lindsey gave a one-shoulder shrug. "I'm being serious. You guys are all gooey and in love—that's only going to be adorable until New Year's Day, by the way, then it's going to be intolerable—but I happen to believe that Maya's good-luck streak kicked off when we started hanging out, not when you two started feeling each other up in public."

With a great deal of forced calm, Nick maintained control of his emotions and removed the almond milk from the frother. "How do you figure that?" he asked after several seconds.

"Because I'm the one who was pushing her toward you," Lindsey replied. "I had a system in place. I reminded her that everybody in this town had certain expectations regarding your relationship trajectory, and she would be on everybody's shit list if she didn't get it together."

"That's not how you phrased it," Maya complained. "Let's not exaggerate." She continued to munch on her Danish while she pouted. "Besides, you're not the reason we got together."

"No, I'm the reason you got together," Blaine said. "If it weren't for me, Nick would still be out there doing that man thing where he glares at me from across the road because he thinks I'm moving on his woman."

"Oh, now who is exaggerating?" Nick groused.

"Not me." Blaine gave an impish smile.

In the weeks since he'd told Nick the truth and sent him after Maya, they had struck a grudging friendship. Without Maya fueling his jealousy, Nick had to admit that Blaine was a good worker and friend. But that didn't mean Nick would admit it to anybody but himself.

"The truth is you guys would still be denying you have feelings for each other if we hadn't stepped in and fixed things for you," Lindsey said. "Bear was involved, too, but since I was the one feeding him instructions, I still get credit for being the mastermind."

"Oh geez." Nick choked on a laugh as he finished mixing Maya's coffee. He went all out, adding whipped cream and sprinkles, then slid the latte in front of her. "Drink up, baby, and don't listen to these fools." He flashed her a charming smile. "We did this ourselves, and we should get all the accolades."

"Oh, good grief," Lindsey muttered. "Deluded, party of one, your table is ready."

Nick ignored her. "It's going to be okay." He rested his elbows on the counter and stared directly into her eyes as she sipped her latte. "I swear this is going to work out how you want it to. The cafe is going to be a big success, and in a few years, you're going to be able to start that restaurant you so desperately want."

Maya blinked several times, then nodded. "I'm sorry I'm such a mess. It's just ... part of me didn't think I'd ever actually make it here. I was convinced I was going to screw up somehow and ruin everything before I even started."

"Maya, you were born for this." Nick gently slipped a tendril of blonde hair behind her ear. "You're going to be okay, and we're going to be with you the entire way. We'll help."

"Yeah."

"I just need you to stop freaking out. If you're a nervous wreck, then I will be too. If we're both nervous wrecks, we're going to be exhausted tomorrow. Is that what you want?"

"No, but it does make me think." Maya turned rueful. "I'm going to have to spend the night at my place tonight. That's where my uniform—that I've so carefully pressed and tried on a million times so that I can model it in front of the mirror—is. All my makeup and hair stuff is there too. I need to look good."

"No." Nick was already shaking his head before she finished. "I don't want to spend the night at your place."

"I don't think she invited you, Sparky," Blaine drawled.

Nick held up his hand to block Blaine's face. "You know I don't like that you're living there. It's dangerous."

"I don't have a lot of options," Maya reminded him. "I can't afford any of the nice places out at the resort or even the mediocre ones on the east side of town. I have to settle for the Sandusky cabins until I can start turning a steady profit."

"Actually, you have one other option." Nick ran his tongue over his lips. He would've preferred having the conversation without an audience, but he was stuck. "You could move in with me."

Maya's jaw dropped. "Did he just say what I think he said?" she asked Lindsey in a loud whisper.

Lindsey nodded, also wide eyed. "He did."

"He realizes we've been dating for exactly two weeks, right?" Maya looked as if she were going to pass out and fall backward off the stool.

"I think he's under the impression that you guys have been best friends since kindergarten and in love with each other since you were teenagers," Lindsey replied. "I don't think the standard timetable works for you guys."

"That right there." Nick snapped his fingers and pointed at Lindsey. "We're not beholden to antiquated dating rules, because we're not like other couples. Also, I can hear you even when you think you're whispering to each other."

Maya gave a hollow laugh. "Nick, we haven't even had our first fight yet."

"Sure we have." Nick refused to back down. "What do you think that whole 'We're not talking for eight years' thing was?"

"Stupid."

He nodded solemnly. "It was indeed stupid. It was also

our first relationship fight. We just didn't realize it at the time."

"But..."

"No." Nick shook his head. "I don't want you at the Sandusky cabins. I understand that I'm coming across as bossy right now. I also know that you're desperate to prove you can do this on your own. Being self-reliant doesn't mean you can't occasionally lean on someone. I want to be that someone for you. Won't you please let me?"

Maya turned to Lindsey rather than answer. "Can you believe this?"

Rather than agree with her, Lindsey squirmed on her stool and avoided eye contact. "Well..."

"Oh, you can't agree with him that this is a good idea," Maya said. "It's not, for the record. It's a completely and totally terrible idea. We've been together for two freaking weeks."

"You've been in love for more than ten years," Lindsey replied evenly. "I don't want to agree with Nick, because we're ovary buddies and all, but I agree with him. The Sandusky cabins are freaking dangerous, Maya. Every shooting we've had in town for the past five years has happened there."

"Well, except for those two hunting accidents," Nick hedged. "But that's neither here nor there."

"It's not safe," Lindsey persisted. "You're the one who told me you push chairs under the door just in case someone wants to kick it in when you're sleeping. You're afraid to stay there."

"Oh, that did it." Nick crossed his arms. "I can be at your place as soon as work is finished today. I bet we can have you moved in three hours."

"And what happens if we get in a fight?" Maya demanded. "What happens if we yell, and nobody has any place to go to take a breath? I don't want to say the wrong thing."

Nick's heart hurt at her earnest expression. "Maya, you

can't say the wrong thing to me. We're going to fight. It's unrealistic to think we won't. The most important thing is we're prepared to work through those fights together."

"He's right," Blaine said. "You need to suck it up." He regarded Maya. "I've been meaning to say something about that place where you're living too. I have no idea if it's too early for you to move in with Nick—although my gut says no—but I do know you can't stay there. I've been looking at places online, trying to figure out a way for you to be safe. This is a much better solution."

"It is," Lindsey agreed. "Not only will you be safe at Nick's house, but I'm betting he'll give you a break on rent."

Nick scoffed. "She doesn't have to pay rent."

"I have to contribute somehow," Maya argued. "I can't just live off you."

"Why not?"

"Because... Because..." Her expression darkened. "You know why."

"Fine." Nick held up his hands in defeat. "You can be responsible for all the groceries. I'll handle the rest."

"That's nothing."

"It's money I would already be spending," Nick reminded her. "It's okay to admit you need help, Maya. One of the things you've got going for you is that I want to help."

"You really should suck it up," Lindsey said when Maya turned to her. "This is the best thing for both of you. Nick is going to have an aneurysm if you stay at that place."

"I totally am," Nick agreed. He gathered Maya's hands and gripped them tightly as he searched her face. "Is there a reason you don't want to live with me? And before you answer, just know the 'We've only been dating two weeks' argument doesn't fly. I've loved you my whole life." He'd felt it even before he said it, but admitting it was like shoving a weight off his shoulders.

Tears filled Maya's eyes, causing his heart to shred.

"Don't do that." Nick brushed the tears away. "I can't stand it when you cry. If the thought of moving in with me is going to make you cry, I guess we'll have to come up with a different solution. You can't stay where you are, though. It's too rough over there."

Maya wrapped her fingers around his wrist. In a raspy voice, she said, "I guess we can try living together. I don't want to mess up your house, though. I'm kind of a slob, in case you've forgotten."

"Well, I'm a neat freak, so it will be fine," Nick reassured her. "Also, it's our house now, Maya. We can talk about decorations and any paint you want to change later. Let's just get through tomorrow and get your stuff moved. The rest of it will work out how it's supposed to."

He believed that to his very soul. Sure, things were moving fast, but they'd been in love with each other for so long that they were actually moving quite slowly. He wanted to keep moving forward regardless. Maya wasn't the only one who had finally gotten everything she'd ever wanted.

After several seconds, Maya nodded. "Let's do it. Let's live together."

Nick beamed at her. "There we go." He leaned in for another kiss, ignoring the gagging noises Lindsey and Blaine made. "Everything is going to work out," he promised as he pulled back. "Just take a breath. We're almost there."

Twenty-Three

NICK

Nick floated through the day. Two weeks of life with Maya in his bed and heart had changed everything about his life. He hadn't known it was possible.

Nothing felt better than waking up with her head on his chest or him wrapped around her or them wrapped around each other in a way that was impossible to know where he ended and she began. He'd never been so happy, and while they still had a few things to work out, he was looking forward to the future.

When his classes ended for the day, the basketball team would come in for practice. Given how nervous Maya was about the opening of her coffee shop, he didn't want practice to stretch late. He planned to do some one-on-one drills and call it a day. Then Bear came in.

"Oh, don't even." Nick wagged his finger. "I don't need whatever crap you're spewing today."

Bear pulled up short. "How do you know I'm spewing crap?"

"Because I've met you."

"I could be here simply because I love spending time with my best friend."

"Is that why you're here?"

"No. Lindsey wants me to pressure you into bringing Maya to the Northern Loves bonfire festival."

Nick scowled. Northern Loves—a play on Northern Lights—was a yearly bonfire extravaganza held by the lake. All the adults in town—and the teens until ten o'clock—gathered around the bonfire and cuddled with their significant others while drinking hot chocolate. The adults' hot chocolate was often doctored with vanilla vodka, but nobody commented on that. The entire thing had been set up as a monument to love, and Nick and Maya had ruthlessly made fun of it as teenagers.

"Why would I go to that?" Nick asked as he dribbled a ball. His team was due to arrive any second.

"Because you're in love."

Nick didn't respond. While the feelings he had for Maya were intense, he was afraid to use the *L* word too soon. He'd dropped it in a way that could be taken as friendship love earlier at the café—casually cool and all that. But he was waiting for the big declaration. He wanted the moment to be perfect, and two weeks was not enough time to achieve that goal.

Bear tried again. "Because you get to drink the best hot chocolate in the world with your friends."

Nick's expression didn't change.

"Because you'll get to cuddle and grope Maya under a blanket, and nobody will be the wiser. Women love bonfires. They feel sexy and romantic around them. That's how I got three of my four kids."

Nick laughed. "I'm not sure we're ready for kids."

"Of course not. You're still in the 'getting sex twice a day' phase."

"Don't tell me that stops. How long have you been suffering from a lack of love?"

"Oh, shut up." Bear made a face, but he couldn't hold it for long. "I get it. You guys are completely and totally gone for each other. Right now, because it's the start, nobody else exists. Eventually, though, you're going to slide into a life that's a little more normal and a little less sexy."

"Bite your tongue." Nick threw up a shot and smirked when it swished. "I happen to think we're going to stay this way forever."

"Oh, look at how cute you are," Bear drawled and rolled his eyes. "I don't want to puke because you're getting way more sex than me at all." He said it just as the first group of boys emerged from the locker room to start practice.

Jake's eyes grew to the size of saucers. "Who is getting sex?"

"Nobody," Nick answered before Bear could. "Ignore him. He's just here to irritate me."

"I'm good at it," Bear agreed. "You guys weren't supposed to hear the sex part, though. Don't mention the sex part in front of your parents. They'll hunt me down, then I'll have to mercilessly mock them until they stop talking to me. There will be tears, prayers to the heavens, and maybe some colorful threats. Nobody wants that."

"We know what sex is." Chris laughed. "We're seventeen, not seven."

"That makes things worse," Bear replied. "Your mothers are picturing you leaving the house next year to go to college ... or getting your own apartment. They want to keep you babies. Trust me. You do not want to mention the *S* word in front of them. I also do not want you mentioning that you heard that word from me. Are we understood?"

The boys didn't initially respond. They seemed to be taking it all in.

Then Jake turned his attention back to Nick. "Who are you having sex with?"

Nick grinned. "Don't worry about it. Where is everybody else? We need to start practice on time because I have somewhere to be later."

"Somewhere that involves sex?" Jake asked.

"No," Nick replied automatically.

"Yes," Bear replied at the same time. "Boys, gather round." He motioned with his hands. They were joined by two more curious faces as they exited the locker room. "I have some bad news for you. Your coach is in love. It's not 'Let's go to Applebee's' love either. It's 'Let's spend the weekend in bed and pretend the rest of the world doesn't exist' love."

"Then that means it's not Ms. Burton," Chris said knowingly. "She's 'Let's go for tea and crumpets' love, and there's no way Mr. Griffith rolls that way."

"Tea and crumpets?" Nick asked.

"Oh, you know." Chris's head bob made him appear far older than he was. "Ms. Burton is what my dad refers to as a high-maintenance chick. He says my mother is high-maintenance, and that's only fun in theory when you're getting regular sex."

Nick slapped a hand to his forehead. "We cannot be having this discussion. I will lose my job."

The boys—and Bear—ignored him.

"My dad says you have to find the right balance," Chris continued. "You don't need someone who is always easy. You don't need someone who argues with you all the time. You *do* need someone who stands her ground on important stuff and doesn't remind you of a doormat."

"You and your dad talk about relationships a lot, huh?" Nick mused.

"He wants me to get it right because he says he got it wrong."

"I hate to break it to you, kid, but your dad *did* get it wrong," Bear replied. "Your mother is a menace. She tried to get all the nail technicians at the salon fired the other day because she says they're illegal aliens, even though they're all locals. She saw some report on *Dateline* or something and decided to take matters into her own hands."

"Yeah, my mom is a nut," Chris agreed. "I mean, she's my mom, so I have to love her, but I don't want to marry her."

"Some people like high-maintenance chicks, though," Jake argued. "Becky Masters is high-maintenance, and she's awesome."

"Becky Masters gives hand jobs under the bleachers," Chris countered. "That's why people put up with the high-maintenance stuff. My dad says she learned that from her mother."

"Your dad says a lot," Nick noted, dumbfounded.

"Your dad *does* say a lot," Bear agreed. "I knew there was a reason I liked him. What else does he say?"

"He says that you and Mrs. Torkelson have a fever that means you're essentially horny monkeys."

"Oh really." Bear crossed his arms. "How does that work?"

"He says you basically eat and fornicate ... and occasionally throw poop at each other, although I didn't get that part. He says you're mated for life too."

"Well, he's not wrong." Bear smiled. "What do you think about your coach?" He inclined his head toward Nick. "Will he mate for life?"

"Of course." Chris shrugged. "He's in love with the woman opening the coffee shop. Everybody knows it."

"They do," Jake agreed solemnly. "My mother says everybody in town has been taking bets since Mr. Griffith and Ms. Markham were kids. She says everybody in town knew they belonged together."

"Is that what your mother said?" Nick asked. "The last

time I checked, your mother was on her third husband. No offense, but I don't think she gets to judge anybody else's relationship."

Jake continued as if he hadn't heard him. "Ms. Markham is hot. I saw her outside the coffee shop this morning. She has people painting the window and she was wearing these black pants that really made her ass look..." He gave a chef's kiss.

Nick agreed but didn't want his students commenting on Maya's ass. "I don't think you should be saying that ... or looking, for that matter."

"Oh, you can't stop us from looking," Chris countered. "Ms. Markham is hot. When she smiles, it makes part of me go squishy."

"Totally," Jake agreed. "If I were ten years older, you don't want to know the things I would do to steal her from Mr. Griffith."

"Hey! Don't say things like that. You need to be respectful regarding Maya. I'll make you run laps if you're crude."

"Maya is going to be around for a long time," Bear explained. "She's not like Ms. Burton."

"Of course not." Chris gave a derisive laugh. "Ms. Burton is going to settle down with a weak man. That's who she is."

"Did your dad tell you that too?" Nick asked dryly.

"He did." Chris didn't seem to understand that Nick was being sarcastic. "He said that high-maintenance women need low-maintenance men, high-maintenance men need low-maintenance women."

"I don't know that I would call Nick or Maya low-maintenance," Bear mused. "But they're not exactly high-maintenance either."

"That's because they're in the middle. They can be low- or high-maintenance depending on the day. In that case, the trick is balance."

"Your father should be a therapist," Bear replied. "What else does he say about me?"

"I don't think we've spent a lot of time talking about you."

"And we shouldn't start today," Nick said. "You guys need to start practicing. We're going to do one-on-one drills first. I want to run the new plays I gave you last week on a man-to-man defense front. We'll go back and forth."

None of the boys scrambled to get into formation.

"You were with Ms. Markham when you were our age, right?" Jake asked solemnly, seeming invested in the conversation.

"Maya and I were friends," Nick replied. "We weren't together."

"But you wanted to be, right?"

Nick hesitated then held out his hands. "Guys, I don't think we should be talking about this. You need to practice."

"He totally wanted to be more than friends with her," Bear volunteered. "He wouldn't admit it, though. They were afraid to leave the friend zone in case they could never get back into it. In a weird way, I think it's best that they held off getting together until now because otherwise, they would've suffered while being separated. Things are 'full steam ahead' now, though." He made a *toot-toot* motion with his arm.

"It's weird to think you were friends with a girl," Jake mused. "Would you change that if you could?"

"No," Nick replied automatically.

"But you spent a bunch of time with a girl who was not allowing you to get to the promised land."

"I don't even want to know what you're talking about," Nick groused.

"Girls are cool," Jake noted. "They're fun when you can do fun things with them. What do you do with them if you're just friends, though?"

"Nick and Maya played basketball and pretended it wasn't foreplay," Bear volunteered.

"And we're done with this conversation. Guys, you need to understand something." He placed his hands on his hips. "Maya has been my best friend for my entire life."

"I thought I was your best friend," Bear lamented.

Nick ignored him. "She's a good person. She makes me happy. That's all you guys need to know."

"But my mom says she's been spending the night at your house for two weeks," Jake argued. "That means she's more than a friend. You don't have sleepovers with girls who are just friends, right?"

"Nick and Maya used to," Bear said slyly. "Nick would sleep on the couch at her house. He lived across the road and could've easily slept in his own bed, but half the time, he didn't."

Nick's stomach constricted. What Bear didn't know was that he spent the night on Maya's couch when his parents were arguing ... which was often during his high school years. Maya's parents understood that and never gave him grief. Maya's father sat him down once and explained that Maya's bedroom was off limits after dark, but that had been the extent of the conversation.

"We're done with this topic," Nick insisted. "I'm being serious. You guys have work to do."

"Are you going to take Ms. Markham to the Northern Loves bonfire?" Jake asked. "My mom says that's a sign of true love."

"Your mom is nailing the mailman," Chris shot back. "Everybody knows it. He takes his lunch at your house every single day."

"Hey!" Jake's eyes flashed. "You take that back!"

"Enough." Nick smoothly stepped between the boys and extended his hands. "This is not a conversation we should be having. Everybody is entitled to their opinion, but this is not the place for this discussion."

Bear leaned in toward Jake and offered a conspiratorial whisper, "Dude, your mom is totally nailing the mailman, but it's okay. Your parents are divorced, and Harvey gets great benefits through that job. He'd make an awesome stepfather."

Jake's horror filled his face. "Mom said he just likes to use our bathroom."

"I'm sure that's it," Bear said automatically. He nodded then mouthed to Nick, "*That's so not it.*"

Nick refused to engage with his friend. "Guys, while I appreciate your interest in my love life, it's not appropriate. Maya is none of your business. We're going to focus on our drills and not worry about the Northern Loves bonfire ... or anything else, for that matter."

"Does that mean you're going to marry her?" Chris asked. "My dad says that everybody in town has started a pool for when you guys are going to get married."

Nick's lips curved down. "This town has way too much time on its hands."

"It's what we do," Bear confirmed. "Just out of curiosity, where did we land on the Northern Loves bonfire? Lindsey is going to be mad if I failed on my mission, and her mother has the kids tomorrow night so that we can spend some quality time together, so I would really prefer it if she's not mad."

A series of wolf-whistles and catcalls filled the gym.

"Enough," Nick growled as Bear puffed out his chest. "Tell Lindsey that Maya and I will decide whether we're going to the bonfire. We'll probably avoid it because it's like being trapped in a fishbowl when we're around people we know these days, but never say never."

"I think he means they're going to skip the foreplay and get right to the main event," Chris offered.

"I think you're right," Bear said.

"Unbelievable." Nick pointed toward the far end of the court. "Line up in two teams so that we can get going. I mean it." His phone dinged in his pocket before the kids could acquiesce ... or argue, which was far more likely, and he frowned when he held up his phone. The caller ID said the call was coming from the hospital. "That's weird."

He answered, though he normally wouldn't during practice, and as he listened to the nurse giving him a rundown of what was happening, his stomach sank to his knees, and his heart started pounding.

"What is it?" Bear asked when Nick disconnected. He no longer looked keen to mess with his friend. He was a pain when he wanted to be but was loyal to a fault, and he knew Nick well enough to understand that something terrible had happened.

"My father has been in an accident," Nick replied quietly. "He was driving."

"Oh man. Is he okay?"

"They're not sure. He's en route to the hospital. They want me to meet them there. They say the police are requesting my presence."

"Uh-oh." Bear rubbed his cheek as the ramifications set in. "Well, go." He inclined his head toward the door. "I'll run practice. Go and take care of your father."

"Are you sure?" Nick didn't know whether he should be grateful for his friend or furious with his father.

"I'm sure. Go. I'll call Maya for you too."

"You don't have to."

"Yes, I do. She'll want to be there."

Nick didn't offer another word of complaint. "Thanks. You're a good friend."

"I'm the best friend. You owe me one bonfire appearance as thanks."

"I'll consider it."

Twenty-Four

NICK

Nick's heart pounded as he hurried into the hospital. His father had been transported to Traverse City—Bellaire was too small for a hospital—and all he'd thought during the white-knuckle drive was that he hoped his father hadn't killed someone. He knew beyond a shadow of a doubt what had happened, and he felt sick to his stomach. Despite that, he calmly walked into the hospital and informed the woman at the front desk who he was.

"Hank Griffith is your father? He's on the third floor."

"Thank you." Nick started toward the elevator, but she called out to stop him.

"The police are up there."

Nick gulped. "Thank you."

He balled his hands into fists during the short ride to the third floor. When he arrived, it wasn't hard to find his destination. Two police officers—both from Bellaire, so easily recognizable—stood talking to a doctor. Nick didn't stand on ceremony when approaching.

"Is he alive?" he asked the officers.

Chet Wilkins, who had been four years ahead of Nick in school, nodded. "Yeah. He's pretty banged up, though." He gestured toward the doctor. "This is Dr. David Perkins. He's handling Hank's case."

Nick extended his hand to shake the doctor's. "What happened?"

"Your father was driving drunk," Mike Wilcox barked. He was older than his partner, Chet, and looked ready for a fight.

"But he's alive?" Nick asked.

"He is." Chet bobbed his head, much more subdued than Mike.

"Did he ... kill someone?" Nick asked, terrified to know the answer.

Chet replied, "Hank swerved off the road—we're not sure why—and hit a tree. Nobody else was involved."

Nick released a shaky sigh. "I guess that's something." He pressed the heel of his hand to his forehead. "Give it to me straight."

"Your father has three broken ribs and a concussion," Dr. Perkins replied. "He's still drunk. His blood-alcohol level came in at point-one-seven."

Nick frowned. "That's like ... really drunk, right?"

"It's not good. He needs help," Dr. Perkins replied.

"Right. Can I see him?"

"Of course." Dr. Perkins's eyes were filled with sympathy. "I know this seems like a lot, but there are some programs I can recommend. I have some literature." He hesitated for a beat. "It's probably best if he goes to an in-treatment facility. They're more rigid."

"He's got other problems too," Mike added. "He's facing charges."

"What can I expect there?" Nick asked. He had an orderly mind and wanted to start making lists of things to do.

"He's going to have to go before a judge," Chet offered. "If you can get him into a treatment program, his court date can be delayed. He's being arraigned here."

"That's a thing?"

Chet nodded. "Yeah. They're getting the video monitor ready right now. It will be quick."

"You need to get him a lawyer," Mike said. "Try Jed Connor. He handles drunk-driving cases."

"It's your father's first offense, so he's likely to get community service and alcohol programs," Chet explained. "He's going to have a lot of fines too."

"I think that's only fair. I'm going to go see him. Then I'll take that literature." He paused. "I just don't know what to do here. It seems like a lot."

"You might want to tap your mother for help," Chet suggested.

Nick shook his head. "That is not going to happen."

"She's already been called." Mike didn't look sympathetic in the least when delivering the news. "Don't look at me like that. She's still his wife. The first call went to her. She's on her way."

"Well, great." *As if things weren't bad enough.* "She doesn't need to be here. She's done enough."

Chet seemed to want to argue but instead flashed a flat smile. "We'll have the video monitors ready in ten minutes for the arraignment. You should go in and see him."

"Thanks." Nick started for the door.

"Just be forewarned—he's feeling belligerent," Chet added. "He doesn't believe he's at fault here."

"Oh, of course," Nick muttered. "Nothing is his fault these days." He squared his shoulders and made his face blank before entering the room, where his father's bruised face shocked him. Anger swiftly followed. "Dad."

Hank looked up from the bed, a wave of resentment flowing forth. "Good. You're here. I want to go home." He didn't move to stand, instead gesturing toward the bed railing. It appeared one of the officers had cuffed him in place. "Get me out of here."

"That's not going to happen," Nick replied as he moved closer. He felt more helpless than he could ever have imagined. "You're being arraigned in ten minutes."

"Arraigned?" Hank's eyebrows rose. "For what?"

"Are you kidding me?" Nick had to bank his anger to keep from ripping his father's throat out. "You drove drunk. You were more than twice the legal limit. The only thing saving you right now is that you didn't hurt anybody but yourself."

"Then I shouldn't be charged with anything."

"That's not how it works." Nick gritted his teeth and debated how to proceed. Finally, he realized being straightforward was the only way to go. "You need help."

"You mean rehab." Hank made a face. "I'm not going to rehab."

"Yes, you are. Chet says your court case can be delayed if you go into a program. I'm guessing that will help when it comes to your sentencing. I'll call Jed to be sure, though, and get him on this."

"I'm not going to rehab. I don't have a problem."

For several seconds, Nick could only stand there and blink. "You do have a problem."

"Your mother—"

"Did not make you get behind the wheel and drive drunk!" Nick snapped. "Yes, she left you. Yes, she broke up our family. But all the choices you've made since then are on you, not her. She has her own ghosts to vanquish. These demons—the ones that put you in this hospital bed—are yours to exorcise."

"I don't have a problem," Hank insisted. "Stop looking at me that way. This is all your mother's fault. And I'm not going to rehab. This is all a mistake, and it will work itself out. You'll see."

"No, you're the one who will be seeing. A rude awakening is coming your way, Pop, and I don't know how to help you." Nick turned toward the door. "They're going to come in and arraign you now. I'm heading to the lobby to look at the treatment options the doctor is providing us. I'll be back when you've sobered up."

"Nothing will change," Hank hissed as Nick pulled open the door. "I don't have a problem. I'm not going to rehab."

"I guess we'll just see about that."

NICK STUDIED THE BROCHURES THE DOCTOR HAD GIVEN him, feeling all at sea. He sat on one of the stiff couches and flipped through them, debating what options were best for his father. The rehab facilities were expensive, but if he could get his father back—or at least a semblance of the man he remembered—it would be worth it. At least, he hoped that was true.

"Nick?"

A soft voice made Nick's head jerk up. He'd been alone so long that he'd managed to tune out the rest of the world. When he saw Maya, some of the rough edges he'd been struggling with smoothed, if only minimally.

"Maya."

He started to stand, but she waved him off and crossed to him, opening her arms for a hug as she sat on the couch next to him.

Nick didn't even know he was going to cry until the sob was already wrenching free. "He could've died."

He buried his face in her neck as she stroked the back of his head. Her mere presence was soothing, although the realities of his situation couldn't be banked for long.

"I know. He didn't die, though." Maya was always considered the more dramatic of the two when they were growing up —and Nick had witnessed some fantastic meltdowns—but when a crisis popped up, she was often the one who handled it. "Listen, I'm not saying this is a good thing." She pulled back to stare into his eyes. "But it's a reality check. We'll figure this out. Together."

The "together" made Nick's stomach unclench. Until her return, he'd felt alone in the world, despite the lifelong friendships he'd built and enjoyed. With her there, with them together, things were different. He wasn't alone. Their bond was stronger than ever.

"I don't know what to do." Nick forced himself to be calm, even though the thing he wanted most was to curl up with his head on her lap and shut out the rest of the world. "He says he doesn't have a problem. He won't go to rehab."

"Oh, he's going." Maya's tone brooked no nonsense. "He's wasting his life. I'll talk to him."

For some reason, her determination struck Nick as funny. "You're going to force him into rehab?"

"Yeah, and it's going to be easier for me than it is for you because he can't push my buttons. You're his son, so he knows exactly how to play you. He can't do that with me."

"What if it doesn't work?"

Maya shrugged. "Then we're going to have to take a 'tough love' approach. That means no contact until he addresses his issues."

Nick balked. "I can't do that. I'm all he has."

"He has to be enough for himself. You can't carry that burden. You're the strongest person I know, but this is too much. You can't live your life and fix his at every turn. He needs to be responsible for himself."

"What if he can't?"

"He can. He just won't. He wants to blame the world for

his woes, but it's time for him to take some responsibility." Maya took the brochures and looked at them. "I'll make a list of the pros and cons. We'll rank them, then call to see who has beds."

Nick couldn't believe how much better he felt because of her simple presence. Warmth suffused him as he regarded her, and in that moment, he realized he didn't just love her. No, he was completely devoted to her, and there would never be anybody else. *Have I always been in love with her? Were the others right?* It felt like a legitimate possibility. Before he could tell her what he was feeling, however, the sound of high heels on tile drew his attention ... right to his mother's concerned face as she appeared in the waiting room.

Nick's back went ramrod straight. "You don't need to be here," he said automatically.

"I'm still your father's wife," Melanie replied calmly. "That means I do. This is a bad situation."

"That you caused," Nick muttered.

Maya shot him a quelling look. "That's not going to help." She turned her attention to Melanie. "I talked to Chet before I found Nick. He says that Hank needs to go to rehab. It's better for him ... and his court case. The judge will think he's serious about sobriety if we can get him in a program."

"We need to keep him there too," Melanie said as she rolled her neck. "He's going to be a pain. Even if we can get him there, he's going to flee as soon as he gets the chance. I know him."

"You left him," Nick countered. "I think you screwed up a word there."

Not until Maya slid in front of him did Nick realize he'd stood. "It's okay," she insisted. "We're going to figure it out." Her hand landed on the spot above his heart. "Don't freak out. We will take this one step at a time. We'll do it together. I promise."

Nick blinked back tears when he saw the compassion in her sky-blue eyes. His hand automatically covered hers. That love he'd been shocked to feel only minutes before was back with a vengeance. He'd never felt anything so overwhelming.

"You guys are together," Melanie said. "Like ... *together* together."

Nick bristled at the observation. "So?"

"So I always knew it was going to happen." A bright smile appeared on her face, which only made Nick all the more edgy. "How long?"

"Only two weeks," Maya replied. "We're still ... figuring things out." She shot Nick a serious look. "We realized that everybody had been right. We were burying our true feelings for each other. Apparently, once we were back in the same town, that was no longer an option."

"It's wonderful." Melanie beamed at Nick. "You finally got everything you've ever wanted."

"Not everything," Nick shot back, his tone biting enough that Maya's shoulders drooped. He regretted that instantly, but his anger refused to be quelled in the face of his mother's sudden happiness. "I don't have my family back."

"Nick, you never had the family you thought you had," Melanie argued. "You looked at your father and me and assumed that because we shared a roof our entire marriage, we were happy, when that was the opposite of the truth. We were roommates, not partners. Heck, if I hadn't gotten pregnant with you, I would've left him a year into our marriage. I knew we were doomed then."

Nick reacted as if he'd been slapped. "Are you blaming this on me?"

"Of course not." Frustration lined Melanie's features. "You're my son. I love you more than anything."

"You just don't love my father."

"I don't know if I'd phrase it exactly like that." Melanie's eyes drifted to Maya, perhaps searching for help. "I loved your father. I was just never in love with him."

"Then perhaps you shouldn't have married him!" Nick pulled away from Maya and glared at his mother with fury. "You caused this situation. You're the reason he started drinking the way he did. He's responsible for getting behind that wheel—I would never say otherwise—but you ruined his life. That's why he's been drinking this way."

"Nick, I know you're upset, but maybe you shouldn't be yelling at your mother this way," Maya interjected nervously.

"Butt out, Maya," Nick snapped. He instantly regretted his tone, but he couldn't throttle his anger. He was too far gone. "This is between my mother and me."

"I couldn't agree more." Melanie planted her hands on her hips. "I stayed with your father because it was the right thing to do for you, Nick. I couldn't live my entire life for you, though. When it was finally time, I decided to live my life for me. I'm sorry that makes you so unhappy."

Nick didn't like the picture she was painting. "You cheated on him!"

"Oh, Nick, your father and I hadn't been intimate in years. I was too young to give up that connection with someone. You feel it with Maya. I see it. Heck, I've always seen it. I wanted to feel it with someone myself. Your father wouldn't even consider going to counseling or trying something new like travel. How much of myself was I supposed to give him?"

"You pledged to love him forever!"

"And I wanted to keep the promise I made, but I was unhappy." Tears shone in Melanie's eyes. "I just wanted a piece of happiness for myself."

"We're not here to talk about the separation," Maya said in a low voice. "We're here to talk about Hank. We need to get him into rehab, deal with the charges against him, and figure out his stuff before we can tackle anything else."

Nick didn't immediately respond. His mind—and heart—were going a mile a minute. After several seconds of clenching and unclenching his fists, he shook his head. "You know what? I'm done with this. *All* of it." His fierce eyes landed on Maya. "I'm not dealing with any of it. I'm leaving."

Maya's jaw dropped. "What do you mean, you're 'leaving'?"

"I don't want to deal with this. I didn't create this problem. I'm leaving it up to the 'adults' to fix. It's their mess." He didn't look over his shoulder as he started for the elevator.

"Nick, you can't just run away," Maya called. "That never fixes anything."

"Oh yeah? That's not what my mother says. She ran away, and her life is finally perfect. I think I'm going to try it." With that, he disappeared into the elevator. He didn't even bother to spare Maya a glance before the doors shut and whisked him away.

Twenty-Five

MAYA

Maya wanted to chase Nick—her heart actually ached at his absence—but she knew him well enough to recognize he needed to cool down. Of course, she was concerned. *Did he mean he's done with me when he said he was done with everything else?* Pushing him would only make things worse. Besides, she had things to do at the hospital.

"He's always been a little dramatic." Melanie gave a hollow laugh.

Maya slowly slid her eyes to Melanie. "It's too much for him right now. This is his worst fear."

"He shouldn't be taking all this on himself," Melanie argued. "Hank's problems are Hank's problems. They're not Nick's."

Incredulous, Maya asked, "How can you stand there and act surprised? This is who Nick is. He needs to help. He's always needed to be the one who swoops in and saves everybody. When you left Hank, he was the only one who could fix things."

Melanie reared back as if Maya had struck her. "You cannot blame me for wanting to be happy."

"Of course I don't." The frustration Maya was trying to keep locked in a box took control. "I love you, Melanie. I always have. But you know you didn't do this the right way, right?"

Melanie didn't respond other than to gulp.

"I get that you were always unhappy," Maya continued. "I saw the things Nick missed when he was growing up and knew you and Hank weren't going to stay together forever. But you don't cheat on your partner. Of course Nick would take his father's side. Hank was the wounded party."

"I didn't physically cheat," Melanie argued.

"You did emotionally, though, and it doesn't really matter now. You left Hank, went straight to another man, and paraded your new relationship all around town." Maya lifted a finger to still Melanie's response. "I get it. You were finally happy and wanted to celebrate it. But it was pure torture for the two men you left behind."

"I never left Nick behind. I just ... couldn't take it any longer."

"Well, you did what you wanted to do, and now we're stuck here." Maya planted her hands on her hips and glared at the door that led to Hank's room. "I don't begrudge you happiness, Melanie. I just want to make sure Nick gets that same happiness."

Melanie nodded. "You should go after him," she said softly. "You're the only one who can make him feel better right now."

"No, that would be a mistake. He needs to calm down. If I go after him now, he's going to vent all over me. I'll be upset. He'll be upset. And it could set us back. I'm not going to allow that to happen."

"So what are you going to do?"

"Handle Hank. I mean, I need to ease some of the burden on Nick's shoulders and prove he's not in this alone. The only way I know to do that is to handle Hank."

Melanie balked. "Nick has never been alone."

"Yet that's exactly how he's felt as he watched his father fall off an emotional cliff. Nick can't abandon people. So he's been the one living in the fallout of your bomb. I don't say that to be mean," she added quickly when Melanie stared at the floor. "It's just the truth. Nick can't abandon his father. It's never going to happen. That means we have to handle Hank."

Melanie gripped her hands together so tightly that her knuckles turned white. She nodded when finally meeting Maya's gaze. "Let's do it."

Maya squeezed Melanie's shoulder before sighing and turning. She didn't bother knocking on Hank's door and instead strode in as if she owned the place. Letting Hank dictate terms would be a mistake. She had to take charge and tell him how things were going to be, whether he liked it or not.

"I think it's time we pick a rehab," she said as she held up the brochures Nick had left behind.

Hank's eyes, red-rimmed and glassy, were full of resentment. "I'm not going to rehab. I don't have a problem."

"Oh, but you do." Maya sat on the side of Hank's bed—the side where he wasn't handcuffed—and held up the first brochure. "This one has a pool."

"Nobody cares about a pool," Hank shot back.

"It's indoors."

"I still don't care. I don't have a problem. This was an unfortunate accident. I'll handle everything. It's not a big deal."

Sadness threatened to overwhelm Maya, but she forced herself to remain cold. Coddling Hank was what had gotten him in trouble in the first place. "I love you, Hank."

"Oh, here we go," Hank muttered.

"Nick loves you too," Maya continued, not missing a beat. "You're his father. When we were kids, he told me he wanted to be just like you. He wanted a family to take care of. He wanted to take his kids camping like you used to take us camping. You were always his hero."

Hank blinked twice. "I..."

Maya waited. When Hank didn't continue, she pushed forward. "You're not much of a hero right now, are you?"

Hank's jaw dropped. "What did you just say to me?"

"The truth. You're a drunk, Hank, and you're ruining your son's life. I'm not going to let it continue. That means you're picking a rehab ... and you're going."

"You're not the boss of me," Hank hissed. "You're not even a part of this family. You abandoned Nick eight years ago. You broke his heart. You're a user, and you only came back into his life because you needed help launching your stupid coffee shop. We don't need you."

The words were like a hard slap, and Maya had to suck in a breath to keep from bursting into tears. She'd always loved Hank and couldn't imagine him ever saying anything like that to her.

"That will be enough of that," Melanie said as she appeared in the doorway. Maya hadn't even realized she'd followed her into the room.

Hank's face reddened as rage took over his features. "What do you think you're doing here?"

"I'm handling the problem." Melanie managed a smile as she met Maya's uncertain gaze, then moved toward the bed. "We have some things to discuss." She grabbed one of the chairs and pulled it closer to the bed. Perhaps wisely, Maya mused, Melanie opted to settle on the side of the bed where Hank was handcuffed. "I was not kind to you when I left."

Hank let out a derisive snort. "Oh, you think?"

Melanie ignored the sarcasm. "I fell in love. It didn't happen overnight. It was a slow process. He listened to me and cared about the things I cared about. He didn't pretend I was another piece of the furniture in the room to be ignored."

Hank sputtered. "I brought home the money. I paid the bills."

"And you ignored me."

"You're not twelve, Melanie," Hank snapped. "What is the matter with you? You're too old to be coddled."

"I'm not too old to need to be loved, though," Melanie shot back. "I never felt loved with you. I was just an accessory you trotted out at the Elks Club when you bothered to go out for the spaghetti dinners once every six months. Otherwise, you sat in that easy chair and ignored me. I needed more than that."

"Well, you left me. I guess that means you got what you needed from someone else."

"I did," Melanie confirmed. "We're not here to talk about me, though. I made mistakes, and I'm sorry for them. I should not have done things the way I did. I hurt you, and you didn't deserve it."

"It's a little too late for apologies," Hank growled.

"Maybe so, but it's not too late to save yourself. Hank, you can't keep doing this. You can't keep drinking yourself to death. It's not fair to you, and it's certainly not fair to Nick."

"What does he have to do with this?" Hank demanded. "Where is he? Why is he allowing you guys to tag team me? I want to talk to him right now."

"He left," Maya replied quietly. "He fell apart when Melanie showed up, said he was done with it all, and ran away."

Surprise filled Hank's features. "What's he done with?"

Maya held out her hands and shrugged. "I think he meant

he was done with everything he's been dealing with, including you and me. But I'm not sure."

"He didn't mean he was done with you," Melanie said hurriedly. "Maya, he's been pining for you for years. Even before you guys lost each other. He just didn't realize it."

"Yes, well..." Maya blew out a breath. "I'm not letting Nick go. That makes me sound like a crazy stalker, but it's not happening. I want him, and I know he wants me. This situation just threw him for a loop. That's why I'm going to fix it." She tapped the brochures she'd dumped onto the bed. "Pick one."

"No." Hank jutted out his chin. "I don't have a problem."

Maya leaned forward, her face only inches from Hank's, and he had no choice but to meet her gaze. "You wrapped your car around a tree. You pass out from alcohol every night. You aren't living your life. Instead, you're bitter because you think something was stolen from you.

"I have a newsflash for you, Hank," she continued. "Nothing was stolen from you. The things you believe were stolen were lost ... by you. It's time to suck it up and be a parent. Nick deserves that."

"Who are you to tell me what my son does and doesn't deserve?" Hank snapped. "You left him."

"Oh, Hank, that's not fair," Melanie chided him. "They were barely adults. They didn't know how to grapple with the feelings they had. They did their best, whether you believe it or not."

"She left him. She broke his heart, just like you broke mine."

"The difference is that they belong together, and you and I didn't." Melanie crossed her arms. "I don't regret our time together, Hank. You were a good provider and a wonderful father to Nick."

"But I was a shitty husband to you, right?" Hank's eyes gleamed with irritation.

"Yes, and I was a shitty wife to you in return. We are not going to turn into shitty parents on top of being shitty partners. That means you're going to work with Maya and me. You're not going to fight rehab. You're going to do this for Nick because it's the right thing."

Maya spoke softly again. "You need to become the father he remembers. It's what's right for him."

Hank sniffled, and for a moment, the set of his jaw told Maya he was going to argue. Instead, his shoulders slumped, and he focused on the brochures. "I don't care about a pool. I want someplace where I can have a room to myself. I'm too old for summer camp."

Maya grinned. "Sure." She flipped open another brochure. "This one has private rooms. You have to go to daily sessions with your group to talk about the reason for your addiction, though."

"Oh geez." Hank threw his hands into the air. "I'm not an addict."

Maya leaned in to snag his gaze again. "You are. But that doesn't mean you can't be the man you used to be. You have to commit to this." She gripped the hand that wasn't cuffed to the bed as hard as she could. "Do it for Nick."

Hank blinked twice then nodded. "Fine." He looked as if he was in physical pain as he turned back to the brochures. "Just get me a private room."

"We'll help you," Melanie insisted. "*I'll* help you."

"I'm not sure that's smart," Hank replied, avoiding her gaze. "You've been living in my head rent free since you left. Giving you more space will be a mistake."

"But ... I want to do what's right for Nick too," Melanie insisted.

"This is a balancing act," Maya interjected. "We need to

get this entire family healthy. I think that means you guys need to get divorced and officially put the marriage behind you. You also need to be good parents to Nick and stop treating him as if he's the one who has to constantly make the effort with the two of you. He needs breathing room."

"And what are you going to do?" Hank asked Maya. "How are you going to help Nick?"

"I'm going to love him," Maya replied. "I'll be there for him no matter what. I'm going to make those stupid cheese Danish he loves beyond reason, and I'll listen when he talks, if he ever talks to me again."

"He will," Melanie said earnestly. "When he left, he said he was done with all of it, but he didn't mean you. He was just frustrated and upset."

"I hope so. But it doesn't matter if he did mean me. I'm not going to let him go. I'll fight for him."

"You should," Hank said in a low voice. "That's what he needs more than anything. He wants to be worth fighting for."

"He's always been worth fighting for," Maya replied. "I just didn't realize it. I made too many mistakes when we were younger. I didn't see what was right in front of me."

"If it's any consolation, he didn't see what was right in front of him either," Melanie offered. "It worked out for the best anyway. You guys were too young. The distance would've broken you, then one of you—probably you—would've given up your dream. That would've resulted in too much bitterness for you to survive. That you guys came together of your own volition is good for both of you."

"Yeah." Deep down, Maya believed that. "It's going to be okay. I'll stalk him later if I have to. He needs a bit of breathing room right now, and we have to relieve some of the pressure, so that's what we're going to do." She focused on Hank, practically daring him to start arguing. "You are going to pick a rehab, and I am going to secure a bed for you today. You're going to put your all into the program, and we'll make things better for Nick as a group. You got me?"

Despite his predicament, despite the fine hanging over his head and the criminal charges he would have to face, Hank smiled. "I think you and Nick are going to make it work in a way his mother and I never could."

"We are," Maya agreed. "It's going to happen. You're not going to give me any grief, right? You're going to go along with the program."

"I'm going to do what's right," Hank agreed. "For Nick."

Maya had never been more relieved in her life. "For Nick. He's worth it."

Twenty-Six

NICK

Nick was upset with himself as much as anybody else. Snakes wriggled in his stomach, and he'd made a mistake when storming out of the hospital. Despite that, he didn't go back. Instead, he returned to Bellaire and proceeded to mope.

His father was a mess after his mother had imploded their family. His head was in a terrible place. He started to wonder if he was as poisonous as the people who'd raised him, and if he was, maybe it meant he was bad for Maya. The thought made him want to hurl ... and cry ... and maybe throw something. With that in mind, oblivious to the cold settling over the town, he went to the basketball court. He didn't play, though. Instead, he sat and remembered better times.

Maya—his Maya—was in every good memory he had of the place. He didn't want to let her go. But that small, niggling part of his brain that couldn't accept what had happened to his family kept telling him he had no choice but to set her free. He didn't want to listen to the voice, yet he couldn't completely ignore it either.

"What are you doing here?" came a male voice, jolting Nick out of his reverie.

When he jerked his head around, he found Bear getting out of his truck. He hadn't even heard the vehicle pull up. "What are *you* doing here?" Nick asked, absently wiping away the few stray tears that had coursed down his cheeks. "I'm not in the mood for a game."

"Good, because it's freezing." Bear crossed his arms. "Word is spreading about what's happening at the hospital. Some of our former classmates work there."

That pang Nick had been trying to ignore returned with a vengeance. "Oh yeah? How is Maya?" The question came out chillier than Nick had anticipated.

"She's with your parents. They're picking out a rehab facility together."

"*What?*"

"You heard me." Bear moved directly in front of him. "Maya took control and talked your father into rehab. She even called to find a bed. Apparently Kim Smith helped her cut through some red tape at your mother's request. He's going to Rustic Pines in Traverse City. They're taking him at five o'clock, sending transportation and everything."

Nick had no idea what to make of that. "He says he doesn't have a problem."

"Well, apparently, he's changed his mind."

"If Maya thinks she can force him when he doesn't believe..." Nick considered what he should say next.

"Maya is a grown woman who understands how to get things done," Bear replied. "How else could she be opening her own business at such a young age?"

"Fair point."

"Mike Donahue is over there and says she's upset."

"I might've been a little too much to handle at the hospital earlier," Nick acknowledged. "It was a lot to deal with."

"I heard." Bear managed a smile. "You're usually the calm one, but when you do explode, it's always a big deal. According to what your mother told Mike, Maya is worried. Apparently, you said you were done with it all, and even though she's trying to hold it together, she's wondering if you were including her in that statement. She didn't confide that in anybody, just for the record, but your mother mentioned it to Mike because she was afraid. Mike being a good guy, he sent me to check in with you."

"And if I did mean to include Maya in that statement?" Even saying it hurt Nick's heart, but he wasn't in a good headspace.

"Then to head off a meltdown from my wife later, I have to beat you up."

Nick wasn't in the mood to laugh, but he couldn't stop himself. "Is that a fact?"

"Yup." Bear bobbed his head. "I'm here to keep my wife happy." He lifted his fists and cocked an eyebrow. "Don't make me destroy you."

Bear was Nick's best friend for a reason—well, after Maya, who was so much more than that. Despite his size and his "Hey, man, let's hang out" attitude, Bear read people better than most. He could handle almost every mood, and Nick relied on him more than he'd ever realized until that moment.

"I take it Lindsey will be upset because Maya's upset," Nick said when he'd managed to curtail his laughter.

"Lindsey will be frustrated," Bear countered. "She loves you. Not in the same way she loves me, mind you, because I'm a god, but she loves you and Maya too. She wants you two to be happy."

"She's a good friend."

"Yes, she is. What she wants doesn't matter right now, though."

"That you're out here in the freezing cold, trying to talk me down from a ledge, seems to suggest otherwise."

"True." Bear pursed his lips, then sighed. "You're doing this all wrong." His voice was so soft that it barely carried over to Nick. "You love Maya. I know you do. Even if you haven't come to that conclusion yourself, part of you recognizes that you want her more than you've ever wanted anything in your entire life."

"I *do* want her," Nick conceded. "I ache for her right now." He buried his face in his arms as he rested them on his knees. His ass had gone numb from sitting on the pavement, but he didn't get up. "But what if I'm damaged? What if she deserves better than me?"

"There's nobody better than you. Well, me, but she can't have me. I'm devoted to that mouth I married, just like you're devoted to Maya."

"I yelled at her."

"She'll be fine. She told your mother she's not going to give you up. Right now, she's just giving you the space she thinks you need. She doesn't want to chase you before you're ready to be caught."

Nick laughed again, and that time, he felt lighter in the aftermath. "That's such a Maya thing to say."

"It is. She's always been strong." Bear crouched to be at eye level with Nick. "You're strong together. How about you let her help instead of pushing her away, huh? You finally got everything you've ever wanted. Don't ruin it now because your dad is a lush and your mother takes no responsibility for her marriage imploding."

Nick sucked in a steadying breath. "I never knew they were unhappy when I was a kid," he admitted. "I just ... never knew."

"I know."

"Everybody else did."

"We had an inkling. But we didn't live under your roof, so we couldn't *know*."

"Maya did."

"Yes, well, she practically lived under your roof at times. It makes sense that she would know more than the rest of us."

"I want to hate my mother." It was hard for him to get out, but he was exposed, and there was no stopping it. "I want to blame her for everything."

"But you can't."

"It's not *all* her fault. She could've done things differently —way differently—but not all of this is her fault."

"It's not," Bear confirmed. "Listen, we want our parents to be perfect. That's not reasonable, though. They're never perfect. You can't live your life for your parents now. They need to get their own lives together—it sounds like Maya is putting that into motion as well, if Mike is to be believed— and you need to focus on your life."

"I don't know what to do."

"Of course you do. Your life is Maya. You need to fix things with her and move forward. Let your parents handle their own problems for a change. Build the life you want."

"What if she wants something better?"

"Dude, I hate to break it to you, but she wants you. If you break up with her, it won't last, because you guys won't be able to stay away from each other. You will wedge a fair amount of resentment and mistrust into your relationship, though. Do you want her wandering around, wondering if you're going to break her heart again?" he continued, barely taking a breath. "Does she deserve a life of walking on eggshells? I don't think so. Neither of you do. Lean on each other and build your relationship that way. You're destined to be together. Embrace it."

He makes it sound so easy, Nick mused. But everything

Bear said was what Nick wanted to believe. "I screwed things up."

"It's not unfixable. She's helping your parents. Maybe you should suck it up and join the party."

Nick rubbed his hands over his face. "I don't want to lose her. I just ... need to be the sort of man she deserves."

"Then be that man. Tell your parents where to stick it and pull it together. Tomorrow is Maya's big opening. Don't you want to be part of that?"

Nick nodded. "More than anything."

"Then I think you know what you need to do."

MAYA WASN'T AT THE HOSPITAL WHEN Nick returned, and he had to tamp down a pang of disappointment when he found his mother and father in Hank's room together. They were talking in low voices—talking, not arguing, for a change—and Nick stood in the open doorway to watch them for several seconds.

"You can keep the house," she insisted. "I don't expect anything from you monetarily, Hank. I don't want you to have to give up your life because I want to live mine in a different way."

"With Clark," Hank said bitterly.

"Can we not go there? I think it's best we keep this divorce as amicable as possible. It's what Nick needs."

"I know." Hank sounded resigned. "It's fine. Whatever you want, I'll agree to."

"No, that's not how it works." Melanie shook her head. "I'm not taking advantage of you. When this is over, when you're finished with rehab, you're going to have your house and a life to go back to. That's important to me."

"Thanks. I guess."

Nick cleared his throat to draw their attention. "What's this?"

"I believe it's us being adults," Melanie replied, flashing a smile. "I wasn't certain you would come back."

"I wasn't certain I would either," Nick admitted. Even though Maya wasn't there, he searched the room's corners yet again. "Where is she?" He didn't have to say her name—it was obvious who he was referring to.

"She helped us get a bed for your father at Rustic Pines," Melanie replied. "Transport has already been taken care of, and I volunteered to sit with him until the van gets here. There was no reason for her to stay."

Nick pressed his lips together. "Did she say anything about me when she was leaving?"

Melanie's lips curved in amusement. "I believe there might've been mention of a 'stubborn ass' she was going to hunt down when he wasn't feeling so sorry for himself. But I get the feeling that hunt isn't going to commence this evening."

"No?" Nick rubbed his sweaty palms over the front of his jeans. "Why is that?"

"Because she opens her first business tomorrow, and apparently, she was supposed to spend all day today baking to get ready for it. She was determined to find you when she left, but I told her she should let you come to her."

"Because I need to grovel?"

"A little. I didn't know what state she would find you in, though, and I didn't think it was fair for her to be in tears all night when she has such a big day tomorrow. I thought maybe you would be ... um ... difficult if she approached you."

"Difficult?" Though the situation wasn't funny, Nick couldn't help emitting a strangled laugh. "I've totally screwed this up." He dragged a hand through his hair and turned to look out the window. "I'm mad at myself."

"Well, join the club," Hank offered. He was no longer drunk although obviously suffering from a hangover. "I believe that's the common feeling among everybody in your family today."

"Oh yeah?" Nick crossed his arms. "Why are you mad at yourself?"

"Because I've been a crappy father."

Nick shook his head. "That's not true. You were a great father."

"Maybe back when you were a kid. I haven't been so great the past year and a half or so. I'm sorry about it."

"And I'm sorry I threw the family into a tailspin when I put my needs above everybody else's," Melanie added. "I'm not sorry I decided to make myself happy, but I am sorry that I did it in the absolute worst way possible."

"We're going to do better," Hank promised. "It won't be easy. In fact, I'm pretty sure the next few months of my life are going to suck. But we acknowledge that we let our problems drag you down."

"And that's not fair," Melanie added.

"Not that I'm not happy to hear you guys say that, but may I ask what propelled you to suddenly decide you needed to clean up your acts?"

"Maya had a few opinions we hadn't considered," Melanie replied.

"She's got a mouth on her," Hank acknowledged. "She wasn't wrong, though, and she was mad enough that she got fired up. When she laid things out for us, well, it became obvious that we'd made some poor decisions where you're concerned."

"And we're concerned," Melanie added quickly. "We don't want to hurt each other any longer. But we especially don't want to hurt you."

"It's time for you to get what you want for a change," Hank added. "I'm pretty sure that's Maya."

"I love her," Nick admitted.

"You always have," Melanie supplied. "Even when you were kids. I saw the confusion on your face when you were about fourteen or so and knew you were going to love her in every way possible before it was all said and done."

"You knew I was in love with her when I was fourteen?" Nick's brow furrowed. "I'm going to call foul on that because I know I didn't feel that way about her when I was fourteen."

"No, but remember the weekend Catherine and I took you down to the Detroit Zoo? We went shopping, too, but the main trip was because we wanted you to see the zoo."

"I remember." Nick bobbed his head. "It was as hot as hell, and we were sweating like crazy."

"Yes, and in the polar bear exhibit, there was a tunnel," Melanie volunteered. "One of those clear tunnels where the bears can swim all around. You and Maya were laughing and having a good time, but she jumped when one of the bears landed in the water directly next to you."

Nick's heart warmed at the memory. "I remember. She let loose this little squeal then got mad at herself because she said it was a girly response. She was in a phase when she just wanted to be one of the boys because all the girls in school were mean to her."

"They were mean because they were jealous that she was accepted so easily by the boys," Melanie replied. "I watched that entire moment play out, and what I saw was you reacting to her as a woman, not a friend. You decided to be protective ... and I know darned well you accidentally touched her breast when she jumped."

Nick's cheeks burned. "You saw that?" he choked out.

"I did. Maya felt it and decided to pretend it didn't

happen. You, however, acted as if you were on fire, and I was afraid you might suddenly combust."

"How do you know I didn't act that way because I'd touched my first breast?" Nick demanded. "That's possible. It could've been the breast and not her."

Amusement lit Melanie's face. "A mother knows these things. In that moment, you realized there could be something more between you and Maya. You were nowhere near mature enough to accept it or act on it, but you realized it was possible, and you wanted it to be true."

Nick gulped. "I didn't realize I wanted her until she came back into my life."

"You were always a little slow," Hank teased, grinning when Melanie shoved an elbow into his arm. "There's a reason everybody in town could see what you two couldn't."

"And what's that?"

"That you were destined to be together."

"No, what's the reason?"

"Because you were afraid to be the man she needed. You're not afraid any longer, though. Be that man. Let her be the woman she wants to be for you. Don't think about what happened to your mother and me. You're not going to be us. Just think about what you want to happen ... and it will happen."

"How can you be sure?"

"Because some things are meant to be."

Nick pressed his eyes shut, willing away the tears. "I don't know how to fix this."

"Of course you do," Melanie countered. "Search your heart. The answer is right there."

Twenty-Seven

MAYA

"I s anybody out there?"

Maya stood behind the coffee bar, wringing her hands, and watched Lindsey pull back the curtain to peer outside.

Opening day had finally arrived. All her hopes and dreams —well, her professional ones, at least—revolved around it, and she was a nervous wreck. The shop had come together just how she'd imagined. Despite Nick storming off the previous day, she'd managed to focus long enough to get all her baking done. She was officially ready, yet there was a hole in her heart.

"Not yet, but it's not even seven o'clock," Lindsey pointed out. "Relax." A calmness that Maya wasn't used to surrounded Lindsey, and it set her teeth on edge.

"We open in thirty-five minutes," Maya countered. "If nobody comes—"

"People are going to come," Lindsey insisted. "It's going to happen. You need to ... not do whatever it is you're doing." She crossed back to the counter area. "You're so worked up. I've never seen you this way."

"It's a big deal," Maya snapped. "I've been saving for this ... and building for this ... for a long time. If it doesn't work, then what am I going to do?"

Lindsey blinked several times, then shook her head. "Good grief. It's going to work. You need to take a pill."

"Whatever." Maya knew better than to get angry with her friend, but she couldn't help it. She was worked up, and it wasn't just the grand opening freaking her out—it was Nick. She'd waited for him to call her for hours the previous day, and when he didn't, she shut off her phone while baking so she wouldn't be distracted. When she turned the phone back on, there were no texts or voice mails. He could have called and hung up, but there was no way for her to know.

"Maya, I think you're worked up over more than one thing here," Lindsey offered as she hopped onto one of the stools. "Do you want to talk about it?"

Maya refused to make eye contact. "I have no idea what you're talking about."

"Oh, right." Lindsey rolled her eyes. "You're a terrible liar. Has anybody ever told you that?"

"Not that I recall."

"Well, you suck." Lindsey blew out a breath, ruffling her bangs. "How's Nick?"

Maya cringed at the question and kept her back to her friend as she wiped down the sink area. It already gleamed, but she needed something to do with her hands. "He's fine ... I'm sure."

"But you don't know?"

"He had some stuff going on yesterday." Though Maya was being purposely evasive, it wasn't just to protect herself. She doubted Nick wanted the specifics of Hank's accident spread around town. That would just make things worse.

"Some stuff, huh?" Lindsey sighed. "It's a small town, Maya. Everybody knows about what happened with Hank.

That news spread early yesterday. I hear he's going to rehab. I even placed a call to find out which ones had openings but found out you already had that covered."

Maya's forehead creased as she turned. "How did you manage that, anyway?"

"Bear's sister is a nurse at the rehab, and she told me. She's responsible for arranging the vehicle the rehab sent to pick him up."

"Oh." Maya had thought she knew everything about how things had played out. Apparently, that wasn't the case. "Well, that's good."

"It *is* good. Hank has needed rehab for a long time. I'm sure he's only going because it will look proactive to the courts, but if he's stuck there anyway and opens himself to getting help, that's good for Nick."

"Yeah." Maya had questions regarding Nick's current status, and she glanced at her phone screen. She wanted to call him desperately but didn't. She couldn't push him before he was ready. "I hope it's what Hank needs."

"I hope so too. Just out of curiosity, were you there when all this went down yesterday?"

"Maybe for a bit."

"Uh-huh." Lindsey sounded as if she was strategizing. "Did something happen with Nick?"

Maya was starting to think her friend knew more than she was letting on.

"I don't know," she replied. "You should ask Nick about that."

"And here we go," Lindsey grunted. "What happened?"

"Does it matter? He's not here. He said he was going to be here, and he's not. Let it go."

Lindsey touched her tongue to her top lip. Maya could practically hear the gears of her mind working.

"Stop looking at me that way," Maya hissed. "I can't

control Nick. If he wants to melt down and walk away because he can't deal, there's absolutely nothing I can do about that."

"Is that what he did?" Lindsey asked gently. "You were vague on the phone when we talked yesterday. You just said there'd 'been a thing,' which could mean almost anything. Melanie was careful not to say too much as well."

"Yes." Maya was beyond covering for him. "His mother showed up to help, Nick melted down, and now I don't know where he is or what he's thinking."

"You could call him."

Maya shook her head. "I can't push him before he's ready. He's stubborn. He'll dig his heels in."

"He *will*," Lindsey agreed. "The thing is, in this particular instance, at least, I think it's possible he reacted, then freaked out after the fact because he recognized he overreacted."

Maya frowned. "Meaning what?"

"Nick has been dealing with a lot, and when it comes to his parents, he reverts to being a teenager. That's kind of normal when you're an only child, or so I've read."

"He said he was done with it all," Maya argued. "*All* of it. I think he was including me in that."

"No, he wasn't."

"He was. I was there. You weren't."

Lindsey crossed her arms. "He wasn't including you."

Her stubborn nature was cause for amusement on most days, but Maya wasn't in the mood to corral Lindsey on top of everything else. "You weren't there. You don't know. I saw him. He just ... stormed out. He didn't even look back. He's clearly done with me."

"Or you're making up stuff in your head because you're dramatic," Lindsey argued. "Which scenario seems more likely to you?"

"The one where I'm right, and you're full of it."

Lindsey snorted. "I see your head is in a good place today." She tapped her fingers on the counter and sighed. "Bear saw Nick yesterday," she blurted as if yanking off a bandage.

Maya froze and gripped the rag more tightly. "What did he say?"

"Bear won't share the intimate details, even with me." Lindsey looked annoyed. "He's too loyal, even though I had it written directly into our vows that he had to share gossip with me if he wanted to keep being able to visit the honey pot."

It took Maya a moment to work out what Lindsey was saying. "Oh, you guys are so gross."

"No, we're pragmatic," Lindsey countered. "I need my gossip. But he wouldn't say much yesterday. Just that Nick was struggling."

"Nick *was* struggling," Maya confirmed. "He didn't want to struggle with me. He wanted to struggle separate from me."

"That could be taken to a kinky place if you're not careful."

"I would rather be kinky than tied up in knots," Maya replied, frowning when she realized she'd made another unintended double entendre. She decided to ignore it. "I don't know what to do. I miss him so much."

Lindsey nodded. "I get it. The thing is you guys are used to dealing with problems on your own. Becoming an 'us' takes a bit of time. You'll get there."

"How can you be sure? He hasn't called me. He hasn't texted. He's just ... disappeared. I think he might actually be done."

"He's not done."

"How do you know?"

"Because you're the thing he's wanted more than anything else for his entire life. He's not letting you go. He's just struggling."

Maya shut her eyes, then forced a smile. "I hope you're right. Either way, I can't focus on that today. I need to focus on the shop. We open in thirty minutes."

"This place is going to be a hit," Lindsey said. "It'll be fine. I promise. As for Nick ... everything is going to work out with him too. Just you wait and see."

"I hope you're right, because I'm not sure if I can take losing him twice."

"Oh, Maya." Sadness permeated Lindsey's expression. "He doesn't want to lose you either. He just needs to take a breath. He'll come to his senses before the end of the day. Trust me."

THE SHOP OPENED TO A SMALL LINE. Maya would've preferred people lining up around the block, but the town was small, and the temperatures had dipped into the teens overnight. Not many would line up, even for coffee and cheese Danish, when it was that cold. Despite her earlier trepidation, Maya managed to calm herself relatively quickly. The coffee shop saw a steady stream of traffic, to the point that it was easy for Maya to keep up, with only minimal help from Lindsey. As for the reviews—everybody raved that the coffee was good, and the pastries were to die for. The shop was a bona fide hit.

That meant all Maya had left to worry about—at least for the moment—was Nick.

"I'll be right with you," she called from the kitchen, where she was opening another tub of pastries, when she heard the bell over the door jangle. She'd thought she'd gone overboard baking the day before, but she was already halfway through everything. "How can I help you?" she asked when she emerged with the tub of cheese Danish. Her eyes widened when she realized the new customer was her old best friend.

"I'll take that." Lindsey swooped in and grabbed the tub of pastries before Maya could drop it.

"Nick," Maya rasped. He had a vase full of roses decked out with brightly colored balloons, and he looked so sad that Maya was afraid her legs would go out from under her.

"Maya." He seemed to have trouble saying her name because he had to repeat it to make sure she heard it. "Maya. I'm so sorry."

So carefully that she wasn't even sure she was moving, Maya reached out to take the flowers. "Are these for me?"

Nick arched an eyebrow. "Do you think I would come to the opening day of your coffee shop with roses for somebody else?"

"I don't know." Maya froze with her hands still open. "Maybe."

"Of course they're for you." Nick looked pained as he finally handed over the flowers. "I just thought I should bring you something."

"When groveling, it's always best to bring something," Lindsey agreed as she placed the pastries in the glass case. "I would've gone bigger than roses, though."

Nick shot her a quelling look. "Lindsey, do you mind if Maya and I have a moment alone?"

"Do I mind?" Lindsey cocked her head as if actually considering it. "As a matter of fact, I do."

"I need to talk to Maya."

"Yes, and you picked a great time for it," Lindsey supplied. "What with her opening her business for the first time and all. Someone needs to be here to wait on the customers, dumbass. That's going to have to be me. If you want to talk to Maya, perhaps you should do it in the kitchen."

Nick took several seconds to absorb the information, then nodded. "Right. I... You're totally right." He turned back to Maya. "Do you want to go in the kitchen with me?"

Maya didn't know how to respond. "I have to be here to welcome the customers," she said finally. "That's my job. I only get to do this once. I have to do it right."

"Of course you do." Nick looked momentarily lost.

"You really are a dumbass," Lindsey muttered. "Just tell her how you feel, Nick. There's nobody in here right now. Blurt it out so that she can stop worrying about throwing up and start worrying about what's supposed to be the most important day of her professional career to date."

Nick blinked again. "You want me to say it in front of you?"

"Yes, that's what I want more than anything. I'm a busybody, and Maya has had a very rough twenty-four hours. I think it's only fair that you tell her in front of me so that I can bear witness to your groveling. If it's not good enough, I'm going to make you go out and try again."

"Oh geez," Nick said at the same time Maya grunted out a "Can you not?"

Maya and Nick laughed in unison. When Nick lifted his head again, he was much more together than he had been when he entered the coffee shop.

"You'll never know how sorry I am," he started, frowning when the bell over the door jangled, signifying another customer entering.

Jake from the basketball team walked in. "Hey, Mr. Griffith." Jake gave him a lazy smile. "I'm here for one of those Danish things you're always raving about."

"You want coffee, too, right?" Lindsey asked.

"Of course." Jake acted as if that was the most ridiculous question he'd ever heard. "Who doesn't want coffee? That's like a crime against nature or something."

Maya gulped when she realized Nick's attention was focused on the teenager. He wasn't going to say what he'd come to say, which meant she would suffer the entire day, and they wouldn't be able to talk about things until the coffee shop closed ... hours from then. Though she should focus on business, she felt sick to her stomach where Nick was concerned.

Nick seemed to be having some sort of inner struggle. Ultimately, instead of leaving the coffee shop to regroup and try again later, he pushed forward ... with heightened gusto.

"I love you, Maya," he blurted, causing everybody in the shop to jerk their heads in his direction. He ignored everyone else and kept his eyes on her face. "I made a mistake yesterday. It was all just too much, and I ran instead of dealing with my problems."

Maya licked her lips, her eyes burning. "I don't expect you to be able to take everything on yourself. That's why I was there. I wanted to help."

"I know, but it was too much. My mother— "

"Is still your mother," Maya finished. "She might not have done everything exactly how you wanted her to do it, but that doesn't mean you have the right to cut her out of your life. She's a human being. Human beings make mistakes."

Nick let out a hollow chuckle. "She pretty much said the same thing to me when we talked late yesterday afternoon."

"You talked? Does that mean you made up?"

"We are ... taking it one day at a time, the same as my father." Nick stepped closer to the counter. "He's in rehab even as we speak. My mother and I are going to have lunch this weekend. But I'm not here about them. I'm here about you."

"And what about me do you want to address?" Maya asked primly.

"That's the spirit," Lindsey encouraged her. "Make him work for it."

Nick held up his palm to blot out Lindsey's face. "I've

always loved you. When we were kids, it was friendship love, but somewhere along the way, it changed. I didn't realize it was changing. Or if I did, I refused to acknowledge it. I was too afraid."

Maya gulped. "Because you didn't want to lose the friendship."

"Yeah." Nick managed a wan smile. "Sweetheart, I kept thinking that I couldn't lose you, but because I was so stupid, I lost you anyway. I don't want that again. I want to be with you."

"Are you sure? You didn't act like that yesterday."

"That reaction wasn't for you. It was for my mother, and I was wrong. But that doesn't change the fact that I was stupid. I promise to be better about that. The stupid thing."

"Because you love me?" Maya suddenly felt bold. "You've said that twice now."

"And I'll say it a million times over the course of our lives, if you'll let me. I do love you. I never stopped. When we fell out of touch, I was angry, but I get it now. It was too painful for both of us to keep yearning."

He moved to step behind the counter, never breaking eye contact with Maya. "We were protecting ourselves when we broke apart. But we don't need to do that now. We're together … and we can be together forever."

"This is like a Lifetime movie," Jake whispered to Lindsey. "My mom watches those, and she loves them. She's going to be so mad when she hears she missed this."

"Word." Lindsey bumped fists with Jake. "For once, I'm going to have all the gossip when people ask. I'll be a witness and everything. It's going to be glorious. We're two very lucky people, Jake."

Maya had to force herself to block them out, or she would lose it. "Are you saying you want to be with me forever?" she asked.

Nick nodded as he cupped her chin. "Yes. I've always wanted you to be my forever, but I didn't know it. I want to get better at this. I want you by my side when things pop up. I don't want to be alone again."

Maya wrapped her hands around his wrists as she debated how to respond. "I don't ever want you to be alone. But I'm afraid. What if we screw this up?"

"Oh, we're going to screw it up." That time, Nick's smile lit up his face. "The trick is to get back up when we've been knocked down. That's the thing we're going to need to do together."

"Yeah?" The waves of unease that had been rolling through Maya since Nick stormed out of the hospital the previous day start to smooth. "I guess that makes sense."

"Yeah, as long as you want to be with me too."

"Of course I do. I love you too."

Warmth enveloped Nick's face. "Of course you do. You've always loved me, just like I've always loved you."

"We're going to figure it out together this time."

"Yeah." He moved in for a kiss but stopped when his mouth was an inch away from hers. "I think I know exactly how to start."

"Oh yeah?" Maya asked breathlessly.

"Yeah. Maya Markham, will you go to the Northern Loves bonfire with me?"

That wasn't the question she'd been expecting. "Seriously? We made fun of the bonfire when we were kids."

"We're not kids any longer."

"I would love to go to the Northern Loves bonfire with you."

"Good. I was going to cry if you said no." Nick swooped in for a kiss before she could say anything else, and as their lips touched and their hearts collided, the world that had seemed so frightening fell away for both of them.

"Oh, your mom is going to be so mad she missed this," Lindsey said to Jake.

"Yeah, she said it was going to be a big deal when it happened," Jake replied. "It feels like a big deal."

"It is. It was totally worth the wait too."

Epilogue

NICK - SIX MONTHS LATER

"Move your hips," Nick demanded as Maya backed into him while dribbling the ball.

After a long winter, one that had seen Maya's coffee shop flourish as Nick's family slowly repaired itself, they were finally able to visit the basketball court again. Their primary focus was dusting off Maya's rusty skills.

"I *am* moving my hips," Maya shot back, her nostrils flaring. "Can't you tell?" She swung her hips to prove her point. "I can't actually drive to the net without moving my hips."

"Well, you're not moving them very well." Nick edged away from her and rubbed the sweat on his forehead with his forearm. "You're shuffling."

Maya's jaw dropped. "I am not shuffling!"

"You're a shuffler. You do it when we're home too. You wear those ridiculous slippers that are too big for your feet and shuffle from room to room."

"Those slippers are my thing," Maya fired back. "I didn't hear you complaining when I put them on for the first time after we moved in together."

Nick smiled at the memory. "As I recall, you were *only*

wearing the slippers that day." He still considered the day Maya had finally agreed to move out of the Sandusky cabins and into his house the best day of his life. Sure, the day they admitted they loved each other was also grand. But things had only gotten better since then. They were even looking for a new house to buy, and he couldn't wait until they found exactly what they were looking for. Until then, he was fine with naked days in front of the fireplace ... slippers being optional, of course.

"That's neither here nor there." Maya used her most imperious tone. "I'm not a shuffler."

"Of course you're not." He smiled softly. God, he loved her so much. If he'd thought that finally admitting what he was feeling meant that those feelings were done growing, he was wrong. He loved her more than he had then, and that shouldn't have been possible. "Let's take a break." He moved to where he'd left a huge bottle of water and his duffel bag. "You need to get your mind in the game."

"Oh, stuff it," Maya groused. She didn't follow him, instead dribbling the ball and glaring at the net. "I'm practicing. Let me practice."

"Fine." Nick downed some of the water and watched her slide left and right. Her ball-handling skills had always been sloppy, but that was fine. She wasn't going to join the WNBA. Her determination was what had always turned him on. With that in mind, he reached into the duffel bag and retrieved the ring box he'd been carrying with him practically everywhere since he'd left the jewelry store with it two weeks before.

"Look at me move my hips," Maya called out as she swung her cute behind back and forth. "Look at them sway. It's a sight to behold."

Nick smirked. It *was* a sight to behold. It was ... magic. He felt it whenever he looked at her. Magic, love, and contentment. They were three things he'd always yearned for. She gave them to him in spades.

Maya, clearly oblivious to what he was thinking, threw up a shot. Then she pumped her fist when it swished. "Ha!"

Nick opened the ring box without realizing he was doing it. He'd thought long and hard when making his selection, ultimately deciding on a princess cut in a platinum setting. She was his little basketball princess, after all. He'd gone for two carats, so it was decent sized without being ostentatious. Since she'd never gone for fancy jewelry, he thought it was perfect ... just like her.

"Who's the baddest basketball bitch around?" she chirped as she made another shot. "That's right. It's me. I'm the queen of the court." She smiled as she turned. "And the queen of your heart." All her bravado slipped when she realized Nick was standing there with a ring in his hand. "W-What...?"

Nick's grin broadened. "I love you," he said softly.

Maya worked her mouth like a guppy, apparently unable to form words.

"I love you more than anything," Nick continued. "I love you more than cheese Danish, and I didn't think that was possible."

"Nick," Maya rasped.

"You're my whole heart, Maya Markham." He moved closer to her and held out the ring box. "I was wondering if you might want to wear this." It wasn't the proposal he had planned. He'd been running a few huge productions through his head, considering making a spectacle out of it and involving all their friends and family. But that didn't feel right.

"Are you asking me what I think you're asking me?"

"No, I thought I would give you this ring and ask you to play one-on-one with me."

Maya's throat moved as she swallowed over and over again.

"Although now that I think about it, marriage is kind of

like a game of one-on-one, huh?" He took another step toward her. "We're going to be navigating the same space, trying to score on a regular basis." He shot her an evil grin. "Both working in tandem with each other to achieve a certain outcome."

"Nick." Maya seemed to be struggling to make her heart and lungs work correctly. Her face was so red. "Are you sure this is what you want?"

He nodded. "I've wanted this since we were fourteen and you told me you were going to bake every single day for your husband."

Maya's brow furrowed. "Every single day is a stretch."

"I've wanted this since the first time I saw you in a dress in high school and realized you were more than just a basketball buddy," Nick continued, barely taking a breath. "I've wanted it since we shared a bed together in college, and the first time I woke up with you, I wondered if there was such a thing as a perfect moment."

Maya's eyes went glassy. "You said I snored that morning."

"And you do. That doesn't mean they're not perfect little snores." He closed the rest of the distance between them and extended a shaky hand to brush her hair away. "I want you forever. I've always wanted you. I'm just not afraid to say it now."

Maya finally managed an even exhalation. "Are you still going to want me when I save up enough money to open that restaurant I've always wanted, and the first year is full of long hours and a crabby me?"

"I'm going to want you even more then."

"How do you know?"

"Because with each breath I take, I think this is the moment when I've finally hit the ceiling of my love for you. I think this is the moment when I can't love you any more. Do you know what I always find?"

Maya shook her head.

"There's always more." He leaned in to rest his forehead against hers, slanting his mouth over hers but not touching lips. Instead, he just breathed in and out, filling himself with her exhalations as she did the same with him. "There's always going to be more."

"Forever is a long time," Maya noted. "Are you sure you're ready for it?"

"I'm ready for you. Forever is just part of that."

"Yeah."

"Yeah," he echoed, slowly pressing the ring box into her hand. "You still haven't said yes," he pointed out when they'd been quiet for a long time.

"Yes." Her face broke into a grin. "It will always be yes with you."

"Even if I want you to fill the bed with cheese Danish and play a little game with me?"

"Even then."

"Awesome." He kissed her, all the love he'd thought temporarily sated rumbling through his chest. When he pulled back, he thought he might burst with happiness. "Do you want to keep playing basketball or go home and play something else?"

Maya gave a wicked grin. "What do you think?"

Nick didn't bother with the ball. He simply joined their hands and started tugging. "Great. I'll grab the Danish when we hit the kitchen, and we'll go from there."

Made in the USA
Columbia, SC
24 July 2024

39274005R00176